KILLER Lies

THE CHAOS CREW
BOOK TWO

EVA CHANCE
& HARLOW KING

Killer Lies

Book 2 in the Chaos Crew series

First Digital Edition, 2021

Copyright © 2021 Eva Chance & Harlow King

Cover design: Temptation Creations

Ebook ISBN: 978-1-990338-28-1

Paperback ISBN: 978-1-990338-29-8

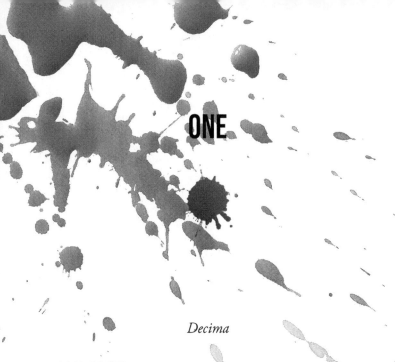

ONE

Decima

I WASN'T sure I'd ever seen anything quite as horrifying as the videos Blaze had loaded onto his phone.

They weren't disturbing in a gory, blood spewing everywhere kind of way. That, I could have stomached no problem. Instead, I watched a child—no more than four years old—learn to fight like a professional killer. I could see the way she put all of her efforts into training for the sake of appeasing her tutors. She wielded a knife with her right hand and repeated the motions that she'd been taught only once.

She moved unlike any other four-year-old I'd ever seen. Which made sense, considering that this video was two years into her training. She would have given an experienced soldier a hard time despite the little hands and the angelic face that was occasionally whipped by the long braid of dark hair that ran down her back.

She was deadly. Fast. Strong.

She was *me*.

In the past two hours, I'd watched dozens of these videos. They'd started when I was around two years old, crying for a mother I didn't remember. By four years old, it looked like I'd completely forgotten her, which I guessed also made sense. Most people couldn't remember their earliest years. I'd been *so* young when they must have taken me.

It hadn't taken long before Noelle was both my family and trainer in one.

Now and then, I still struggled to wrap my head around the fact that the little girl in the videos was me, especially when I didn't remember that entire chunk of my life. But she was. Even the video files were named "Decima" with a date and series of numbers attached. If they hadn't been, I still would have recognized myself in that childish face. As I got farther into the videos, I started to come across training sequences that had stuck in my memory from way back then.

As the video I was currently watching came to an end, I decided I'd had enough. What more could I learn from them? The household had stolen me from my parents when I'd been a toddler. They'd instructed me in fighting arts and stealth for reasons I didn't understand. No explanations were given in the video records. Noelle must have carried them on her for some kind of reference if she'd needed to push on a specific part of my training.

It wasn't just physical training in there, after all. A few of the videos had shown the psychological conditioning I hadn't even realized I'd gone through. The conditioning that had embedded the awful phrase that had let them take over my free will: *Garlic milkshake*. And programmed me with other innate responses through hypnosis and punishment too.

Suddenly I understood why I'd always felt uncomfortable about the idea of turning on the TV in any of my hotel rooms while on assignment unless I had to in order to gather information. Why I'd never been the slightest bit tempted to step outside my rooms in the household without explicit permission. Why I'd barely asked any questions about my role in the household until I'd finally escaped it.

They'd honed my body and shaped my mind into the exact tool they'd wanted me to be. A shudder ran through me at the thought.

I shifted on the picnic bench and reached across the space between that table and the one where the guys were sitting, handing the phone back to Blaze. We'd come to this secluded corner of a park in the wan early morning light so that he could show me more of what he'd discovered. We hadn't wanted to linger at the scene where Noelle had attacked me—and where she and her men had met their deaths.

I was still wary of the four hitmen eyeing me from across the distance between the tables, but I couldn't resist flopping back on my own and closing my eyes, trying to put a cap on the emotions that were roaring through me.

Who was I really? Were my parents still out there? Why had Noelle and the others treated me like this?

The strongest emotion by far was confusion. That and queasiness at the awareness that I had no idea who I'd been before I'd been kidnapped or who I'd have grown to be.

But that part didn't matter, really. I was Decima now, and nothing would change that.

The yawning sense of loneliness I'd never understood before opened up inside me. I'd been missing my real family this whole time without knowing it. My fingers itched for my stuffed tiger toy—the one I'd seen myself clutching in the earliest videos before I'd become more compliant. I must have brought it from home.

No wonder I'd had such a hard time leaving it behind. It'd been my one connection to the home I'd lost.

Blaze's foot tapped against the pine boards of his picnic bench. He'd been stirring restlessly since I'd started watching the videos, but so far he'd managed to keep his energy contained enough to avoid peppering me with questions. Apparently the hyperactive hacker's patience had run out.

"How much of all that do you remember?"

I pushed myself into a straighter sitting position, eyeing the guy. The breeze tossed through his floppy, pale red hair until he pawed it behind his ear.

What could it hurt to be honest? I cleared the lump from my throat. "I know that I was trained all through my childhood and teenage years. I remember a few of the sessions I saw in the videos, as I got a little older, but none of the really early stuff. And I have no idea about anything before the household. But there has to be a before, right? I wouldn't have been crying for my mom if there wasn't. I was so young…"

Blaze gave a sympathetic shake of his head. "You couldn't have been older than one and a half or two in the first videos," he said with a flash in his eyes that was unexpectedly protective. Then he paused. "What were they training you for?"

They still didn't know that part. Well, they could probably guess, given the training *they* must have received for their own line of work. No one learned to wield a knife like child-me had just to carve up a turkey. And the guns…

I drew in a breath and hesitated. Four pairs of eyes remained locked on me. I still barely knew these men, even though I'd been living with them for several days. I hadn't been aware that they were contract killers rather than cops until last night. That was a pretty major deception.

But then, I'd lied through my teeth to them when it came to so much about myself. They were brutal killers… and so was I. If anyone could understand the life I'd been living, maybe it was them.

There was still so much I didn't know about who I was, and they might be the only people who had a real chance of helping me figure it out. They'd come to back me up when I was in trouble. And I had to admit that even with *their* initial kidnapping taken into consideration, they'd treated me with more respect than anyone in the household truly had.

"What do you think it was for?" I said. "You've seen

how I can fight. I was learning how to kill. Once I was older—starting when I would have been around eight or nine, I think—they started sending me on missions. Small local ones at first, then farther out." I wrapped my arms around myself instinctively. "They told me I was taking down bad people—that the world was an awful place and almost everyone in it was awful, and getting rid of the men and women they pointed me at would make things a little better. Make the household a little safer. I never saw any reason to believe anything different…"

Because the people who'd taught me hadn't allowed me to. Until now. Until their carefully constructed façade had crumbled when *these* men had blasted into the household and blown them all away.

I still didn't totally understand that either, even if I believed the guys that they'd been hired by a client to do it, that it hadn't been personal for them.

I sealed my lips as I looked over the four imposing men at the picnic table parallel to mine. Blaze was still jiggling his knee. Garrison sat on the bench, his ankles crossed as he watched me intently with his piercing hazel eyes. In the sun, they appeared lighter than usual—a pretty, almost green color.

Julius leaned against the side of the table with one foot propped on the seat, his massive, muscular frame giving off a typically commanding air. With his military short hair, he looked every inch the ex-soldier. Talon was poised on the far bench with his elbows braced against the tabletop, his icy blue gaze fixed on me beneath the sheen of his pale, shaved scalp. The coldest killer of the bunch had the look of a lion ready to strike, but I didn't think any of his animosity was directed at me.

"It makes sense that they could have convinced you," Garrison said, somewhat grudgingly. The lanky blond man had tried to rankle me with his snark nearly every time we'd spoken to each other in the past couple of weeks. I didn't think he liked offering any sympathy. "You had them brainwashing you from when you were so young. Even older kids are pretty impressionable." Then he shut his mouth tight as if he'd said more than he thought he should.

Blaze frowned. "They started sending you off to *kill* people when you were still just a kid? That's—"

His voice halted abruptly at a sudden movement from Julius. The crew's leader straightened up. He took a step closer to me, peering at me with his deep blue eyes. Something in them sent a weird but not totally unpleasant shiver over my skin.

"I knew we'd met before," he said with a startled expression that looked odd on his normally assured face. "I helped you once."

I blinked at him, and a twinge of the unexpected sense of familiarity I'd felt here and there before rose up inside me again. "If we'd actually interacted, I would have thought I'd remember that."

"Maybe not, given the circumstances." His surprise faded away, replaced by his usual confidence—and a warmth I wasn't totally used to. "It was more than a decade ago, not long after Talon and I had started the crew. Blaze and Garrison weren't in the picture yet. The two of us were working a job in Miami one night. I had a bike back then—a Triumph. I was just getting on it in the alley where I'd parked when this girl who wouldn't have been more than eleven or twelve came running down the alley toward me. It was dark—you were frantic—but it must have been you."

Talon lifted his head to look at his boss. "*That's* what really happened to the Triumph? You told me you totaled it."

Julius shook his head. "She was bleeding from a cut on her side, and I could hear people running after her. The alley was a dead end. I wasn't going to leave some kid for a bunch of creeps to find. So I told her to wait there and marched out, told the people who were charging over that I'd seen her running off in a different direction. And right when I went back to check on her, the bike came roaring out of the alley with her perched on it. She left me in the lurch." He chuckled, seemingly unoffended in hindsight. "I figured I could always get another one. She obviously really needed it."

My mouth fell open. I *did* remember him now that he'd pieced the details together. I'd partly bungled a mission, caught a trip wire on my way out of the house where I'd made the kill and gotten several guards on my tail. One of them had shot at me and nicked the side of my chest. It was the first time I'd had a mission go haywire, and I'd been freaking out underneath. In the darkness and the haze of my panic, I'd barely registered the facial features of the stranger who'd protected me.

Then cool logic had kicked in thanks to my training,

and I'd made use of the resources available to me. A.k.a., his bike.

"I did," I said. "Need it. Thank you. I probably would have figured out how to get out of that mess one way or another, but… you made it a lot easier."

Once I'd left the city well behind, I'd ditched the bike at a junkyard and called the household to orchestrate my pickup. I'd never mentioned that anyone other than me had been responsible for getting me out alive. Julius couldn't have known that story unless he'd really been there. And studying him now, I could easily superimpose his authoritative presence over the shadowy impression in my memory.

And now we'd somehow stumbled back into each other's lives when it turned out I might need him again— in a much bigger way. The realization brought a strange mix of relief and unease.

Garrison let out a light snort. "What kind of mission did they have you on at eleven years old? Did you kill your mean science teacher?"

My gaze darted to him, and the uneasy sensation within me expanded, twisting around my gut. "The household never told me any details about the people they sent me to kill other than what I needed to know to get the job done. That one… That one was a rich man who had a big house guarded by men with semi-automatic rifles. He kept a pet bearded dragon in his bedroom. I slipped in through a back window, dodged all the guards, and cut his throat in his sleep. I just… ran into a little trouble on the way out. I didn't have as much practice then."

Garrison blinked at me, his smug smile vanishing. "Okay, I stand corrected."

Blaze's eyebrows leapt up. "Twelve years ago in Miami? Was he an older man, in his 60s, with a house in North Beach? Big stucco number with bizarro gargoyle mounted over the door?"

I stared at him. He hadn't even been in the crew yet then—how did *he* have any idea about this? He couldn't have been out of his teens back then himself. "Yeah… How did you know?"

The hacker let out a disbelieving guffaw. "That hit still gets talked about in the circles we run in. That was Milo Evangelez—the gemstone baron of the southeast."

Something shifted in Julius's expression. He cocked his head. "What are some of the other missions you carried out? The particularly memorable ones?"

My skin started to itch with a deeper discomfort. Noelle had drilled it into me that I wasn't supposed to talk about anything I did outside the household. And… a gemstone baron… Why would they have wanted to kill him?

Suddenly I wasn't so sure I wanted to hear what else the guys might tell me.

But I couldn't be a chicken about this, and Noelle didn't dictate my life anymore. I wracked my brain for missions that stood out more than the others and forced my mouth to move.

"Like I said, I wasn't told things like names. Even if I

overheard information like that, I put it out of my mind." Probably thanks to all Noelle's hypnotic suggestions, I realized now with a grimace. "There were three businessmen in Italy who always went everywhere together. That made them difficult to take out. They acted all jovial and friendly in public, but in their hotel room, they were assholes to each other. I half-expected them to kill each other themselves before I poisoned them. Managed to sneak some special ice cubes into the drinks in a room service order they placed."

I paused for just a second, pulling my lower lip under my teeth before I continued. "Another of the harder ones was this man in Osaka. I had to kill the guy in a bathhouse, and he was as big as a sumo wrestler. Do you know how hard it is to strangle someone who outweighs you by five hundred pounds with nothing but the towel they walked in with?"

The guys were staring at me in silence. It was kind of unnerving. Even Garrison the Indifferent was gaping at me.

Unsurprisingly, Blaze lost the ability to contain himself first. "Are you hearing this?" he said, glancing around at the others with an awe I wouldn't have expected from my sparse descriptions. He met my gaze again. "The man in the bathhouse—the sumo wrestler type—that would have been Akio Nakamura, the founder of Nakamura Tech. The Italian brothers must have been the co-founders of the aerospace center in Rome—a big source of political debate."

Those... didn't sound like the horrible criminals

Noelle had made them out to be either. My stomach started to knot. "How can you be so sure?"

"It all makes so much more sense now. Holy crap." Blaze clapped his hand against his knee. "*You're* the Ghost."

I stared at him. "The what? What are you talking about?"

Julius cuffed his younger associate lightly on the shoulder. "What Blaze is doing a very bad job of explaining is that the mercenary underworld has been tracking certain high profile and highly skilled kills for years, trying to figure out who's pulling them off. People started referring to the mysterious assassin they assumed was responsible for most—if not all—of them as the Ghost, since the assassin never left a trace. The three hits you mentioned were all attributed to the Ghost."

"Somehow I don't think anyone would have predicted it was a teenage girl," Talon remarked in his deep baritone. I couldn't tell from his tone whether he was impressed or merely stating a fact.

"Everyone's been incredibly impressed by your work— and curious as hell about who you are," Blaze said, *his* eyes shining with unrestrained excitement. "Holy shit, we've had the Ghost staying in our apartment for days and we didn't even know it."

Garrison recovered from his shock enough to look me up and down with a skeptical expression. "From what I've seen during that time, I wouldn't say you quite live up to the expectations we all built up."

I rolled my eyes at him. "I'm sorry if I couldn't

immediately overpower four highly trained hitmen while on my own with no preparation and multiple injuries. Also, FYI, I probably *could* have killed you at least five times if that was what I really wanted to do, but I was waiting you all out to see what you knew about the murders at the household."

"So, your excuse is that supposedly you were going easy on us?"

I shrugged, leaning forward on the bench. "You could try me right now. I think I'm ready to take off this brace." I tapped the plastic structure around my arm that'd been shielding my previously sprained wrist. "One-on-one, let's see who comes out on top."

I didn't really mean the challenge, but even Garrison of the many masks couldn't stop uncertainty from flickering in his eyes as he looked me over again. Facing me—a woman with an immaculately deadly reputation—scared him in a way that he wouldn't admit.

The entire crew was *impressed* by my kills and the reputation I'd built up with them—a reputation I'd had no idea about. The idea that mercenaries all around the world might have been discussing each of my hits and comparing notes and theories made me want to squirm. All I'd been doing was following orders.

With that thought, the knots in my stomach turned into a dull ache. "The people I mentioned," I said tentatively. "And whoever else it seems like I killed, that you attributed to the 'Ghost'… Were they involved in illegal activities as well as the legit businesses? Were they some kind of criminals?"

Julius sobered in an instant. "Some of them definitely had questionable ties," he said quietly. "But many of them, as far as any of us knew, were sticking to at least the letter of the law. We assumed they were being taken down by competitors or people with a personal beef, not for any real crimes."

I dragged my gaze away from him to stare off through the trees. Why had Noelle really ordered me to kill each of my targets, then?

I'd been surrounded by lies my entire life, so was it really a surprise if the people I'd killed weren't as deserving of their horrible fates as I'd been told?

I'd been nothing but a tool for the household, a tool for their own selfish ends. *They* were the bad guys in this scenario, not the heroic underdogs they'd painted themselves as.

Nausea trickled through me, and I had the sudden urge to march right back to the mansion and kill them all over again.

Within a few seconds, the flare of rage faded into more queasiness. I rubbed my face. I'd learned so much, and all of it only made my life and the mission I'd given myself more complicated. Where the hell did I go from here?

And how was this crew of hitmen going to factor into it?

"What now?" I asked, focusing on Julius, since ultimately it'd be his decision. "You know who I am, I know who you are…"

He contemplated me for a moment. "That's up to you.

What do *you* want to do with everything you've discovered?"

I'd never heard those first four words before—never been given the freedom to do whatever I wanted. What *did* I want to do?

I felt my answer out slowly. "I want to know who I really am—or who I was before I was taken. I want to find out why the household took me and trained me, and why you were ordered to kill them. I need to understand where I fit in and why they want me back."

Blaze was the first to speak. "We can help you with all of that." He glanced at Julius for confirmation.

Julius nodded. "Whether you like it or not, we're all tangled up in this mess together. After everything we put you through getting to this point, maybe we owe it to you to find you some answers. And frankly, I'd like to know what those answers are too."

With his dark eyes on me, I couldn't help wondering how much he was seeing me, the fully grown woman with fifteen years of kills under her belt, and how much the scared eleven-year-old girl who'd been briefly in over her head all that time ago. But I wasn't going to argue against his decision, not when it benefitted me so much.

I couldn't help checking Garrison's expression. He didn't exactly look thrilled, but he only scowled without a word in protest. Talon gave a brief dip of his head as if it didn't matter much to him either way. I studied him next, searching for a sign of the man who'd turned so intense when we'd collided in the exercise room days ago.

As far as I could tell, he wanted to pretend we'd never

had scorching-hot sex up against a wall. I guessed if he preferred to avoid the subject, I would too, even though I wasn't sure I'd mind a repeat of our encounter.

At least he didn't seem to feel he needed to avoid *me*.

I leaned back on the bench, taking the crew in as a whole. Julius may have agreed to help me, but I still had a choice. I would never sacrifice my free will again—not for these men or anyone else. I could still go off on my own to find answers if that suited me better.

What good would sticking to my own devices do me, though? I had little money and fewer resources. The contacts I'd known were all tied to Noelle, so I couldn't trust any of them.

This crew was the best resource I'd found by far. Was I really going to throw that away just because I still cringed a little at the thought that they'd been the ones who'd torn the household apart?

I had no loyalty to the people who'd lived there. Noelle and her colleagues had kidnapped a toddler, brainwashed me, and controlled me for years. They'd sent me off to kill people for no reason but their selfish gain.

The men in front of me had connections and skills... and they'd also offered me something nobody else ever had: freedom. They were *more* than just a resource.

Resolve unfurled through my chest, steadying me. My mouth curved into a small smile. "What are we waiting for then? Let's get started."

TWO

Julius

WE SAT around the dining table, Blaze's usual spot filled by Dess as he squeezed in at the corner, too close to Garrison for either of their liking. If I had to hear another second of bickering from them…

"You eat so much pasta that you smell like it," Garrison chided, taking a bite of his chicken.

My mouth became a thin line as I awaited Blaze's comeback.

"You eat so much chocolate that… you know what? You don't smell like chocolate." Blaze smirked. "You smell like a heaping pile of dog—"

"You both fucking stink," Dess cut in, her mouth full as she spoke. My spine straightened as she said it, and I couldn't help but chuckle a bit. Having someone else break up the constant heckling between them was a blessed relief.

She looked at me with a glint in her dark eyes. "Don't think that you smell any better."

Everyone looked at Dess for a moment, and she smiled at us. "Talon's the only decent one here, isn't that right?" she added, giving him a wink.

Talon, for all it was worth, looked pleased with her announcement. He continued eating with a hint of what might even have been amusement on his face, but he didn't reply.

I looked around the table again, noting the homey feel that had settled over our group even with a relative stranger in our midst. Of course, the truth was that Dess barely felt like a stranger now. We knew who she was on a level she'd shared with almost no one before, and the same for her with us. I didn't need to watch her from the corner of my eye every few seconds, checking for hostile moves.

It was so much better this way, having everything straightforward and clear. It would make our jobs easier, and we'd be able to help her more when we weren't blinded by lies.

Dess stood up from the table and took her plate to the sink. Now that I knew what she was—what she'd been trained to do—I could pick up on the strength and agility that marked even the simplest movement, every motion she made deliberate and coordinated. Everything about her screamed "dangerous" if you knew how to look right.

But there was still so much about her that none of us knew, her included. So many things about her past that could prove more dangerous than she was.

Who was she? Who was after her? We could obviously

expect further threats to arise, but where and when and to what extent?

Not knowing how to prepare left me on edge. I dealt in certainties and absolutes, planning our missions and our overall security down to the smallest detail. Anything left to chance could pop up and bite us in the ass at the most inopportune moment.

I didn't have much choice, though. The only other option was turning her loose, which she didn't want... and neither did I. Every particle in my body said both she and we were better off with her among us.

I *wanted* to help her.

The thought of those people wrenching her from her family and forcing her to become their murderous tool brought a bitter taste to my mouth. Fury flared to the surface at the memory of the fight in the sewers this morning, when her former trainer had sicced all those men on the woman she'd raised since early childhood. I'd like nothing more than to rip through every person responsible for Dess's imprisonment, and I'd be counting the days until we found them.

My hand dropped to the military-issue Beretta M9A1 at my hip. The feel of the cool, smooth metal settled my nerves, even though there was no one in front of me to shoot just yet.

"I think we need dessert," Blaze said, cutting off my train of thought.

Dess laughed lightly as she rinsed her plate at the sink. "Do we? Let me guess, you have a sweet version of pasta for that."

Blaze snorted. "If only. How's this for an idea? We have ice cream, and I know that Garrison keeps a tub of chocolate syrup in here somewhere. To celebrate your newfound freedom, why don't I whip you up a chocolate milkshake?"

I doubt any of us had failed to notice Dess's enthusiasm for all things cocoa-related. Her face lit up the second Blaze mentioned the syrup. But as he finished his suggestion, an uneasy twitch ran through her slim frame. The eagerness in her expression dimmed.

"That's all right," she said, her voice oddly stiff. "I'm actually pretty full."

I studied her for a second, my brow furrowing with confusion, before it hit me.

In the videos, her bitch of a trainer had used the phrase "garlic milkshake" to completely control Dess as a child. She must have unpleasant associations with that combination of words—and maybe with each of them on their own as well. *Very* unpleasant, if it'd shaken her adoration for chocolate.

"Thanks anyway," Dess added quickly, and headed to the exercise room that'd become her honorary bedroom in the apartment. Blaze started after her, puzzled and apologetic. "But... she *loves* chocolate," he murmured to himself after the door shut behind her.

Garrison scoffed and cuffed the back of his head lightly enough for the gesture and the words that followed to come across more teasing than hostile. "For someone supposedly so smart, you can be one dim motherfucker."

Blaze scowled, and I stepped in before they got going

again. "You remember what her control word was at the household?"

Blaze's eyes flickered the way they always did when his brain was moving at a million miles a second putting the pieces together, and then he smacked himself in the forehead. "I think we need a codeword for milkshakes."

"Maybe we should simply avoid them for the time being," I remarked dryly, but afterward, my gaze slid to Dess's door. There might be other ways to start solving that problem—ways that got right at the source. If she wanted that.

There was only one way to find out.

As the others finished clearing the table, I walked over to Dess's room. After a second's hesitation, I knocked.

"What?" Dess asked from the other side.

"It's me," I said. "Can I come in? There's something I'd like to talk to you about."

"Sure, come in," she said, sounding normal enough. But when I opened the door and saw her sitting on her cot, I couldn't help noticing the slight slump to her shoulders and the pensive crease on her forehead that she managed to smooth away a moment later.

I considered asking the most obvious question: *Are you okay?* But I knew how quickly *I'd* deflect an expression of concern like that. And I was coming to see that Dess and I had a lot in common.

I sat across from her on the workout bench, spreading my legs as I leaned my elbows into my knees. "Do you want to talk about it?"

She sighed and made a face. "Not really."

I nodded. "I get that, but I might be able to help if I know what's going on. We heard the phrase your trainer used in the videos. I'm guessing it still bothers you?"

Her mouth twisted tighter, a little of the pain I didn't think she wanted to admit showing through. "It doesn't just bother me. It can *control* me." She swore under her breath and pressed her palms to her forehead. "What if I can't fix what they broke? Not completely."

My heart ached for both her and the girl I'd encountered all those years ago. What if I'd taken her under my wing then? Not that I could imagine she'd have let me, but her life... it could have been different. Better.

All we had to work with was where she'd ended up in reality, though.

I shook my head. "You're not broken. You just have some interesting features."

She raised her eyebrows at me, and a small smile curved her lips. "That's one way to look at it, I guess."

"Maybe all those features will come in handy one day."

Her eyes sharpened. "If this situation doesn't get me killed first." She sucked a sharp breath in through her teeth and held it for a few seconds before releasing it. "During the fight, Noelle used the code word, and it almost worked. I followed her halfway to the exit before I could stop myself."

I winced inwardly. No wonder that wound was raw for her. "Noelle's dead now," I reminded her.

"Yeah, but she didn't work alone. Anyone else who knows or gets ahold of that phrase could use it to give them enough time to take me down. Even one second of distraction in a fight could cost me my freedom. You don't know how it feels to have someone else in control of your body, screaming at yourself to stop and getting nowhere."

Her breathing quickened as she spoke, and she was right. I had no idea how that felt, and I didn't even want to imagine it. But that didn't mean I couldn't offer her anything.

I clasped my hands together in front of me, holding her gaze. "In my special ops training, we learned a variety of techniques for avoiding mental conditioning. It's easier to put up those barriers before the conditioning happens, but the exercises can help to fight off the compulsions too. Mental conditioning is dangerous, and it's a testament to your strength that you broke through it so quickly. Most people could never hope to do that, especially when they've been programmed since early childhood."

Dess tilted her head with a curious expression. "Did anyone ever try to condition you in that way?"

"No," I admitted. "Nobody ever caught me for long enough. But I practiced the techniques all the same, and I talked to guys who were held prisoner who managed to resist."

"I guess it can't hurt to try." She straightened up, the new resolve in her stance already reassuring me that she wasn't shaken too badly. "Can you teach me those techniques?"

"That's what I was thinking. I can give you the grounding, but what's most important is that you make sure to practice them regularly on your own once you've got the hang of them."

"Oh, if there's one thing I've got in spades, it's self-discipline." Dess's mouth quirked into a more genuine smile, one that brought the beauty in her face into clearer focus. Damn, this woman was gorgeous when I let myself notice.

But now wasn't the time for thinking about her looks. She needed guidance, not ogling.

I motioned to the floor. "We need to sit for the first exercise. It's a meditative experience, and it's best to get centered on a flat surface with nothing to distract you."

She lowered herself to the ground and crossed her legs, pulling them in tightly as I followed her. "Is this how you learned that you like to meditate?"

I blinked at her. "How did you know I meditate?"

She shrugged. "Blaze mentioned it. He said he learned how from you."

"I practice yoga," I said. "Meditating is the only part Blaze enjoys, so that's what he does. I do it all. There's a lot more to it."

A sly glint sparked in Dess's eyes. "I bet that makes you flexible."

Damn it if my dick didn't start to harden just with that brief remark, as if she meant anything like *that* by it. I gritted my teeth against the pang of arousal and evened out my breathing.

"Yes, but that's not what you want to be focused on right now. There are two main strategies that we can use, but before we attempt either of them, you need to be relaxed. I suspect that's going to take some work. I can feel your tension from here."

"I'm not sure I know how to relax," Dess admitted.

"You've got to learn, or none of this will help you," I said, and she huffed. I watched as she willed her shoulders down. "Good. We'll work on relaxing you more, but first I want to tell you the two things we're going to try. Visualization and disassociation."

"Those sound like fancy words for sitting on my ass. Is this really all that meditation is?"

I took a deep breath. "Do you want to learn or not?"

She winced. "Sorry. Continue."

I took in the way her black hair tumbled across her shoulders. Her spine remained straight, her slim figure on lovely display within her fitted tee and sweats, but her pert chin dipped in concentration.

Then I mentally swatted myself across the head for leering at her. Maybe I shouldn't be lecturing *her* about staying on topic.

I reined in my other impulses and thought back to some of my earliest lessons. "The conditioning is in your head, so you're going to need mental tricks to deal with it. That's why it's best to clear your thoughts as much as possible first. With visualization, you can imagine that the conditioned commands are a wave that simply washes over you without catching hold. Picture yourself holding firm while the words roll over you and slip away. Can you try that?"

Dess nodded, her movements already slowing as she sank into the sort of mental zone I was familiar with. She did pick up training fast, didn't she? She stayed still for a while, her chest rising and falling within her cotton shirt, and I definitely wasn't noticing how well her toned curves moved beneath that fabric.

"You said the other way is disassociation?" she prompted after a few minutes. "What does that involve?"

And so eager to learn. Another thought that shouldn't have sent a twinge of desire to my cock but did.

I pushed those emotions aside yet again. "That's right. You can disassociate yourself from the girl who went through the conditioning—convince yourself that it happened to a different woman, separate from who you are now. If you aren't the one who was conditioned, then the effect can't work on you."

Dess hummed to herself. "That makes sense. I like that one. I *feel* different already."

"That's a good place to start, then."

She inhaled and exhaled even more deeply than before. I could see the loosening effect spreading through her entire body. Gradually, more of the tension fell from her posture and her face. A softness crept over her features, totally at odds with her usually tough exterior.

Not many people would have gotten to see the vulnerable side of this woman. I was honored to witness it.

What was passing through her head right now as she sat there, a goddess of death incarnate? She looked so breakable, but I saw the illusion for what it was. I knew how *un*breakable she truly was.

The two factors in combination made her all the more appealing. When had I ever known a woman like this in my entire life? A woman who could hold her own against me in so many ways...

But as lust flickered up from my belly, a memory snuffed it out. The memory of the eleven-year-old girl with desperate eyes, dashing into an alley.

Dess needed help now just like she had back then, not to be treated like a conquest. I wasn't going to take advantage of her while she worked through her tangled past. Maybe when she'd healed more—

No, I wasn't even going to let myself think about that.

Other questions about the future lingered in the back of my mind. She could be here with us for quite a while. With her deadly precision and strength, she'd be an incredible asset in our line of work. Having the Ghost as part of the Chaos Crew? We'd be even more unstoppable than we already were.

Would she even want to join us? I couldn't see broaching the subject just yet. But while she was with us, I'd get the chance to see just how well this cunning assassin could fit within our ranks.

The rest we'd have to take from there.

THREE

Decima

AFTER A RESTLESS SLEEP that stretched into the afternoon, the first thing I saw when I opened my eyes was that damned stuffed tiger.

The thing that used to bring me so much relief and comfort now felt like another lie that I would never be able to fully trust. I scowled at the plush creature even as my fingers itched to wrap around its soft, well-worn fur and pull it close.

Was it something that Noelle had gotten to soothe me as a child? No, she'd never cared about my emotional wellbeing, and I'd hidden the toy from her over the years. I'd always had the sneaking suspicion that she'd throw it away if she knew how much I treasured it.

Anna, the only emotional comfort I'd ever had at the household, had never said anything about the tiger that I could remember either. I'd caught a glimpse of it in a couple of the earliest childhood videos...

Did that mean it'd come from the life I'd had before the household? It could be a clue—or simply a tool my kidnappers had used to placate a distressed toddler in the moment.

I didn't allow myself to dwell on the thought as I got up from my bed and quickly changed, but I couldn't help brushing two fingers across the striped fabric of the tiger before I strode out of the room.

I found Blaze sitting at the dining table, a half-devoured plate of fettuccini alfredo poised at his left and his laptop propped open at his right. He rapidly typed with one hand as he forked pasta into his mouth with the other.

I suppressed a laugh. "You take multitasking to a new extreme."

Blaze's head whipped toward me. Rather than turning the computer from me or closing it, he gestured to the seat at his side. "Come and sit down. Maybe you can help me."

Something in my chest tightened at the welcome with a startled pang. He trusted me enough to share whatever he was working on.

Of course, what he was working on was *me*. As I dropped into the chair, the window open on the laptop's screen jittered with an occasional flicker of an image. As I watched, one of those flickers flashed into a folder at the bottom of the display.

"What's all this?" I asked as Talon emerged from his

bedroom and headed to the refrigerator behind us. "Who are you looking for?"

Blaze shot a smile at me, his knee bouncing with his usual frenetic energy. "Technically, I'm looking for you. Or anything that could lead us to your birth family."

Talon grunted. "Why bother with your fancy software? Wouldn't one of those DNA sites do the trick faster?"

I sat up straighter in my chair. "Is there a website that'd connect me to my relatives by my genetics?" I had a vague sense that I'd heard about something like that before.

Blaze studied me. "I keep forgetting how much you've been out of the loop the last twenty-or-so years." He turned to include Talon in his answer. "Any of the public companies that run DNA matches come with too many problems. To start with, it'll only help us if one of Dess's relatives has already gotten a test with them too, so it won't even necessarily turn up anything. And they *are* totally public. If the people hunting for her have set up flags in any company's systems, we could inadvertently lead them right to us."

"So do it privately then," Talon said.

Blaze rolled his eyes. "I don't happen to have the skills to sequence her DNA, so unless you took a secret course in microbiology, that's not happening. There aren't any significant private databases that I'm aware of that would give us a decent chance of finding a match anyway."

I peered at the laptop screen. "What *are* you doing, then?" He'd clearly come up with some kind of solution. The tech genius seemed to have an answer for everything. Compared to my minimal computer skills, the stuff he could pull off might as well have been DNA sequencing.

Blaze gulped down another mouthful of pasta before answering. "I took a bunch of stills from the videos of you right after you were taken and now I'm having my facial recognition app run them against all the missing child reports it can dredge up from around the right time period for kids around the right age. Since we don't know how much global reach this organization had, I'm taking them from all around the world. There are a lot—it's going to be a slow process."

My heart sank. "You haven't found any matches yet."

"Nothing definite. I'm having it pick out ones that are somewhat close in case they did something to your appearance before any of those videos were taken. And if this doesn't pan out, there are plenty of other strategies I can try."

His optimism took the edge off my disappointment. But after I'd plowed through a bowl of cereal, I found myself wandering through the apartment, desperate to hear a *ping* of an alert that might mean a match. When it didn't come, I finally planted my hands on the other side of the table.

"I can't just sit around and wait for something to happen. There's got to be a way I can investigate too."

Talon let out a doubtful sound from where he'd moved to the couch and dragged out his knitting bag. I was never going to get totally used to the sight of that musclebound killer weaving the needles back and forth with their yarn, as close as the movements might come to the jerk of a knife.

"Whatever bad idea you're about to suggest, the answer is no," he grumbled.

I made a face in his direction. "Who says it's a bad idea?" Even as I said that, an actual idea occurred to me. One that had the potential to be dangerous, sure, but leaving the crew's apartment would always be a risk. I wasn't going to find the answers that'd reduce the danger if I stayed cooped up in here.

"I don't know," Talon replied in his typical impassive voice. "The last time you took off, you nearly got kidnapped again. Whether it's bad or not, I'm pretty sure it'll be hazardous to your health."

"Hey," Blaze piped up. "We should at least hear what she's got to say. It is *her* life we're trying to piece together."

"Thank you." I folded my arms over my chest. "I could go talk to the contacts I know in this city. They were connected to the household. Maybe they know more than I do about where else this organization operated or who they really were."

Despite his earlier support, Blaze frowned. "Because they're connected to the household, they could be under surveillance. You might be walking into a trap."

"I'd be careful about it. This isn't my first rodeo, remember."

"I don't think you want them knowing you're even still in town," Talon put in.

I threw my hands in the air. "Fine. Then I'd just spy

on them from a distance and see if they lead me anywhere useful. Happy?"

His mouth still slanted in at a skeptical angle. But thankfully, at the same moment Julius strode into the room. "Since you're arguing loud enough for me to hear you through my door, I'm going to weigh in." He nodded to me. "You obviously understand the risk."

Relief started to trickle through me at his confident tone. "Yes. I *am* the one who almost just got kidnapped and then found out that my whole life has been a lie. Believe me, I'm not going to be giving anyone out there the benefit of the doubt."

"Good." He gave Talon and Blaze a look as if to remind them that he was in charge here and then returned his attention to me. "I trust that you'll be discreet, and you should be able to take an active role in this investigation. Like Blaze said, it's your life. And we're not your jailors anymore."

My shoulders relaxed. "Good. So you're not going to make a fuss about me leaving?"

The corner of his lips twitched upward in a subtle smile that shouldn't have been so sexy. "I hope you'll come back of your own accord this time, but no, I won't. I don't want you going in and out of this building alone like you did two nights ago, though. It's too visible. If the people searching for you haven't connected you to this place, I'd like to keep it that way. I can escort you out through our private route and meet you when you get back, if you'll agree to those terms."

"Sure," I said, my spirits rising. I didn't know if I'd

totally believed until this moment that the men really were going to treat me like an equal among them rather than a prisoner. "That's fair." I didn't want anyone involved with the household tracing me here either.

"Excellent." He dug into his pocket and handed me a wad of cash for good measure, with a glint of amusement in his eyes. "And I can't let you go out there without proper resources. I'm guessing you'll find a way to spend this wisely."

———

I leaned against a light fixture a few shops down from the bakery, a light brown wig covering my tightly concealed locks of black hair. The hat that I wore atop it hid any irregularities to the wig, and sunglasses masked the rest of my face. I knew from my observations of Blaze's software that revealing my full face even for a second put me at risk of being captured by a street camera and IDed.

So far, I hadn't been able to find any sign of the guy I was looking for. I'd strolled past the bakery a couple hours ago and again a few minutes ago, and Jay's curly hair hadn't been anywhere to be seen through the front window.

It wasn't a big shop. If he'd shown up for his usual late afternoon shift, I should have spotted him.

A waft of the sweet, doughy scent carried on the breeze and set my mouth watering. It was too risky to go right inside and ask after him, but man, what I wouldn't have given for one of those chocolate chip cookies to hop its way out here.

Maybe Jay had taken today off? Maybe he'd changed his schedule? Leaving the apartment had been enough of a hassle that I didn't want to give up on my quest without getting some idea of when he'd actually be here. Julius might have been willing to escort me out, but he'd insisted on keeping part of the route secret, leading me blind. As a precautionary measure in case I was captured, which I couldn't blame him for when it'd already nearly happened yesterday.

I got a break when one of the women I *had* seen working behind the counter emerged from the alley. She must have left through the side door. She was just running her fingers through her billowy hair, which was creased from being trapped in its net for however many hours.

As soon as I clocked which direction she was headed in, I ducked through a nearby shop, darted around to the end of the block, and ambled toward the bakery as if I'd only just arrived in the area. When I came up on Jay's coworker, I made a show of stopping in my tracks.

"Hey!" I said brightly. "You look familiar. You work at Moe's, don't you?"

The woman halted abruptly and then laughed. "Now I feel like a celebrity. I do."

"I was just heading over there. Best cookies ever." I didn't have to fake the enthusiasm in my voice with that comment. I groped for the right impression to give to sell my next question and settled on slightly coy, as if I had a crush. That was a normal reason for asking about a guy, right?

I dipped my head and twisted my hands in front of me with feigned nerves. "Say… is that guy with the curly hair and the goatee working today? I was hoping I'd get to say hello."

The woman started to grin, but then the smile faded. "You mean Jay. He *was* supposed to be in today…" She bit her lip.

My pulse hiccupped. "What? Did something happen to him?"

Enough real distress must have come into my voice to convince her to reveal a little more. "Oh, I'm sure he's fine. Just being flaky. I heard he's missed his last couple of shifts. The manager couldn't reach him today. He's probably just not answering because he knows she'll chew him out."

"Oh! Well, at least I'll get to have those cookies," I said, and gave her a little wave to let her carry on her way.

I didn't go into the bakery, of course, but walked right by it, my forehead furrowing. Sure, Jay hadn't seemed like the most dedicated worker ever, but I didn't like that he'd suddenly "flaked" on his job within days of me reaching out to him.

It was probably a coincidence. I hoped it was a coincidence.

Shrugging off my uneasiness as well as I could, I flagged down a cab and gave the driver the address of the old mall on the other side of town.

Jay had just been a grunt worker. He'd had no stake in

the bakery. Scarlett had *owned* the electronics store where I'd talked to her last time, as far as I knew. Noelle had said she'd worked there for years, usually on her own. She couldn't just flake out and not bother to show up.

She'd know more about the household than Jay would have too.

I had the cabbie stop a couple of blocks away from the mall, handed him a good chunk of my remaining cash, and meandered along the street toward the low building while giving the area a careful scan.

No one I passed looked like anything other than a regular pedestrian who didn't give a crap about me. I didn't notice any new cameras mounted nearby or other signs of surveillance. Even if I'd missed them, nothing about my appearance right now should tip anyone off to my identity.

I ambled through the dingy mall haphazardly, as if I didn't have any particular destination. Just window shopping, whatever the hell that really meant. But when I came into view of the electronics shop, my stomach knotted.

All the other stores were still open. The mall didn't close up until well into the evening. But Scarlett's shop was fully shuttered—not like she'd just stepped out for a moment. Like she'd closed up for the day.

Swinging past it as close as I dared, I noted the faint dusting of grit along the bottom of the shutters where it'd been sprayed by last night's cleaning crew working over the floors. She hadn't opened up at all today, at least. Possibly the shop had been closed for longer.

The memory wavered up of the way she'd talked when I'd come to her store last week, the edge of nervousness in her voice and body language. I'd wondered who she was worried about.

Maybe she'd been right to worry. Jay *and* Scarlett— that couldn't be a coincidence, could it?

I kept my pace casual as I headed back toward the mall entrance, careful not to draw any attention, but my heart was thudding. When I'd made it several blocks from the building, I stopped and dragged in a deep breath. My pulse kept racing on.

The last two people I'd had contact with outside of the crew were missing. What had happened to them—and had it happened because of me?

FOUR

Decima

BLAZE STILL SEEMED cheerful when I returned to the apartment, led by Julius, but he mustn't have had any exciting news, because he nudged his laptop aside and asked, "Find out anything interesting?"

I scratched my hairline, which was still a bit itchy from the wig, and frowned. "They were gone."

Garrison's head snapped up from where he'd been flicking through his phone in the kitchen area while waiting for the kettle to boil, and Talon set down his knitting. "Gone?" the bigger man repeated with a frown.

"Vanished from the face of the Earth. The guy at the bakery hadn't shown up for his shift in at least a couple of days, and the other woman's shop was all closed up." A frown of my own tugged at my lips. "I don't like it."

A laugh tumbled out of Blaze. When I narrowed my eyes at him, not understanding how the situation was funny in any way, he waved his hand. "The bakery, huh? One of your sources works there?"

"Yeah, so what?"

The words had barely left my mouth when I realized the tidbit of information I'd revealed. It hadn't been that long ago when I'd been hiding as much as I possibly could from them.

Garrison had arched his eyebrows, his tone more sardonic than Blaze's. "It wasn't the chocolate chip cookies you wanted out of that place after all."

I rolled my eyes. They knew I'd lied about a hell of a lot of other things. This one wasn't a big deal.

"It was at least as much for the cookies," I retorted. "I know you thought they were amazing too. Anyway, it doesn't matter. My contact there is gone, and anything he could have told me is gone with him. And I have no idea what happened to him or my other contact."

Julius ran his hand along his chin. "It could be that once you'd made contact with them, the household called them in to find out what they knew about *you*."

"Maybe." But how long would that have taken? Why wouldn't they be back sooner?

I shoved those uncomfortable questions aside and focused on Blaze. "I've got nothing. Did you come up with anything here?"

"You mean did his fancy app come up with anything," Garrison remarked.

Both Blaze and I ignored him. Blaze looked back at the computer and made a face. "We might need to move on to plan B."

My heart sank. "The program's gone through all the missing kid reports and didn't get a single match?"

"Well…" He pulled the laptop back to him and started clicking on files. Talon came over and Julius drew closer as I did for a better look. Garrison, being his typical nonchalant self, stayed where he was like he didn't give a shit, but his gaze lingered on us anyway.

"These are the sorts of things I got in the loose matches," Blaze said, motioning to the screen.

I snorted at the first one. "The household didn't change my ethnicity."

One girl in the image—young, no more than two years old—did have gray eyes and black hair like mine, but the shape of her features marked her as clearly East Asian in heritage. I guessed mine weren't *that* different, but they were different enough to set our ancestors continents apart.

"Yeah, I know." Blaze clicked open another, which showed a girl whose eyes, nose, and chin mimicked my toddler self so closely I could see how the software might have picked up on the similarity… but her wavy hair was bright red, and freckles dappled her cheeks. "And this obviously isn't you either, unless they managed to inject permanent dye receptacles right into your hair follicles."

I stared at him for a second. "That's not actually possible, right?"

He chuckled. "No, thank God, or my job would be a lot harder. Anyway, the others are all like this—specific details that make it clear they're not you—and there were no exact matches. I *did* end up connecting one missing toddler to her adult self living out in Des Moines... I'm not sure she has any idea her dad stole her away from her mom after they separated... I sent a tip with the information to the police department who handled the original case so hopefully they can finally set things straight."

He grinned with satisfaction at the victory that had nothing to do with our original mission. It was hard to feel too frustrated about it in the face of his delight at solving some problem, even if it hadn't been ours. He hadn't needed to go to the trouble—he could have shuffled aside that case and moved on—but it'd mattered to him to give the woman and her mother some peace.

There was a lot more to Blaze than the incisive hacker and gleeful backup shooter, wasn't there? As he tapped away at his keyboard to bring up whatever he wanted to show me next, I couldn't help noticing the way his head tilted to the side and his bright brown eyes sharpened with concentration. The late-afternoon sunlight streaming through the apartment's tall windows highlighted the planes of his smoothly handsome face and the light red hair that fell nearly to his shoulders.

Before, his regular flirting and gestures of affection had put me so on guard that I hadn't really appreciated how attractive he was. But when he was caught up in a puzzle, eagerly putting the pieces together, there was no denying he had a certain appeal.

Maybe I should give kindness another chance.

The thought provoked a memory of honeyed words

and a vicious smile that sent a shiver through me. Thankfully, Blaze redirected my thoughts.

"My best guess is that your kidnapping wasn't reported," he said. "Possibly you were taken in a country with an incompetent police force."

"Or she wasn't kidnapped at all," Talon said.

Blaze cocked his head at the other man, and I knit my brow. "What do you mean? The household obviously—"

"They were connected to human trafficking operations," the former military man interrupted, firmly but more gently than I'd usually expect from him. "We found that out during our initial research. Kids who get trafficked aren't always taken from unaware families. It's possible you were sold."

A chill washed over my skin and condensed in my chest. I'd had a vision in my mind since seeing the videos of me as a child—a vision of a happy family who'd loved me and tucked me into bed every night. I'd assumed that it was the only explanation. People didn't just *sell* their children to random criminals, right? My parents wouldn't have looked at me and decided that loving me wasn't worth it.

But they could have done just that. Now that the possibility had been presented, I had to admit it was plausible, especially with the lack of a missing child report. I was coming to recognize that Noelle had been correct about one thing: the world was a dark, brutal place for anyone who didn't have the means to defend themselves.

"It's possible," Blaze admitted, looking between me and

Talon. I could tell that he didn't want to admit it—not with me here. My heart dropped into my stomach, and he drummed his fingers on the table in front of him. "It's more than possible. There's no way to trace the connections if that's the case, though. Even within the organization, any trail of records would be long-destroyed by now."

I swallowed hard. What was the point in searching for my birth parents if they hadn't cared enough to hold on to me to begin with? We didn't know for sure, but did I really want to know if it was? I tried to push down the painful emotions rising through me, but a tendril of hopelessness twined around my gut.

Before I could dwell any longer on the thought of a family who'd purposefully given me over to be trained as a murdering machine, Blaze switched gears, clicking through to a different set of photos—these ones of Noelle. I recognized her emerging from an alley near the entrances to the sewer system where we'd met, and another of her through the windshield of a vehicle stopped at a red light, dressed in the same sleek clothes. A flash of anger burned through my momentary despair.

Whether my family had wanted me or not, the household still had to account for the way they'd treated me. The lies and the training I'd been forced into. The freedom they'd stolen from me. *That* mattered.

"I managed to get these screenshots from traffic and security camera footage from yesterday morning," Blaze said. "They should be clear enough to run the facial recognition on. Since we can't trace your origins, we can see what we can find out about the people who took you, and she's our best lead." He tapped on the touchpad, and the screen started flickering with its search.

I folded my arms over my chest. The idea of spying on Noelle brought out a kneejerk refusal that I tamped down on. The household didn't get to decide what lines I shouldn't cross now. But all the same—

"She's dead. How much are we really going to learn this way?"

Blaze smiled at me and the men flanking me. "I'm hoping that we'll turn up some other associates who are less dead. She's probably had meetups in public places for various reasons. When you don't trust anyone outside your own organization, that's the way to go. And who knows what other connections she might have?" His smile widened. "Silly question. In a few hours, *we'll* know."

"How much can you even search?" I asked, watching the screen. Images streaked into new folders every few seconds, much faster than when he'd been running the search for my childhood face. Of course, most of them were probably loose matches that wouldn't turn out to be Noelle at all.

"My software can crawl through all the still images and video footage that's ever been uploaded onto the internet, from social media sites to news outlets," Blaze announced, his voice warm with pride. "And it'll peek into more private avenues too where I've opened up access. She might be dead, but she'll still give us some answers. And this kind of interrogation is a lot less hassle than the bloody type."

He paused and glanced up at me. "Is this bothering you? I know she was… important to you."

That was probably the best way of putting it. I wasn't sure Noelle had ever cared about me, at least not for anything other than how well I could carry out her assignments. And after finding out that and how thoroughly she'd programmed me to be her tool, I wasn't sure I cared about her either. But her death and my discovery of her betrayal were still so fresh, maybe it made sense that my emotions were a little muddled.

An assassin couldn't afford to focus on emotions. I needed a clear head and a steady hand. Noelle had been right about that too, no matter how many other ways she'd been wrong.

"It's okay," I said. "I want the answers too, as fast as we can get them."

"It looks like we've already got a few exact matches. Let's see what we've dug up…"

He opened a folder and clicked on the first file. A slightly grainy image filled the screen.

It was a selfie, a blond girl posing in front of an old stone statue with her mouth pursed into duck lips. She didn't look remotely like Noelle. I was about to ask Blaze if his software needed a tune-up when my gaze caught on the figures in the background.

Just beyond the girl's shoulder, a woman with dark brown hair was walking along a park path. I could only see her face in profile, but every nerve in my body jangled with recognition. It was Noelle.

And she wasn't alone. She was talking next to a skinny

man with graying hair whose mouth was open in animated conversation. I narrowed my eyes at him, straining my mind.

"Do you know him?" Julius asked.

I shook my head as I committed the details of his face to my memory. I *would* know him if I saw him again. "I didn't usually interact with anyone other than Noelle and Anna within the household. There are probably all kinds of people they worked with who I'd have no idea about."

"It doesn't matter," Blaze said, chipper as ever. "I'll save him and send him through the scans later. Leave no stone unturned."

The next one was a video clip. We had to watch it three times, me leaning closer to the screen with each iteration, before we picked out Noelle in the bottom of the frame at the left side. From the length of her hair, I could tell this footage was from at least a couple of years ago.

She'd briefly turned to glance at something behind her, but around her a mass of other people were gazing toward something up ahead. Several of them were waving signs and banners. I studied them all, not sure what to make of this. "What's going on there?"

Talon pointed to a podium that showed at the upper corner of the shot. "Looks like a political rally. Damien Malik."

Julius made a thoughtful sound. "This must be from when he was running for re-election a few years back."

"Damien Malik?" I said. "Should I know who that is?" I was aware of the current president of the country and various other major figures, but that name sounded familiar only in the vaguest of ways.

"He's a congressman," Garrison spoke up from his spot on the other side of the room, where he wasn't even doing a show anymore of not following our search. "Current majority whip in the House of Representatives. Kind of a big deal for anyone who hasn't been living under a rock."

I glowered at him, half-heartedly wishing I had a rock to toss at his head, and turned back to the screen. Unfortunately, I had to ask, "What exactly does a majority whip do?"

"He's supposed to rile up the rest of the representatives in his party to pass the legislation the president wants," Julius said. "Although there've been murmurs about Malik pushing his own ideas a little harder than people would prefer."

That didn't sound too ominous. When the household wanted to "push an idea," they obviously knocked off whoever was standing in their way rather than just talking about it. I'd presumably helped them do so more times than I wanted to think about.

"Should we read anything into her being there?" I asked.

Blaze shrugged. "I wouldn't think so. A rally would be a good place to blend into the crowd and carry out some kind of surreptitious transaction that has nothing to do with the purpose of the gathering. Can you see if she's reaching out to anyone there?"

We squinted at the recording again, but the part that'd caught Noelle only showed her making that brief turn. We couldn't even see what or who she'd been looking at. I blew out an irritated breath.

"Hey," Blaze said reassuringly, "we've got lots more to get through. Those answers are in here somewhere."

We checked out a few more photos, none of them very enlightening. Here was Noelle walking down a sidewalk alone. Here was Noelle exiting an organic grocery store with a shopping bag over her arm. Here was Noelle sitting at a patio table with a different man from the first picture, but one who was equally unfamiliar to me.

Blaze set that one aside for further investigation and opened the next file, which was another video. The three of us behind him leaned in automatically to take a closer look. But I immediately recognized the scene, so definitively that my heart skipped a beat.

It was a different day. Noelle wore different clothes, and the cast of the light was different, as if the sky had been overcast rather than cloudless. But there was no mistaking the signs and the banner by the podium.

She was at another Damien Malik rally.

Blaze hummed. "Well, that's starting to look like a pattern."

Julius's forehead furrowed. "I'd say."

I stared at the screen—at Noelle, who turned her head to stare straight toward the stage with her usual implacable air.

Was Damien Malik tangled up with the household somehow? And if so, what kind of part did he play in this mess?

FIVE

Garrison

I HAD to admit that it was impressive how quickly Blaze could dig up information, not that I'd ever tell him as much. The last thing he needed was me swelling his head even bigger.

So when I finally let myself come over to join the group discussion after he'd dug up Dess's former trainer at a third Malik rally, I watched him replay the clips without any overt reaction. My gaze slid to Dess instinctively. She was good at hiding her emotions, nearly as good as I was if not better, but even she couldn't stop the tension from showing through right now. Didn't the other guys see it?

Maybe they did and they were just giving her the space to work through her emotions on her own. Why did her response have to itch at *me* so strongly?

As I refocused on the laptop's screen, Dess shifted on her feet. "How could this Malik guy be connected to the household? Does he have some kind of stance that's friendly to criminals?"

I couldn't help snorting at that suggestion. When she gave me a baleful look, I shook my head. "Couldn't be more obvious how out of touch you've been, sweetheart. Anyone who knows anything has heard about how strict Malik is on crime."

Blaze nodded. "He's constantly pushing for harsher sentencing, as well as increased funding and authority for law enforcement."

Dess frowned. "Yeah, that doesn't sound like a guy who'd support kidnapping toddlers and murder for hire. Maybe he was a potential target."

I shrugged, still studying the video recording. It was hard to make out much of this Noelle woman's body language in the mass of the crowd, but she wasn't giving anything away with what I could see. Other than her brief glance backward, she was simply watching the stage where Malik must have been speaking. Was she preparing for some kind of gambit? Standing guard?

I couldn't tell with so little to work with.

"You don't know much about how politics work," I reminded Dess. "People can be total hypocrites, and I'd say that's twice as likely when it comes to our dutiful representatives."

"He's kept a pretty consistent façade if it is one," Julius remarked.

Blaze tapped at the keyboard of his own initiative and brought up a recent news clip of Malik answering questions at a press conference. A twinge of apprehension ran through me. Whenever I saw the guy with his implacable face and his gray hair slicked back impeccably straight, he set off warning bells in my head. That face was a mask—I'd have bet all the money I had in the bank on it.

Of course, every politician wore a mask, just as much as I did. But I couldn't remember ever seeing Malik's so much as waver. It was as complete and unshakeable as those silvery strands smoothed over his skull. Either he didn't have much to hide anyway… or he was so used to hiding that he could do it effortlessly by now.

In my experience, the second possibility was way more likely.

"There's got to be *some* connection, right?" Dess said. "We've found Noelle at three different rallies now, all in different states. And we haven't found her image at any *other* rallies. Just his."

I arched an eyebrow at her. "Maybe she was just a big fan."

Dess glowered at me again. "Of a guy who'd want nothing more than to shove her behind bars for the rest of her life?"

I couldn't hold back a smirk. "Hey, some weirdos get off on that kind of thing."

Dess let out a huff, but the upward twitch of the corners of her mouth suggested she wasn't completely impervious to the joke. "I guess it takes one to know one," she shot back, and it was my turn to restrain a laugh.

As irritating as I sometimes found her ability to snark back at me, I had to admit I kind of enjoyed it as well. She knew how to give as good as she got, and she never got her back up too much about it the way Blaze sometimes did. I wouldn't have dared to say some of the jabs I'd aimed her way at Julius or Talon for fear of my life.

Maybe she did bring something a little bit refreshing into the honed dynamic the four of us had formed.

That thought brought a flash of memory to the front of my mind: her mouth colliding with mine, our brief crash of passion on the rooftop deck. I wet my lips instinctively, lust unfurling in my groin imagining *her* tongue flicking over the same terrain.

She could bring as much heat to her touch as to her banter. Even looking at her gorgeous face and the curves of her slim but powerful frame stirred my dick. Fuck.

I clamped down on those sensations as hard as I could and shoved them away. The fact that I couldn't completely erase the flare of attraction set my teeth on edge. She shouldn't have been able to get under my skin like this. Any emotional pull I couldn't shut off was a weakness.

While I'd been grappling with my dick's desires, the gears had obviously been turning in Blaze's head. "I'll start searching for the other people we've found with Noelle in the photos. That'll help us get a fuller sense of the big picture."

Julius nodded and gave him a brisk pat on the shoulder. "Get to it. And let us know as soon as you find any leads that the rest of us can follow up on."

I inhaled deeply and found my nerves were still jangling too much for comfort. I needed to gather myself and get my head on straight again before I could get back in my element. There were a couple of things that could help with that.

I moved to the kitchen, flicked the kettle on, and grabbed one of my favorite instant cocoas from the cupboard. Just looking at the spread of boxes and tins sent a twinge of nostalgia through my chest that was reassuring despite the pang of homesickness mixed in.

Mixing up a mug of hot cocoa had always been my mom's favorite way of unwinding after a stressful day, and she'd never minded sharing. I liked thinking that every flavor and brand I sampled was in her honor, as if she wasn't missing out on them after all.

"I'll be on the rooftop thinking deep thoughts if anyone needs me," I informed the others, shaking off those remnants of the past.

Dess's gaze had followed my movements. At the sight of the mug, her eyes lit up. She glanced toward the stairs that led to the deck with unusual hesitance and asked, "Do you mind if I join you?"

Did I ask for company? I thought automatically, but I caught the acidic reply before it fell off my tongue. She was grappling with a hell of a lot more than I was. It was a big deck. I could still get my space—and maybe a little more banter with her would bring me back to myself better than solitude. I just had to keep my mind on what mattered.

"As long as you keep your paws off my telescope this time," I said, and grabbed another mug.

By necessity, I'd gotten a very efficient kettle. It was singing in less than a minute, and I filled both of the mugs with a practiced stir to dissolve all the powder and a dollop of cream in mine. I'd noticed Dess preferred hers as unadulterated in its chocolatey-ness as possible. Not that I'd been taking notes or anything.

When I nudged the mug across the island toward her, she scooped it up with an expression of childlike delight. The gleeful glow in her face contrasted with the hardened killer I knew her to be so completely that it tugged at something in my chest. I couldn't tell whether I was relieved or regretting that I'd agreed to include her.

I opened the door and let her climb the stairs to the deck ahead of me, definitely not ogling her pert ass in those well-fitted jeans. When we came out into the cool evening air, Dess stepped off to the side. She gazed up at the moon as she took another sip, and then closed her eyes with a smile of absolute bliss that made me want to lick the cocoa right off her mouth.

"I never thought I'd find someone who enjoys this stuff as much as I do," I said, to stop myself from simply standing there drooling over her. "Somehow you've got me beat."

"I've been chocolate-deprived," Dess replied. "Got to make up for lost time." She took a gulp followed by a pleased hum that went straight to my groin and then fixed her dark gray eyes on me with a glimmer of mischief. "I assume this cup isn't going to knock me out?"

I winced inwardly. I'd never admitted to drugging her first drink with us, but it wasn't surprising that she'd clued in. "You were hiding a lot from us back then," I reminded her. "We were taking necessary precautions."

"Well, at least those precautions came with a whole lot of chocolate-y goodness, so I guess I'll forgive you that one transgression."

"Thank you so very much," I muttered. "If I'd known we were dealing with the Ghost, I might have spiked it with something stronger."

She laughed. "I'm an assassin, not an elephant."

The humor in her voice set me at ease again. "Are you sure?" I asked. "We do know you a lot better now, but I'm not assuming there aren't a few things you're still hiding."

"If I decide to take off my human suit, you'll be the first to know." She paused, breathing in the steam from the mug and returning her gaze to the sky. The amusement faded from her face. "*I* didn't even know how much I was hiding from you back then. I had no idea how complicated my situation was."

The trace of anguish in her voice made my chest constrict. "We'll figure out the truth," I assured her. "There's nothing Blaze can't ferret out. Just don't tell him I gave him that vote of confidence."

This time, the joke didn't budge her pensiveness. She swiped her hand across her mouth. "I know. It's just... weird. I feel like I've been playing a role all this time without even realizing it—and I have no idea who I really am beyond that role. I want to be someone real, not just what Noelle and her associates sculpted me into. But I don't know where to start finding that person."

Most people would never understand the desire to stop pretending and start being herself. *Most.* Her words struck a chord deep inside me, somewhere that I hadn't been affected in far too long.

I'd built my life around playing roles and being the person my crew and my clients expected me to be. Being real—yeah, that was the tricky part.

But I could tell she was talking genuinely with me right now, offering more honesty than I was sure I'd earned.

"You're getting there," I said, with the urge to match her openness with my own. "The real you is clearly a chocolate addict."

Her smile came back, a minor victory. "Okay, I'll give you that."

"And simply recognizing that you feel a little lost— that's something real too."

Her attention settled on me, and I had the impression she was evaluating my own motives. "Do *you* really think so?" she asked. "Or are you just trying to get me to open up about my secret elephant nature?"

A chuckle tumbled out of me. "I guess you'll never know."

She grimaced. "I'm not sure I can even tell with myself. Putting on a front has become so automatic."

I knew what she meant there too. Her candor loosened my tongue more than before. The question fell out before I could second-guess the impulse. "Were you being real when you kissed me up here before?"

Dess considered me intently enough that heat washed over my skin without her even moving. "It was strategic," she said finally. "I was using the kiss to get something I wanted. But if it makes you feel better about it, I did like it too." The corner of her mouth quirked upward. "Didn't you?"

From that coy smile, I had to assume she'd been able to tell how much I had. But I hadn't expected her to answer so honestly on that subject either. For a second, I lost my voice.

"I don't know," I heard myself saying, with the same automatic defensiveness she'd admitted to in herself. "It was over awfully fast."

The sly gleam came back into Dess's eyes. She set her mug down on the nearest table and stepped toward me. "Well, I guess there's one easy way to confirm."

Then she grasped my shirt by the collar and bobbed up to capture my mouth with hers.

I'd been lying when I'd said I didn't remember whether I liked the last kiss, and this one brought that lie into sharp relief in an instant. I liked this—hell yes, I did.

I ran my fingers along her jaw and tugged her just a little closer to deepen the kiss, savoring the tart sweetness of her mouth the way she'd reveled in her drink. Her arms wound around the back of my neck, and I couldn't resist bringing my other hand to her hips and pulling her flush against me.

She let out a little growl that electrified me from head to toe. When she ground her groin against mine, I just about spontaneously combusted.

Holy hell, this was some woman. Why had I wanted to avoid getting tangled up in her again?

My cock had hardened in an instant, straining against

the fly of my jeans. I kissed Dess harder, flicking my tongue between her lips to duel with hers. Her fingers curled against my scalp with a flurry of sparks, and I nudged her backward so she was pinned between me and the wall. The way her body molded against mine, somehow soft and tough all at once, had my nerves clanging with need.

Just how long could I wait before I buried myself right inside her?

No sooner had that question crossed my mind than footsteps thumped on the steps leading to the deck. With a mumbled curse, I tore myself away from Dess. I jerked my shirt straight and willed the flush on my skin to cool just as Talon appeared at the top of the stairs.

He looked from me to Dess, who'd propped herself against the wooden wall with her arms folded over her chest as if nothing at all unusual had been going on. The moonlight shone off his shaved head. His icy blue eyes gave no sign of suspicion, but Talon might not have cared even if he could guess what we'd been up to.

"Dinner's here," he said. "Steffie brought takeout from that Greek place down the street."

Dess straightened up. "Great. I'm starving."

Talon nodded and headed back down. Dess started after him, but as she passed me, she brushed her hand across mine.

"So," she murmured. "Do we have a verdict?"

It took a second for my brain to catch up. My cocky attitude snapped back into place over the walls I'd dropped for just a moment.

"I liked it just as much as you did," I replied dryly, and ignored the pang of longing that resonated through me at the flash of her smile before I watched her graceful form move down the stairs ahead of me.

Maybe even more. And that right there still felt like a problem.

SIX

Decima

I KNEW something was up the next morning the moment I entered the kitchen and saw all the guys talking around Julius's card table of army figures. They spoke quietly, not even glancing over as I grabbed a glass of water. I lingered for a moment, trying to catch a snippet of conversation.

Then it clicked.

This scene looked familiar. It was exactly what I'd seen when they'd been planning their last mission. I watched as Julius moved a few figures across the board, and Talon readjusted one, saying something in his usual low tone. Blaze shifted from foot to foot as he added a few lines to a sketch on the whiteboard, and Garrison monitored the expressions of his friends rather than the board itself.

I itched to go over and find out what they were up to

now, but... this was their work. If they'd wanted me involved, they'd have asked me, right?

They were doing so much to help me without my even asking them to, without my having any hope of repaying them in any material way. I didn't want to overstep and sour the budding peace we'd made.

The restless itch didn't leave with those thoughts, though. I turned and headed back to my room, which held both my cot and the guys' exercise equipment. Working out was always my go-to method of burning off tension.

As I stepped onto the treadmill, I paused. How much was this habit my own, and how much was it simply something Noelle had drilled into me?

My hesitation only lasted a few seconds. My trainers had pushed me to stay strong and lean, but when I'd decided that I needed a release in the middle of the night, it hadn't been Noelle who'd compelled me to do sets of cardio exercises. I'd turned to that outlet of my own accord.

I set the pace slow to start, a brisk walk that transformed quickly into a jog. When my legs felt warm and supple, I turned the jog into a sprint and finished the last quarter of a mile. As the second mile rolled around, I sprinted half of it and slowed to a jog. By the time I finally slowed to a walk again, my breath was coming a little rough. Good.

I took myself through some stretches, and then I jumped into a weight training rotation that had me sprawling on the floor, breathless and satiated. The rush of exhausted exhilaration after a good workout was something that I'd never be able to top any other way.

Well, maybe I'd found at least one other way recently. My attention settled on the weight rack for a moment, remembering Talon's firm hands hefting me up there, his body scorching against mine, his cock filling me. A giddy flush rose over my body.

I stood and strode toward the cabinet against the wall, pulling out a scratchy towel and wiping away my sweat. When I brushed the towel over my face, I caught a hint of laundry detergent, but it had been overpowered by the reek of male perspiration. Despite being clean, the towel still smelled of musk from overuse.

I couldn't stop myself from running it over my face again and breathing in the scent deeply. It reminded me of Talon—of how sweaty we'd gotten during the collision of our bodies in that very atypical workout the other day.

The exercise hadn't totally burned away my restlessness, though. My nerves still twitched with uncertainty. I needed something more.

I stalked out into the common room to find the guys had vanished while I'd been working out. Steffie had arrived and was wiping down the kitchen sink. Giving her a wide berth, I paced from one end of the apartment to the other. That didn't help. I clearly wasn't going anywhere.

"Full of bees," Steffie said in her dry voice.

I turned toward her. "What?"

She swiped her cloth across the kitchen island. "Full of bees. It's what my mother always used to say when I couldn't sit still. Like I had a hive riled up inside me. A frequent problem of Blaze's, you might have noticed. Seems like you've got the same difficulty at the moment." She shot me a crooked smile that didn't totally fit with the grandmotherly vibe of her gray-and-white streaked bun of hair and softly plump figure.

"Yeah…" I wasn't sure how much to say to her. The guys had introduced me briefly to the woman who took care of their cleaning and errands, but I'd barely spoken to her before. Did she even know what they'd found out about who I was and why I was here?

I ambled over and started unloading the dishwasher, which was both something to occupy myself and a show of solidarity. Joining someone in their work was one way of forming a connection. I'd mostly used that trick with targets I was planning to kill, but there was no reason it couldn't work with a potential ally.

Steffie raised her eyebrows but didn't shoo me away. When I was halfway through sticking the dishes back in the cupboards, I judged it safe to venture, "How long have you been working for the crew anyway?"

"Oh, years and years," she said. "I watched them train Garrison in. But obviously I have seniority over all of them." She winked at me.

"So, what, they put up a job application online or something?"

She burst out laughing: a rich, vibrant sound that spoke of a big personality within her subdued exterior.

"That wouldn't do for work like this. No, I was… part of a job, and they decided it was a good idea to keep me on to do jobs for them."

It was hard to keep my jaw from dropping. I had a sudden image of Steffie stalking through dark corridors alongside the guys with a gun in her hand, which would have seemed totally ridiculous if not for the glint in her eyes. "A job? I mean—I know what kind of jobs they do."

"Yes, they mentioned that the air had been cleared." She moved to start wiping down the front of the fridge, scrubbing hard at a few stray splatters of food. For a minute, I thought she might have decided she didn't trust me enough to say anything else. Then she sucked in her breath.

"They're good boys—you should know that. I'd been sold to the people they were hired to go after. People who used me as a slave. I'd been with them for years too. I hardly remembered… I didn't have anything but my name when Julius set me free. But he saw something in me and he knew I'd been cleaning for the men who'd 'owned' me, so he suggested that I could look after this apartment for them. And then when that worked out, other properties they wanted kept up. And other responsibilities on top of that." She shot a glance at me over her shoulder with a quirk of her lips. "I know a good situation when I've got one. I made myself as useful as possible."

The thought of Julius extending that offer of kindness to her wasn't too hard to believe after he'd opened his home to me too, but hearing her explanation sent a waft of warmth through me. These men were killers, but they weren't *just* that, any more than I was.

"You have your own place now and everything?" I asked.

"Oh, yes." Steffie beamed with obvious pride. "Blaze found the perfect apartment for me nearby. I pay for it all myself with my earnings—a woman needs some independence. Now I have a space just for me."

I could tell how much that mattered to her. Maybe I understood that emotion more than she realized. I'd had a space of my own in the household, but even those rooms hadn't really been *mine*. Everything that'd belonged to me in the household had been constructed around their needs and what they wanted from me.

"I'm glad you got out of that awful situation," I said honestly.

Steffie nodded and went back to her cleaning. "They didn't have to offer their hands to help me up, but they did without hesitation. I'd do anything for them. I'd kill for those boys."

Her faint accent that I couldn't quite place thickened her words, and I could hear the slight warning behind them. *Hurt them, and you'll regret it.* But after the rest of her story, I respected her more for her vehement devotion.

"They've earned it," I said, and she smiled again.

With the dishwasher empty and Steffie reabsorbed in her tasks around the apartment, I meandered over to the television. I hadn't had much chance to make use of it in my past life. Maybe it could provide the stimulation my body insisted I still needed.

I picked up the remote and flipped through the channels, wishing I knew how to bring up that show Blaze had tracked down for me with the spy lady and her husband. None of the scenes that flashed by me grabbed my attention. I started hitting the button so hard that I'd already switched channels when my gaze caught an image that made my heart stutter.

I flipped back as quickly as I could. The newscast was just cutting away from Damien Malik's face. "With Representative Malik's proposal shut down by one swing vote, it remains to be seen what steps he'll take next to forward the party's agenda," the reporter said in that droning monotone they all seemed to use.

Then she started talking about a heatwave in Alabama, as if I cared about that. I glared at the TV, but the force of my will couldn't make the show switch back to talking about Malik again.

Oh, well. It wasn't as if it'd sounded like what they were talking about connected to the household anyway. It'd just be easier for me to understand Noelle's interest in the man if I knew more about him.

What had his recent proposal been? Something to crack down on criminals, like the guys had said he liked to do?

I shut off the TV and leaned back on the couch with a deep sigh.

A familiar baritone voice carried from one of the bedroom doorways. "You look like you're contemplating the meaning of life."

I jerked straighter on the sofa and turned to meet

Julius's assessing gaze. Something about the boss of the crew always made me want to impress him, to show how together and capable I was—as if I hadn't already proven that in both my dealings with his crew and the history of assignments they'd only just realized belonged to me.

"Not exactly," I said. "Just the meaning of the household."

"Come up with anything?" he asked, ambling over.

I couldn't stop my gaze from lingering on the ample brawn of his massive body flexing beneath his fitted T-shirt and dark jeans. Anyone with eyes could have recognized that he was one prime specimen of manhood. The kindness Steffie had told me about somehow brought that appeal into even sharper relief.

I shook myself mentally. Less than a week ago, I'd hooked up with Talon. Yesterday I'd been admiring Blaze's looks and kissing Garrison. And now some part of me was wondering what it'd be like to have the man in charge pinning me down on this sofa?

Was there really anything wrong with that? If I was interested in all of them, and they were interested in me…

Maybe there wasn't a problem with that, but I didn't actually know that Julius was interested in anything other than maintaining the order in his home now that I'd crashed into it.

"No," I said, remembering his question. "I guess that's the problem." I turned back around and frowned at my hands in my lap. "Every part of my body is clamoring to do *something*. To take action. But I don't have anything *to* do."

Julius leaned against the back of the sofa at the other side, a few feet away but close enough that my skin tingled with my awareness of his presence. "What did you do at the household when you were between missions? It doesn't sound like they had you constantly on the go."

"No," I admitted. "I guess it's just... I'm *not* really between missions, am I? I'm on one right now—the one to figure out where I came from, who exactly took me, and why—but I have no idea how to carry it out. So far Blaze has been doing all the work. I don't have any innovative computer programs I can put to use."

Julius hummed, the warm sound washing right through my nerves. "Well, I'm not sure I can help you with that mission, considering I don't have any action *I* can take toward it either while Blaze is still working his technological magic. But how would you feel about putting your skills to use in other ways in the meantime?"

My gaze shot back to him, a jolt of adrenaline racing through me at the implication of his words. "What did you have in mind?"

Julius smiled, his deep blue eyes brightening at my enthusiasm. "How would you like to work with the Chaos Crew on a job?"

I blinked. It was hard for me to imagine being part of their work. The two jobs I'd witnessed—after or nearly at completion—had been a totally different style from my type of job. The way the crew worked was purposefully messy and, well, chaotic. And they obviously had their roles down in perfect cohesion and cooperation.

He continued before I could reply. "If you're not

comfortable with it or you want to recover more from your injuries before pushing yourself, you're under no obligation, but I'd love to see the infamous Ghost at work."

I bent my wrist, not feeling even a tinge of pain from it anymore. The car accident that had bruised my ribs and sprained my wrist could have been so much worse, but even a wrecked car couldn't get the drop on me for long. I no longer needed the brace, and aside from an occasional twinge of pain in my ribs, I was good as new. No weaknesses to hold me back.

"What *is* the job?" I asked.

"It's a fairly straightforward one. Go in, kill the assholes we've been hired to kill, get out. We're taking care of it tonight." He cocked his head. "Having watched you fight while injured, I expect it'll be quite a show seeing you fully in action."

Was that a flicker of another kind of interest in his eyes? I'd swear I caught a hint of the same heat that was trickling through me at his nearness, but it was there and gone so quickly I couldn't quite tell. Julius didn't hold up walls of defensiveness the same way Garrison did, and he wasn't as impassive as Talon seemed to be naturally, but he kept his emotions close.

"I usually work pretty differently from you and the crew," I had to point out.

Julius shrugged. "It'd be a trial run. Maybe it'll turn out to be a bad idea... or maybe it'll be a brilliant one." He shot me a rare smile that showed his teeth—and nearly melted the panties right off me.

I still wasn't sure about the whole chaos thing, but the prospect of getting to do any kind of work sent a thrill through me. And this was an awfully immense show of trust. Julius had enough faith in me to invite me along and let me take part in the kind of job he staked the crew's reputation on.

That alone felt like more than enough reason to jump at the chance.

I only had one more hesitation. I'd been forced to kill people for years—people I now knew might not have done anything all that wrong. Going forward, I could make those decisions for myself.

I studied Julius's expression. "Are we sure that the people you're taking down deserve it?"

Julius analyzed me right back, scanning my face as if evaluating my motives for asking the question. It really was very simple. The killing itself didn't bother me, but I wanted to know who I killed and why I killed them. The idea of murdering someone innocent—someone who didn't deserve the brutal wrath reaped by the Chaos Crew —made my skin crawl.

Maybe Julius could read some of that with his gaze. "It's important to you that we don't kill innocents."

"Yes," I said firmly. "It is."

He smiled again, slower and softer, but somehow this one sent an even deeper surge of attraction racing through me. "Good. We feel the same way. I believe in dealing out justice alongside the chaos. We require that our clients provide information on the targets' background, and Blaze confirms it independently. We only accept jobs that involve marks who've been doing plenty of destruction of their own."

A sense of certainty clicked into place inside me, as if this was exactly what I'd been waiting for. "All right," I said. "I'm in."

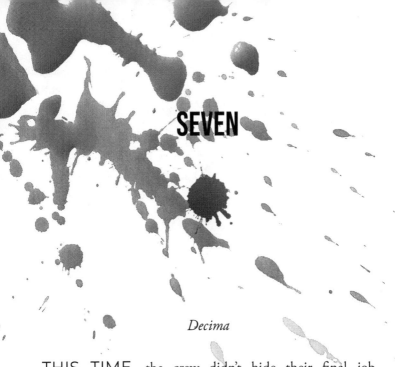

SEVEN

Decima

THIS TIME, the crew didn't hide their final job preparations from me. So I got a clear view of the tactical vests, weapons cases, and other mission paraphernalia they were assembling near the door.

"Did you rob an army surplus store?" I couldn't help asking.

Garrison released a harsh laugh, and Julius shot him a pointed look. I wondered if there had been an argument that I'd missed while they'd been gearing up for the mission.

Garrison cast his gaze over me next. "Better to be overly prepared than not at all," he said, eyeing the exercise clothes I still wore from earlier.

"Where do you expect me to get an appropriate outfit for a job like this—out of my ass? I don't even know what the job is."

Julius spoke up before the younger man could get another word in edgewise. "We've got a few more pieces to see to. We'll pick you up some tactical clothes on our way back. Garrison, you can stay and fill Dess in on the details of the mission."

The blond man's eyebrows shot up. "You're leaving me behind now? What am I, the babysitter?"

His boss looked like he was restraining himself from rolling his eyes. Or strangling Garrison. I could relate to both impulses, as much as I'd enjoyed kissing him last night.

"You're supposed to be the smooth talker in the crew," Julius reminded him. "I think you can handle a little conversation. Your skills aren't required for this last bit of prep."

Garrison grumbled wordlessly under his breath, but he didn't raise another overt protest as the other guys tramped out of the apartment. I studied him, my nerves prickling.

Was he really that annoyed about having to spend time with me? I'd thought we'd made a sort of peace on the rooftop, but maybe I'd been wrong. There was still so much I didn't really get about relating to other human beings, at least ones I wasn't supposed to be either training with or murdering.

It shouldn't have mattered anyway. Caring about things like whether people *liked* me only complicated my life.

But that way of thinking, that forming social bonds wasn't important—that was definitely Noelle's teaching. How could it be anything else when I'd never had the chance to live any other way? Part of me was starting to think I'd appreciate a few complications of that sort.

"Why don't we go up to the deck?" I suggested. Garrison usually seemed more at ease there, and I liked the atmosphere too. "I could use some fresh air."

Garrison marched ahead of me without a word and led the way up. He didn't wait for me, striding right out onto the deck while leaving the door open, and stood with his back to me as I emerged.

"I'm sure that Julius explained that this is one of our easier missions," he said abruptly. "You shouldn't have much to worry about."

I grimaced at his back. "I wasn't worried. It would be nice to know what we're actually doing, though. I can handle whatever it is, but I prefer to go in *prepared*, like you mentioned earlier."

Garrison finally turned to look at me. It wasn't a sidelong glance or a hostile glower. He considered me analytically. "I know you can handle it."

That ounce of approval settled my nerves. I didn't need reassurance when my track record spoke for itself, but it was good to know that Garrison was still capable of moods other than intense snark.

He flopped into a lounge chair near his precious telescope, and I ambled closer. I propped myself against the wall nearby. "So, the job…"

"All right already. We're going to L.A. Via private jet, obviously, since regular airlines won't accept all of our equipment."

I blinked. "You guys own a whole *jet*?"

Garrison smirked. "Well, half wouldn't get us very far." Then he sobered up enough to add, "It's not ours. The client is paying for it. Our skills are in high demand, so we get requests all over the country, sometimes overseas, and for those we require travel in style as part of the payment. They're happy to supply the vehicle in exchange for having us doing their dirty work."

"Wow." I'd never thought about just how much the crew might be getting paid for their work. I'd never seen any money from my missions—and when would I have had a chance to spend it anyway?

Had the household profited from my kills? I'd assumed all my targets were people they personally wanted taken down, but it was possible they'd hired me out to other parties too, wasn't it? The thought made me want to scrub my skin raw.

Just how many ways had they exploited me?

I shook off those unsettling questions and focused on Garrison again. "And who are the targets of this job?"

Garrison lifted his eyes skyward. "We're supposed to shoot up some people on an indie studio movie set. The production's being run by a bunch of gangsters who cast themselves and all their buddies into the roles. From what I gathered in our conversation, not that he admitted this outright, the client is pissed that he wasn't invited to join in. So he's hiring us for revenge."

"Wait, this man is having you kill people because he's jealous? You guys get involved in that kind of drama?"

Garrison laughed darkly. "Half of our jobs are based on this kind of drama. All that matters to Julius is that the people we're taking down are scummy too; the reasons we're getting paid to do it don't really matter."

"You have to admit that this setup sounds a little bizarre."

"It's ridiculous, but it should be a cut and dry job. They're all doofuses, so it won't take long to get in, make a bloody mess of killing them, and get out. Blaze said that there isn't much security from the digital standpoint, as far as he can tell from a distance."

"We're going to go in based on what he can tell from across the country?"

Garrison narrowed his eyes at me. "Of course not. He always takes a survey of the situation on location once we arrive. We're not idiots."

I held up my hands. "I was just asking. I've never worked with anyone before."

"Right, the lone wolf. You should give us a little credit."

His tone had turned cutting again. I frowned. "Do you have a problem with me coming along?"

He propped his arms behind his head. "Why would I have a problem with the famous Ghost coming along for a joyride?"

I narrowed my eyes at him. "I don't know. Why don't you tell me?"

"How about this?" Garrison said. "You don't know who you are or where you belong, so you sure as hell can't know how you'll fit in with us. That kind of uncertainty gets people killed."

"The only people who are going to get killed tonight

are the ones we were hired to kill. I'm absolutely certain about that. I don't let my personal life get in the way of a mission."

"So you say. I'm just not all that keen on giving that theory a test run with real guns and real bad guys."

I pushed off the wall and stepped closer to him. If he was going to try to push my buttons, I'd push his right back. "Is that really it, or are you worried about your *own* performance? You do seem to have a habit of getting a little... distracted when I'm around."

Garrison scoffed. "Now you're just making shit up."

I let a knowing smile play with my lips. "I don't think so. Although if you've forgotten what happened the last time we were up here, maybe you should get that head of yours checked out."

He shoved himself out of the lounger to face me eye to eye. The heat in his gaze scorched through me all the way to my pussy. "I remember that *you* couldn't keep your hands off me. I'd say that makes you the problem more than me."

I snorted. "Oh, yeah, and you were *such* an unwilling participant."

Garrison's tongue flicked across his lips, and the sight sent another wash of heat through me. If he was a complication, then yeah, some part of me wanted to dive right in. Especially if that would mean releasing the tension that'd been building between us since the first time I'd planted my lips on his days ago.

"Why shouldn't I take what's freely offered?" he said.

"It doesn't mean I'm going to be dreaming about happily ever afters while we're getting down to work."

I cocked my head. "Who said anything about happily ever after? Ecstatic right now sounds good to me."

He waggled his eyebrows, taking a step closer. "I'm glad you have so much confidence in my ability to make you scream."

"I don't know. So far you seem to be all hot air and no follow-through."

I gave him a light nudge to the chest, both to provoke him and as an excuse to feel the taut, lean muscles beneath his button-up. Oh boy, did he respond. The next second, I found myself shoved against the wooden wall with Garrison's hands on my waist and his hips pressed tight against mine.

"I'll show you follow-through," he muttered, his breath searing over my lips, and slammed his mouth into mine.

The times before, there'd been a hint of hesitation to his kiss. Even when our mouths had collided and he'd kissed me back with a surge of passion, part of him had been holding back, not quite letting go.

This was different. He was taking what he wanted with every particle of his body where it aligned with mine, and the need radiating through him turned me into a puddle.

His tongue swept into my mouth, clearing away all tastes that weren't *him*. I wound my arms around his waist, pulling him closer as I rose to my toes to deepen the kiss. One of his hands rose to twine his fingers in my hair, hanging loose down my back. He tugged, pulling my head back to expose my neck to him.

Garrison kissed his way down to the hollow of my throat with a force that left me breathless. When he nipped my collarbone, I gasped. His grip on me tightened. I'd known he had a fire in him that could burn us up together, and now that he was releasing it, I wanted nothing more than to go to all the way up in flames.

Garrison nibbled his way over to my shoulder, yanking my shirt to the side to get better access to the crook of my neck. Then he paused, pulling back just enough to speak with his lips grazing my skin. "You're not going to suddenly go all assassin on my ass like you did with Blaze if I get any more handsy, are you?"

A flush that was more embarrassment than desire this time tickled over my skin, remembering the incident all the guys had witnessed—when I'd slammed Blaze into a kitchen counter after he'd flirted with me. I dug my fingers into Garrison's shirt.

"There are certain overtures that I have... bad associations with," I said. "And so they set off a defensive reaction. As long as you don't get too sweet on me, we should be able to manage this without you getting your ass kicked."

Garrison chuckled with a wash of hot breath, but when he lifted his head to meet my eyes, I thought I saw a glimmer of understanding there. Of course the master at reading people would be able to piece together enough from my brief explanation to guess.

To my relief, he didn't pry any further. The corners of

his lips curled wickedly. "You want it rough and hard then, huh?"

A thrill raced through my veins at the promise in his voice. I grinned back at him. "Do your worst."

The words had barely left my mouth when he was slamming me back into the wall. His hand dipped down and shoved inside my sweatpants.

"Do you want to know what I'm going to do to you, Dess?" he asked as the pants tumbled down my legs and only his hand remained against my panties, caressing the spot at the apex of my thighs teasingly. I bucked into his hand, and he laughed. When I looked down at the way he worked me, he gripped my chin and forced me to meet his eyes. The grip wasn't quite bruising, but it showed he understood exactly what I needed. "I asked you a question."

Anticipation unfurled through my belly. "What— what are you going to do?" I whispered eagerly.

He released my chin and tore the panties right off me. Then he plunged one of his long fingers inside of me as he continued working my clit.

"Sweetheart, I'm going to fuck you so hard that you're going to beg for me to slow down." He bent closer to my ear, growling the next part. "But I'm not going to. Not until you fucking *explode.*"

A giddy shiver passed through me, watching him take on an even more asshole-ish persona than the one he usually wore—one determined to get me off by any means necessary. Oh, yes, please. Garrison must have noticed, because he straightened his shoulders and licked his bottom lip. He was so fucking hot when he wasn't being a prick. Or at least, when he was being a prick for my benefit instead of to heckle me.

Speaking of pricks…

I reached forward and curled my fingers around his erect cock through his pants. At the first stroke, he jerked against me with an involuntary thrust. "As long as you explode with me," I murmured. The dark smile that spread across his face fueled my hunger, sending jolts of excitement through my veins.

Without warning, Garrison spun me around. I had to whip my hands out to catch myself against the wall. His fingers didn't miss a beat, one now circling my clit, another delving deep inside me for that even more sensitive place far within. He didn't stop until I jerked and cried out, the sweet spot inside getting more sensitive with every blissful stroke.

"Down you go, sweetheart," he said, slapping my back like a light spank. "You'll take this whether you like it or not."

I'd seen him in action—I knew he could have struck hard enough to hurt me if he'd wanted to. He was finding the balance between giving me what I needed and keeping me safe, and somehow that turned me on even more. My mouth watered as I bent at the waist, my forearms sliding down the wall.

The sound of torn foil told me he'd had protection on hand, thank God—I was so tangled up with need I might have told him to keep going without it. I had a birth control implant, but I had no idea how cautious these men usually were when it came to other possible consequences of casual sex.

Garrison's pants dropped, and there was a soft hiss as he must have slicked the condom over his erection. Arousal flooded my sex. My pussy felt as if it were dripping.

He gripped both of my hips forcefully, tugging my ass back to meet him, and then he thrust into my cunt without a moment of preamble.

I saw stars.

He hadn't lied when he'd said that he'd fuck me hard. His thighs pistoned back and forth, his cock ramming into me as deep as it could go. Pleasure rushed through me with every thrust, and I cried out for him, loud enough that the people way down on the street below might have heard. I didn't give a fuck.

Garrison reached around and grabbed hold of my chin again, grasping it as he pounded into my cunt. I arched toward him as my climax swelled within me. My noises of pure pleasure multiplied until everything came crashing down—rupturing and leaving me shattered beneath him, barely able to hold up my own body with legs that had become jelly.

As my channel clamped around him, he gave a pleased grunt. Instead of continuing to his own release right then, he withdrew with a jerk and tugged me around so fast I swayed. He lay me down on the lounger, prowling over me, his hazel eyes darker than I'd ever seen them.

"I could fuck this pussy all day," he murmured. Then he plunged into me again.

As he fucked me the second time, his gaze held mine, searing with his own desire. His ragged breathing matched mine, carrying through the air around us. With each buck of his hips, I spiraled toward a second release. I barely felt the thick cushions beneath me.

I wrapped my arms around Garrison, digging my fingernails into his back. His chest hitched, and he pushed even deeper inside me, raising my hips to meet him at a better angle. The rush of sensation nearly had me sobbing.

He wasn't being half as rough now as he'd been before, but I was so lost in the moment it didn't matter. I'd have killed anyone who tore us apart before I reached my peak.

Thankfully, it didn't come to that. Garrison plowed into me, and a renewed wave of ecstasy flooded my nerves. My eyes rolled back to take in the light speckling of stars across the evening sky. My moan reverberated off the walls.

Garrison bowed his head over me with a deep groan of his own. He gripped the sides of the lounger as his movements grew choppy. With one final thrust, he sagged over me, barely holding himself up with his elbows.

Before he suffocated me under his weight, he rolled to the side, tipping me with him so we both fit on the lounger together. The cool air licked over my naked legs. Neither of us had bothered stripping off our shirts, but the half-nakedness felt weirdly more intimate than if we'd been totally nude. It was a testament to how desperately we'd needed this moment.

I didn't know what to say, but there didn't seem to be

any need for words. I lay there in the cocoon of warmth we'd formed, savoring the afterglow.

Garrison stroked his hand over my hair and along my jaw. He tipped my chin up just enough to press a kiss on my lips that felt almost tender, especially after the brutality with which we'd initially come together.

If he'd led with that move, my body would have flinched with panic. After what we'd just done, I was relaxed enough with him that it didn't bother me. He'd been nothing like the man who'd violated me so horribly. He *was* nothing like that man.

When Garrison lay his head against the cushions again, I peeked over at him. Curiosity stirred inside me. He hadn't shied away from the role-play I'd asked for— and he'd more than delivered. He must be fairly experienced. More than I was, but then, who wasn't? All the amazing sensations of sex were one more freedom the household had stolen from me for too long.

"Do you get a chance to do this sort of thing—with other women—very often?" I asked, tilting my head to the side to watch his expression. "I mean, I'm guessing it's hard to keep up a relationship in your line of work."

Garrison's lips twitched, whether with amusement or discomfort, I couldn't tell. "Yeah, but it doesn't matter to me. I haven't been looking for a relationship anyway."

I let out a teasing huff. "Who's the real lone wolf then?"

"At least I know how to *work* with other people on a regular basis," Garrison retorted. He kept his tone light, but a trace of tension wound through it.

"I'm sure there are a few emotional—and other— needs that the rest of the crew can't quite fulfill for you. Nothing so strange about that." I paused. "I guess that's a trade-off to this kind of life."

Garrison shifted, easing a little apart from me. "It's not a trade-off. Some people aren't interested in grand romance or becoming a family man. I'm perfectly happy with the life I'm already leading."

I squinted at him in the growing darkness, having trouble believing him. Garrison was a master not just of reading people but of presenting himself to others the way he wanted. I wasn't sure I'd ever seen him without some kind of mask on. How much was he hiding even from himself?

"Is that really true?" I asked without thinking. "Or is it just easier to tell yourself and everyone else that because you don't think you can have everything you'd really want anyway?"

Garrison heaved upright and grabbed his pants. "I'll thank you to save the psychoanalysis for someone who needs it," he snapped, any lingering tenderness wiped away. Before I could figure out what I'd done wrong or how to fix it, he stalked across the rooftop and down the stairs.

EIGHT

Decima

THE FLIGHT to L.A. was far shorter than I'd expected, and once the wheels hit the ground, the guys sprang into motion. By the time the sun had fully set, they had the plan solidified.

The studio was a squat brick building on the outskirts of the city, about as far from actual Hollywood as you could get while still being within the L.A. city limits. I approached the two security guards on the outside of the side door, peering around the street as if I were lost or looking for something. The warehouses nearby were either abandoned or shut down for the night. There was no one around but us and the shadows.

This was my first act on the job, so I intended to prove just how much of an asset I was. I meandered past the guards without a glance at them, pretending to be too distracted to take notice.

"Hey, sweet cheeks," one called out just after I'd passed him.

I was already whipping into action. I swung around and disarmed the guy who'd spoken with a brisk snap of my hands. A second later, I gave him a kick to the gut that sent him staggering toward a darkened alleyway—where Julius yanked him aside and put a bullet across the back of his head with a splatter of blood and brains.

The remaining guard was mine to handle, and I made it quick, dodging his fist and snapping the gun from his grasp. When he threw another punch, I allowed his momentum to drive him forward while I slipped behind him, wrapping an arm around his throat. The crack of his neck took only a sharp jerk of my body, and he fell to the pavement dead.

I turned and looked at Julius—his tactical uniform already speckled in blood. The black material masked it well, but in the hazy glow of the security lights, the liquid glints shone. He'd made a mess of his kill while I'd done mine clean, like I'd been taught. Suddenly my meticulousness wasn't a benefit. A prickle of uncertainty ran through my body.

If I wanted to fit in with the crew, I needed to do things their way. *Expertly orchestrated chaos*, Blaze had recited for me gleefully. The gore made an impact that their clients wanted.

Well, I could learn. How better to learn than on my feet, watching them in action as an immediate model?

Julius didn't remark on the difference between our kills, and neither did the other three men as they converged on us, though I thought Garrison raised his eyebrow with a hint of disdain at my corpse. He'd barely spoken to me since our evening hookup, and he didn't break that pattern now.

We slipped into the studio, where large swaths of fabric hung from the industrial-height ceiling to section off the filming set. Julius, Talon, and Garrison headed to the left, while Blaze and I headed to the right, setting our feet so we didn't make any noise. It didn't sound as if the actors and crew were likely to hear us over the melodramatic shouts carrying from the soundstage.

"All is lost! How can we ever regain our former glory?"

I reached a gap between the curtains and peered through. For a second, I just stared.

The actors were dressed in… aluminum foil? Or at least suits that appeared to be made out of it, with motorcycle helmets coated in silver paint over their heads. One of them swung an elongated gun that wobbled in his grasp, clearly made out of foam rather than metal. Another poked at a small cardboard box covered in blinking lights that didn't appear to do anything in response to his jabbing fingers.

Julius had said this was a low budget production, but this was really scraping the bottom of the barrel. I'd witnessed high school theater productions with better costumes and props than this.

It seemed to be a sci-fi flick. At least, I guessed that the mottled teal and purple surface under their feet and the mauve crepe bushes in the background were meant to be alien terrain rather than a sign that their set designer was colorblind. And the jumble of cracked metallic objects off to the side, which included a couple of cans I could still see torn scraps of soup labels on—that must be their crashed ship, I was guessing?

Confirming my suspicion, the actor with the box started talking. "There is still hope! The conditions on this planet can support our life. Perhaps there are other beings we will encounter, a grand new society we can become a part of."

At his pompous tone, Blaze clapped his hand over his mouth to muffle a laugh. His amusement sparkled in his eyes despite his best efforts. I bit my own tongue, a giggle bubbling in my throat.

"How can you say such things, Robin?" the actor with the foam gun asked, swishing his weapon again for dramatic effect. "Earth is destroyed. *Destroyed*. We shall never set eyes on it again. All we have left are these tools… and our memories."

I caught sight of Julius peeking through a gap at the other end of the sound stage, his mouth twitching at the ridiculousness in front of us.

"We still have each other!" the other actor declared.

"I suppose that is true." The man with the gun swiveled toward the camera. "And if the world is on fire, then I can burn other things too."

I had no idea what that sentence had to do with the story, but I could tell it was meant to be a tagline, one they imagined would be printed on the movie posters and quoted all around the world. Dear lord. We were really doing society a service here by putting them out of their—or everyone else's—misery.

"Cut," the director shouted. "That was the best take yet, guys. Really, you outdid yourselves. Take five and see if you can loosen up for the fight."

Loosening up apparently involved shaking their heads and arms while making baboon noises. I clamped my mouth shut against another giggle. Then a conversation reached my ears from the crew on the other side of the curtain.

"This new camera setup is *sweet*, isn't it?"

"Hell, yeah. And that stuck up jerk at the depot will never miss it."

The first guy cackled. "Not from his grave, that's for sure. Remember how he squealed like a pig going down?"

The other guy snickered without any hint of remorse. "I wish we could use it as a sound effect in the film."

My jaw clenched. They weren't just making a shitty film—they were shitty people. We really *were* doing the world a favor by taking them out of it.

The phone in my pocket quivered with a faint vibration. Julius had given his signal. It was time to get to work.

The others didn't waste any time. Bullets sprayed across the set from where Julius was still concealed in the folds of the sheets. I couldn't help marveling at his precision: every shot, even fired so rapidly, clipped an artery in a neck or wrist or thigh, maximizing the blood that spurted across the soundstage.

But I didn't pause in my admiration. I whipped up my

own gun, already calculating how I'd use my skills to create a similar effect. The challenge sparked a jolt of excitement in my chest.

I didn't have time to revel in the thrill. The plan was for Julius to handle the north side of the set and me the south. *Avoid the kill shot until they've had a little time to stagger around,* he'd told me. *The longer they live, the more they bleed.*

My first few shots slammed into legs and shoulders, hindering my targets without killing them—but not making much chaos either. Although the cast and crew brought plenty of their own chaos to the scene, running and stumbling around with panicked shouts. I caught another guy in the gut and the jerk who'd described his victim's squeal across the forehead, carving a gouge that made *him* squeal.

The men I hadn't shot immediately scrambled for their guns. I blasted their hands and forearms, sending the weapons spinning. One fled toward the exit, and I sent a bullet into the back of his skull. Well, this was my first time out. Julius had also emphasized that the security of *our* crew trumped every other consideration.

My gaze caught on Julius, who'd stepped partly into view among the shadows cast by the sheets. He aimed his gun with an intent expression, and every shot was perfection. Blood sprayed and hissed from every artery he severed. It was painting the teal-and-purple set a brutal shade of red. Damn, the man was good at what he did.

The wounds he inflicted were vicious enough to send his targets crumpling to the floor in agony, clutching at their broken flesh. Some never moved any farther, still sprawled there when he put the final bullet in their brain or heart a little later. Others crawled toward the doorway and were either blasted in their tracks by him or stopped by Blaze, who I knew was lurking around the fringes with his pistol, ready to pick off those who tried to flee.

Talon wove his way through the flailing mass of figures, his serrated knife flashing under the set lights. He dug the blade into the necks of his victims, wrenching it downward across their chest in a zigzag pattern I'd seen before that seemed to maximize the flow of blood, even though it was instantly fatal. He mowed through the bodies with all the predatory grace of a panther. I had to drag my gaze away.

I'd just shot a few more of the men on my side of the room when a big boar of a guy charged at me in a full suit of foil, as if that was going to protect him any. He probably figured he had a chance of knocking me down compared to the guys because I was smaller and, well, female. But he'd learn the error of that assumption just like all the other people who'd fatally underestimated me in the past had.

I pulled the trigger when he was only a few feet away —and managed to hit him just to the left of the most vital part of his throat. Blood sprayed, and the guy staggered and gurgled, but he stayed alive enough to lurch this way and that for another several seconds before he crumpled.

There. I could be messy too. I'd just needed a little practice.

None of these idiots could stop us. We held all the

cards here, and we were dealing out their fate for the equally violent lives they'd lived. All of us, working together in unison. The exhilaration of the collaboration brought an unexpected smile to my lips.

I'd never felt like this on a mission before. I'd gotten satisfaction out of a difficult job well done, sure, but it'd never been a joint effort. Something I was creating *with* other people, something bigger than I could have managed on my own.

I'd thought I preferred working alone, but there was something special about this kind of team effort that it'd never occurred to me I was missing.

Another shot exploded near the front of the room, despite the bodies that already littered the floor. I looked up to where the sound had originated and smiled as Blaze took down another gangster who'd hurtled toward the exit despite the blood pouring from his wounds. True to his assigned role, he was keeping our chaos contained.

Garrison played an active role too, even though he wasn't involved in the killing tonight. I knew he'd gotten information about the filming schedule and personnel ahead of time using his manipulative charms. Now that the bodies all lay motionless or sagging, nearly dead, he stalked between them. He scanned the bodies, checked for pulses, and motioned the rest of us to those that hadn't quite given up the ghost yet. He also emptied their pockets of anything that could be useful or a threat. Like in the job I'd crashed days ago, he tossed all of those items into a sack.

As I delivered one last kill shot, the adrenaline in me

softened from a rush to a pleasant buzz. Blaze pulled out his tablet. "No security has been alerted. I'm not seeing any sign that the police have flagged concerning activity in the area either." He turned. "I'll collect the hard drive that the security cameras are feeding into."

"I'm going to make one final circuit of the building," Garrison said, his hand drifting to the holster he kept at his hip just in case.

If I'd been working alone, all the work of double-checking and securing the scene would have fallen on me. Another benefit of teamwork.

Because my efforts hadn't been quite as bloody as the other main killers on the crew, my clothes had survived relatively unscathed. I simply pulled a hoodie over the fitted shirt with its protective padding. Julius and Talon chucked off their tactical gear in exchange for tees and jeans that'd look more natural moving through the city, wiping off stray streaks of blood with rags. Somehow their well-muscled forms, Talon's more compact and Julius's bulkier, had gotten even more mouth-watering after seeing them fully in action.

Garrison brought the car around, and we all piled in, leaving the chaos behind. The strip where we'd landed the jet was only a twenty-minute drive away. By the time we reached it, the guys had already fallen into the sort of casual conversation I'd gotten used to around the apartment, as if we'd done nothing more than crash a party in the normal people way.

"Could you believe those props?" Blaze crowed, shaking his head. "Those were a crime all by themselves."

"Don't get me started on the dialogue," Garrison muttered. "It couldn't have sounded more wooden if it'd been delivered by a couple of two-by-fours."

Julius gave one of his quietly confident smiles. "I'd say we made a much more interesting picture with what they gave us to work with." He nodded to me. "And Dess more than held her own. You did good out there."

With him, it was hard to tell how much of a compliment that was—mild or ecstatic or somewhere in between. But I'd take it. I scrambled onto the jet with a bounce in my step, still a little hyped up from my earlier rush.

As I sank into one of the posh leather seats and the engine started to rumble, Garrison pulled a bottle of wine out from a cooler between two of the seats. "To a job well done!" he said, raising it and popping the cork.

He took a swig and passed the bottle on to Talon. The older man downed a gulp of his own and clapped Blaze on the shoulder in a rare show of physical comradery, however brief. The hacker let out a whoop when he grabbed the bottle for his turn. Julius watched over them all with his usual penetrating gaze, foregoing a drink himself, but his smile lingered on his lips.

When the bottle finally made its way to me, I let myself have a tentative sip. I didn't usually bother with alcohol unless I needed to put on a show for a job, and then I actually swallowed as little as possible. I wasn't totally sure how the effects might blur my mind. I couldn't help noticing that when Garrison made a grabby motion to get it back, he directed it at Blaze, who passed it over from me, instead of looking me straight in the eyes.

As the plane soared through the sky, the men fell into a discussion about the most ridiculous moments in past missions, pausing to correct themselves or each other and to exaggerate the situations even more. Soon, even Julius was chuckling. I laughed along from my seat, but I couldn't help feeling a little off to the side.

I hadn't been part of any of those missions. I wasn't really a part of the crew, even now. I'd only been a guest star for this job. Who knew if Julius would *want* to have me along again? I'd held my own, but I knew I hadn't been as much in my element as the rest of them.

They knew each other better than I knew... anyone. Maybe they weren't related by blood, but they were a family in every other way that counted. A pang ran through my heart with the longing to be in their midst, just as much a part of it as the rest of them.

I didn't know who my birth family was or how they'd lost me—or given me up. Maybe I never would. But this family right here was something I knew with a sudden certainty I wanted in on. Noelle had made me a lone wolf, but every nerve in my body clanged with the sense that I was meant to be part of something bigger.

As long as I was with the Chaos Crew, I had a chance to form those bonds, didn't I? I'd just have to make sure I proved myself worthy in every possible way they could want.

NINE

Decima

WHEN I WALKED out of my room the next morning, everything seemed completely normal, like we hadn't just blasted away a dozen or so gangsters the night before. Garrison stood in the kitchen over the stove, sipping hot cocoa from a mug and flipping bacon in a frying pan, both sending delicious smells into the air in a mix of sweet and salty. Julius and Talon were sitting at the table polishing off the last bits of what looked like pancakes, and Blaze was cross-legged on the sofa with a typical plate of pasta on one knee and his laptop on the other in an impressive balancing act.

But in a weird way, the fact that it felt normal was the most abnormal thing. I walked over to the kitchen without a single quiver of apprehension running through my nerves. Blaze gave me a little wave of welcome, Julius nodded to me, and Garrison—well, Garrison flicked a brief glance my way and tensed his jaw, which was par for the course. No one made a big deal of my presence.

It was like I belonged here. Like I'd always lived here with them, as much a part of the crew as they were. Was the change in them or in me—or both?

As I grabbed my usual box of cereal out of the cupboard, wondering if I could get Garrison to spare any of that bacon for me and suspecting the chances were nil, Julius motioned to Talon. "They've just gotten a new model of dagger in at our favorite shop. I think you'd like it. The balance is impressive. You should take a look."

Talon grunted. "I'm pretty happy with the one I have."

"You can never have too many weapons," Blaze piped up from the sofa. "Always carry at least two backups, I always say."

"You always say since when—this morning?" Garrison teased.

"I'm sure I've said it at least once before. I've definitely *thought* it." Blaze glanced at me. "Did you sleep okay after the flight?"

"Yeah," I said automatically. "It was good to be ho—"

I cut myself off in mid-word with a sudden, startling realization. I'd been going to say *home*, and… the crew's apartment did feel like home now. I knew where everything important was. I knew what to expect from the guys, at least well enough to relax around them. They were treating me like a standard inhabitant and not an interloper.

It was hard to imagine that the apartment I'd lived in for not much more than a week had so quickly replaced the house where I'd spent more than twenty years of my life, but maybe that said more about how homey the household *hadn't* been than it did about this place.

While my thoughts drifted back to that past period of my life, Blaze checked his laptop and let out an uncharacteristically disheartened sigh. It wasn't hard to figure out why.

"Still no useful results from all those searches?" I asked. The other men looked over as well in anticipation of the hacker's answer.

Blaze frowned. "Nothing that sends us down a longer trail. I keep finding more people to check out but none of them turn up anything suspicious or concerning. I have no idea whether the people I'm looking at now are even remotely connected to your household." He shook himself and shot me a rejuvenated smile. "But don't worry. I'll keep at it. There's got to be a solid lead in here somewhere."

"And if there isn't, we have other avenues we can pursue," Julius put in.

Did we, or was he just saying that to reassure me? I popped a spoonful of cereal into my mouth and chewed pensively.

There'd been so much I hadn't known about my old home and the people living there. But that home could tell stories of its own, couldn't it?

My heart leapt, and my head jerked toward Garrison. "You collect all the wallets and phones and similar things from the scenes of the jobs. Do you still have all that from the household?"

Garrison might not have wanted to make super friendly, but he did meet my eyes and offer an apologetic grimace in response. "We dispose of them within twenty-four hours of finishing the job. It's too risky carrying evidence like that around when it doesn't seem needed. And that early on, we had no idea it would be relevant."

I let out a huff of breath. "Understandable."

But there'd been a lot they'd left behind. Maybe no obvious identifying information, but there could have been mail in a drawer, notebooks on shelves, even a reminder scrawled on a post-it note might point us in a useful direction to finding the larger organization the household had been a part of. The people Noelle had obviously still been working with, since she hadn't come for me alone.

The thought of walking back into the space that I'd last—and only—seen splattered with blood made my gut knot, but with every passing second, my certainty grew that it was my best course of action, if I was going to take any action at all. And damn, did I want to.

"I need to go back to the mansion," I said. "They were working out of that building for decades. There's got to be some kind of evidence left behind."

Talon's attention shifted to me. He didn't speak, but his somber gaze emanated concern.

Julius expressed what all the others might have been thinking. "That'd be pretty dangerous. Our client has been hassling Garrison about the missing 'item' from that job, which we have to assume means you. He probably has eyes on the place."

I shrugged. "You should know by now that I'm aware of how to stay under the radar. I can avoid whatever and whoever I need to."

"We don't know exactly who we're dealing with here or what kind of resources they have," the crew's leader reminded me. "And you might not find anything to make it worth the risk. His people have clearly been through the house since we left for them to have figured out that you're gone. There's a strong possibility they'll have grabbed anything tied to the household's criminal operations already."

I shifted restlessly on my feet. "I know that too. But I need to try. Even a small possibility that I'll turn up the start of a trail makes it worth it."

Julius sighed, but he inclined his head at the same time. "I can understand. This is your life and your family we're talking about, and I've already made it clear that we're not your keepers. You've proven yourself more than capable by any measure."

"Thank you."

When he lifted his gaze to meet mine again, a tingle of heat raced through me. I'd earned his trust, but suddenly I wanted more than that. I wanted to peel back the layers of who *he* was and get at the beating heart beneath that fueled his commanding presence.

I reined in the impulse, but not before I thought I saw a matching spark of interest flash in his eyes—and vanish.

He sucked the last of the syrup off his fork in a gesture that made my panties dampen in an instant and stood up. "Finish your breakfast, and I'll take you through the tunnels again. But once you're out there, you'll be on your own."

"Until I get back," I said, the corner of my lips quirking upward.

The slow smile I was appreciating more every time I saw it curved his own mouth. "Yes, until you get back."

———

I did three circuits as I approached the mansion, first a few blocks away and then getting increasingly closer as I confirmed there were no watching eyes—living or digital —pointed my way. I'd put on a thin hoodie with the hood raised over the wig I'd bought earlier, sunglasses hiding my eyes.

But it seemed that precaution wasn't totally necessary. The mansion was in a sprawling residential neighborhood, and there wasn't a whole lot of activity in the middle of the day. It'd have been easy to spot any suspicious signs.

There were a few cameras mounted around the property's walls, but I simply steered clear of them and scrambled over the same way I'd scrambled out a few weeks ago. On the ground in the yard, I stalked across the lawn even more cautiously. There was a new camera mounted over the front door, one that the average person wouldn't have been able to pick out it was so well-disguised, and another at the back.

That was fine. Noelle wouldn't have done her job right if I hadn't learned how to get in by plenty of means that didn't require doors.

I jimmied a ground floor window open, eased aside the curtain, and peered through the room to check for surveillance or human presence on the inside. The sitting room was totally empty other than the posh furniture. Looking at it gave me an unsettling feeling of déjà vu.

Hadn't I walked through this room on my first prowl through the mansion after I'd left my section of it on the night of the massacre? Hadn't there been a bloody body sprawled across that armchair?

If so, all trace of both the body and the blood had been washed away. You'd never have imagined anything even as violent as a papercut had happened in this room.

I slipped inside and took a quick inventory of the space. It held nothing but the furniture, the drawer on the side table and the surface of the coffee table totally bare. At the doorway, I peeked into the hall.

Ah ha. Someone had mounted another discreet camera at the far end, pointed down the length of the hallway. I pulled back, leapt out through the window, and moved to another farther down.

The dining room I climbed into next I'd definitely seen before—complete with bloody bodies slumped across the table. As with the first room, all evidence of them had been wiped clean. Could that even be the exact same table? I had to think the blood would have stained the pale wood beyond repair.

Who the hell had done this—and why had they bothered with this careful reconstruction? It was obvious the police had never been through. There was no caution tape or chalk markings of bodies. It was as if the household's inhabitants had been utterly wiped from existence... except for me, of course.

My stomach knotted. I didn't know whether to feel relieved that the crew's job here had allowed my escape and freedom or horrified by the callous aftermath. I had no idea who any of these people had been. Sure, they'd all been criminals, but Anna hadn't been all bad. There'd been at least a little real kindness in her treatment of me.

Of course, while treating me that way she'd also enabled me to kill who knew how many innocents. Their blood was on her hands too.

The thing was, whoever had ordered their deaths clearly hadn't had good intentions either. They wanted me for their own purposes, which I hardly thought were good, especially with how cagey they were being with the crew about what they were "missing." They sure as hell hadn't ordered the massacre for my benefit but for some gain of their own.

My jaw working with suppressed tension, I stalked around that room and then the next and the next. With the last, I was able to cross the hall on my belly, below the view of the camera, to reach the staircase and investigate the second floor.

I found no books on the shelves, no papers on any desk, no paraphernalia of any kind in the drawers and closets. The clothes still dangling from their hangers told only the story of people who'd had a lot of money. They were designer label but nothing particularly distinctive.

Once I'd returned downstairs, I crawled beneath the level of the camera into the first room on the opposite side of the ground floor. After determining that it held nothing useful and ducking out its window, I hit my first real problem.

The grand living room, the place where I'd encountered by far the most bodies, had windows that appeared to be jammed shut. No matter what I did or what tools I put to use from the kit Julius had lent me, I couldn't get either of them to budge. Had someone gone out of their way to more tightly secure them?

Did that mean there was something worth finding on the other side?

I clambered back into a room I'd already investigated and studied the camera from a doorway. I couldn't get to the living room without coming into view of it. I also wasn't going to be able to make it to the side hall that led to my old rooms as long as I was avoiding it either—there were no windows into that part of the mansion.

I'd just have to take a gamble and bust my butt finishing my inspection.

Blaze had offered me a slim paintball gun specifically in case I needed it for this purpose. I aimed it at the camera's lens and fired.

A blue blotch hit the lens, obscuring all view of me. If anyone was currently monitoring the feed, they'd know right away that an intruder was in the house, just not who it was. I had to hoof it.

I dashed into the living room. My pulse stuttered at the contrast between the sleek leather surfaces and polished floors now and the carnage that'd been strewn across the space before, but I didn't let that uneasiness slow me down. I sprinted from table to cabinet, pawing through every nook. All I turned up were a few blank pieces of notepaper. For fuck's sake!

As I whirled around, my gaze slid across the ceiling instinctively, even though I'd already checked for cameras. My eyes paused on an odd mark I hadn't noticed carved into the old-fashioned trim in one corner of the room. Between the white paint and the position, it was almost invisible unless you happened to look straight at it from the right angle.

I stepped closer, squinting at it. It looked vaguely spherical, though narrower at the top than the bottom... almost pointed, like a teardrop. A straight line sliced through it on a diagonal. I couldn't remember ever seeing that symbol before.

It wasn't much, but it was something. I whipped out my phone and snapped a picture of it, zoomed in as far as I could go.

Then I whirled around and rushed across the hall to the passageway that led to the small study with the secret bookcase entrance to my old rooms.

Somehow, even after seeing the whole house in its current state, coming up on the spot where I'd left Anna's crumpled body sent a fresh wave of queasiness through me. Even here in this remote corner of the house, whoever had swept the mansion clean had removed all indication that she'd existed too. There was only the desk, the filing cabinet—empty—and the bookshelves, which contained a scattering of not particularly impressive looking volumes.

I glanced over the titles on the spines, flipped open a

few to check for inscriptions, and swept several aside to check the back of the bookcase for a way to access the door behind it. There, I came across the symbol from the living room for a second time. A tiny version of it was carved into the topmost portion of the bookcase that covered the secret entrance to my quarters. The etching was no larger than the pad of my thumb, just above the line of the shelf.

I knit my brow at it and took another photo. My heart was thumping faster. I was running out of time. I jabbed my fingers at the carving and then all across the rest of the bookcase, but nothing made it budge.

Right now, who knew how many enemy forces could be racing this way?

Cursing under my breath, I backed up and glared at the bookcase. But then, maybe it was silly to put myself in any more danger to try to get into the rooms where I'd spent years upon years already. The household people had never left anything in there that'd tipped me off to their true agenda before, so why would there be anything useful in that section of the building now?

My desire to see that space one more time was more nostalgia than anything else, and I didn't have time for foolish emotions in the middle of a mission.

I spun on my feet and hustled to the nearest window. With a leap over the sill and a lope across the lawn, I put the mansion that'd been my home and my prison for far too long—and the ghostly emptiness inside it—far behind.

TEN

Blaze

ONCE DESS LEFT THE APARTMENT, we were all on edge.

I tracked her from the city's security cameras, though with her disguise and her skill at stealth, I could only find her in brief glimpses because I knew exactly where she'd been going.

Julius lingered by his board of army figures, moving them around sporadically as if he had a full mission to plan. He did so with vicious swipes of his hand and a lethal intensity in his expression. I knew he was preparing for the possibility that Dess would be caught.

Garrison strode past me a few times as he paced around the house. He didn't say anything to indicate he was worried, but the fact that he was so quiet at all instead of snarking away at us showed his uneasiness.

Talon shut himself inside the workout room. Every

once in a while, we heard a particularly thunderous sound of his fist hitting the punching bag or the clank of metal weights returning to their racks.

Only when I told everyone that Dess was approaching the covert entrance to the building did they seem to calm down enough to get back to their normal lives. Garrison strode out of the kitchen and toward the roof, almost as if he'd been waiting for this confirmation before leaving the main room. Julius slid his figures back in place and left through the front door, heading down to retrieve her. Talon gave the punching bag a few more swings and then headed into the bathroom to shower.

I couldn't peel my eyes away from the laptop screen until I saw Dess vanish near the entrance, approaching the spot where Julius would be waiting for her. It didn't take long before she came striding through the door. She had a pensive air to her that made it hard to tell whether she'd found what she'd been seeking.

She looked at me the moment she entered the room, and the gray in her eyes seemed to lighten. She veered toward me immediately. Julius, coming in right behind her, looked her up and down as if double-checking that she'd returned in one piece before heading to the fridge to grab one of Steffie's premade sandwiches.

Did he know what Dess had found already, or was she telling me first?

She sat down at the dining table kitty-corner to where I was sitting with my laptop. The guys—well, mostly Garrison—often hassled me about how little I used the workstation actually devoted to my work, but I focused better with the ability to move around as a whim took me.

"I didn't turn up much, but there was one small thing that might lead us somewhere," Dess said. "At least the trip wasn't a total bust."

"You can show me everything you saw there," I told her. "There might be more significance to some item than is obvious at a glance."

She shook her head. "It's not that. There was *nothing*. Everything had been cleaned up and cleared out—I mean, the furniture was there, but the drawers and shelves were pretty much empty. There was no sign of the murders either. But someone was monitoring the place—there were new cameras outside and one inside." She sucked her lower lip under her teeth in a gesture that sent a little flare of desire through me. "All I got was this."

She brought up a photo on her phone and set it on the table for me to see. It was a symbol carved into a molding somewhere in the house—a teardrop shape with a line bisecting it at a diagonal. And maybe a tiny notch at the lower part of the line? It was hard to make out. But something about the design gave me a vague twinge of recognition.

Where had I seen that before?

"It was in the living room, and also on the bookcase that hid the secret doorway into my quarters in the house," Dess said. "Maybe other places, but that's all I found in the time I had. Do you have any idea what it could mean?"

She flipped to the photo of the bookcase with the

symbol carved into the dark wood. Seeing it on that surface made something click in my head. I stared at it for a moment longer and then turned to her.

"It's the same as your tattoo."

Dess blinked at me. "Tattoo? What tattoo?"

I guessed it wasn't surprising that she wouldn't know. She hadn't known about an awful lot of things her "household" had done to her, and the tattoo had been placed somewhere it'd be almost impossible for her to discover on her own.

"Come here," I said, beckoning for her to stand. I walked her over to the full-length mirror near the front door and switched my own phone to selfie mode so it would act as a second reflection. "Lift your hair up from the back of your neck."

Dess looked puzzled, but she did it. And there was the little black tattoo I'd remembered, marked into her skin at the base of her skull where her hair mostly concealed it. Carefully, I parted the strands to reveal the shape a little better, not even touching her skin, and held my phone so she could see the image that was reflected in the mirror.

Dess drew in a startled breath with a hiss. "What the hell?"

"We saw it when we were checking you for injuries after your crash," I told her. "It's hard to make out the details through your hair, but it looks incredibly similar to that carved symbol to me. I don't think that's a coincidence."

Dess let her hair fall. Her eyes flashed. "They did this

to me. The people from the household—whoever took me. They fucking *marked* me like I'm their property."

My chest clenched at her anger—not because it bothered me, but because she was so justified in it. "You're nobody's property," I reassured her firmly. "And you can get it removed. I'm sure there are services that could manage it, just shaving the hair there first."

But in typical Dess fashion, she'd already moved on to the next part of the problem. She spun toward the table with my laptop. "The symbol has something to do with the people who ran the household. It could lead us to more of them."

"Absolutely," I said, glad to have something concrete to focus on that might help. "Send the photos to me, and I'll get some image recognition searches running."

Dess did as I asked and sank back into her chair, watching me type with open curiosity. "This'll work like your facial recognition searches?"

"Exactly. Although it'll probably take a lot longer for the app to complete the search since it has to check *every* kind of image it can dig up, not just ones it recognizes as containing faces. But I can leave it running in the background for however long it takes." I finished the last commands and sat back. No trouble at all.

We sat there for several minutes, both of us braced in case an immediate result came up. When nothing happened, I glanced at Dess with an apologetic twist of my mouth. "Like I said, it could take a while. It's obviously not a very common symbol if we haven't found anything right away, but I guess we already could have guessed that."

She let out a discontented hum, her forehead furrowed. Watching her, the constricting sensation came back into my chest.

I couldn't imagine what she was going through with so many unanswered questions and so few leads left. I couldn't think of a single way to ensure we got the answers she longed for or to fix the trust the people in her past had damaged so thoroughly.

But maybe that wasn't up to me. Maybe she could just use a chance to let some of those emotions out.

"How are you doing?" I asked, nudging the computer aside. It'd notify me if anything popped up, and watching wouldn't make the search run any faster.

Dess's gaze jerked up to meet mine. "Me?"

A gentle smile stretched across my face. "Yes, you. You've had your whole world upended in the last week. How are you hanging in there? I can't even imagine how tough it is, even for someone as tough as you."

The corner of her mouth twitched at the compliment. Then she sighed. "I don't know. How I am feels like such a complicated question now. I hardly know *who* I am."

She paused, and I didn't rush her. When she spoke again, the words came out in a rush. "I do know that I'm grateful for everything that you and the rest of the crew have done for me. Nobody has ever been here for me the way that you guys have. You've welcomed me into your home and done everything you can to help me find answers. It's just even with all that, the sense of how much of my life is still a mystery won't stop gnawing at me. I don't like having all these questions hanging over me with no way to answer them."

"That makes sense," I said. I didn't have any way to hold the gnawing at bay either, though. I made a face at my laptop as if that would encourage it to spew out some results.

But there was one thing I'd been able to offer Dess before that might help now—if not in a concrete way, then at least to allow the time to pass more comfortably.

I stood up again. "It's hard to focus and come up with ideas when you're all tense about the situation. There's nothing else we can do to dig into the problem right now. Why don't you unwind a little?"

She raised an eyebrow at me. "Like how?"

I grinned. "I happen to know a TV show you're very fond of."

Dess couldn't suppress the eager spark that glinted in her eyes, even though she made a show of muttering, "Oh, all right," as she got up. I ushered her over to the sofa and motioned for her to sit down. Then I hustled over to my main computer setup to start the next episode streaming to the TV. I'd already downloaded the entire three seasons that'd aired, as well as a long-lost Christmas special I'd managed to dig up.

There wasn't much that made Dess really happy, and she deserved all the joy I could provide.

By the time I'd returned to the sofa to the theme song of *Spy Times*, Dess had relaxed right into the cushions. She stared at the TV avidly, a little smile playing with her lips.

I'd meant to watch the show with her, but the truth was, I wanted to watch her more. My gaze kept sliding back to her no matter how hard I tried to concentrate on the goofy storyline.

It wasn't really her looks. Yes, she was beautiful, from the dark locks of hair that tumbled down her back to the toned muscles and curves of her body honed by years of training. Even her slender but strong hands, capable of ending a life in an instant, fascinated me. But none of those things were what drew me in the most.

There was a stillness to her that I'd never been able to reach myself, a sense of inner certainty and confidence even in the middle of the storm her life had become that called to me like a beacon. I admired the same qualities in Julius, but somehow Dess exuded them even more than our commander.

Just sitting next to her, I absorbed a little of that calm. Her presence grounded me more than anyone I'd ever known. My knee didn't bounce and my foot didn't jiggle with the urge to stay in motion as I studied her. I could slow down and sink into the moment in a way that so often eluded me.

And here in this space, it was hard to imagine that anything but the woman sitting across from me mattered at all.

That last thought hit me squarely in the heart. I hesitated, feeling it out.

I didn't just admire her. I was falling for her.

But what difference did it make if I was? I'd made a few flirty gestures in the past, and she'd demonstrated *very* emphatically that she wasn't open to those kind of overtures... from me, anyway. I could still vividly remember the clamp of her hand around my throat. I didn't want to push her into feeling she had to defend herself from me ever again.

A laugh burst out of Dess at a particularly comical scene, and she glanced over at me to share the amusement. I chuckled too, though I wasn't totally sure what the joke had been because my attention had been so much on her. But she didn't appear to notice my distraction. Still smiling, she turned back to the TV.

A swell of resolve rose up inside me. Being her friend might be the closest I'd ever get to her, and that meant it'd just have to be enough.

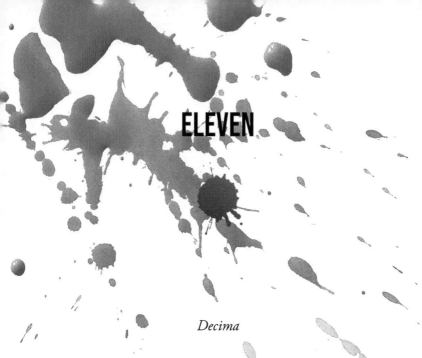

ELEVEN

Decima

JULIUS REACHED FORWARD and tightened the strap of my bulletproof vest. I sucked in a breath. "This isn't supposed to be a high-risk mission," I reminded him, rolling my shoulders to give myself some more breathing room.

"Anything that involves a high-profile target comes with a greater risk," Julius said.

"But Malik isn't a target."

"Malik *is* the target. We might not be killing him, but we are collecting information from him. With any luck, this operation will go smoothly, but we have to be prepared if it doesn't."

I nodded, glancing around the posh hotel room three hours from our usual stomping grounds. Julius had been the crew's leader for years, and his strategies had never led the guys astray. I could trust him on this.

He was the one who'd found out about our current opportunity. Damien Malik had been invited to speak at a political convention being held in the convention center next door to the hotel. Malik and all the other participants were staying here, which gave us the perfect opportunity to dig for information more directly than we'd had the chance to before.

Garrison had sweet-talked the front desk staff until he'd wrangled us the room right over Malik's. Now it was just a matter of making a quick trip down.

"Stay alert, and I'm sure it'll all go fine," Julius said, giving me one last onceover. "Talon and I will be keeping an eye on the convention—we'll let you know if there's anything to be concerned about."

"Right," I said. We'd determined that Malik and his team should be busy until well into the evening, no time to stop back at his room unless there was a sudden deviation from schedule.

I turned toward Blaze, who was already strapped into his harness beyond the open doors to the balcony. "Let's do this."

He grinned at me, the breeze ruffling his hair. "Ready when you are."

As I walked over to fit my own harness around me, Julius and Talon headed out. Garrison watched them go with a subtle frown and poked at something on his phone. He tipped his head toward us, focusing on Blaze rather than me. "Everything still looks good from my vantage point."

The cool air raised goosebumps on my arms, but the

adrenaline starting to thrum through my veins drowned out any discomfort. I grasped the rappelling line, gave it a testing tug, and motioned to Blaze.

We lowered ourselves toward the balcony below in tandem. I knew from experience that my stomach would accept the trip a lot better if I avoided looking at the fifteen-story drop below my feet. I could have made the drop in a few seconds, but I restrained myself to Blaze's less swift pace in case he ran into any trouble. He handled the descent with the obvious skill of someone who'd done it before, but clearly he hadn't made as much a habit of it in past jobs as I had.

"That's better," he said with a rush of an exhalation when his feet touched the balcony railing.

I laughed softly under my breath and sank down in front of the balcony doors. It only took a little prodding and a few twists of my picks to deal with the simple lock. No one expected intruders to be coming from this direction, especially not fourteen floors up.

Leaving our gear attached so we were prepared for a hasty getaway, we slipped into the dark hotel room, our ropes trailing behind us like massive tails. Blaze immediately spotted the laptop on the desk. He opened it, his eyes darting across the screen as it blinked to life.

I took my position by the front door of the hotel room, listening for any sounds of unexpected arrivals while watching Blaze work his magic. He was the one handling most of this mission. I was just here to keep the hacker safe.

Even though technically all he was doing was typing,

he was something to look at. He maneuvered that keyboard like I might have a knife or a gun, his gloved fingers flying with brutal efficiency, his gaze fixed on the screen with total intentness. When he broke past the security, he let out a muted cheer of victory before diving farther in with a sharp grin.

He rarely came across as vicious in his everyday life— not like Julius and Talon, who exuded physical menace with every move they made, or Garrison, who could take a weaker person's head off with a verbal barb. But Blaze clearly had the same killer instinct. How could he not, as part of the Chaos Crew?

He knew what he did well, and he accomplished it with feral intensity.

As I watched him in the partial darkness, the stream of sunlight from the displaced curtains catching on his pale red hair and determined expression, a tendril of wanting unfurled low in my belly. When he wasn't being flirty— when he didn't remind me of that time that I longed more than anything to forget—I couldn't help wondering what it'd be like to have his attention focused on *me* with the same intensity. To have those fingers moving over my body with all that energy and passion...

I shook myself mentally. This wasn't a good moment to be dreaming about hooking up with another member of the crew. If that was something he ended up wanting too, we'd figure it out some other time.

Maybe it was understandable that my sexual urges were going into overdrive when I'd gone so long without the opportunity to fully satisfy them, but I hadn't lost my sense of self-control.

I was being careful not to break Blaze's concentration, but when he leaned back for a moment with a cock of his head, I let myself speak. "Have you found anything?"

"Nothing that would connect him to you so far." He clicked open a few more documents and scanned them. "Malik has his fingers in a lot of pies, but I'm not seeing what would have drawn your trainer's interest to him or anything that ties him to the household."

"And no hints of anything criminal either?"

"There've been occasional murmurs about misconduct in the past, but either they weren't true or he's very good at hushing people up. I haven't come across anything on here that'd point to wrongdoing right now." He glanced over at me. "Honestly, it wouldn't be surprising for the guy to have had a few unstable moments where he got in a bit of political trouble earlier in his career, but I wouldn't read much into that."

I raised an eyebrow. "Why not?"

"Back when he was first making a name for himself, one of his kids died, very young—a car accident that killed her and the nanny. That could throw anyone off kilter. And besides, a lot of people feel he's a little *too* harsh on crime, so for him to be involved in a criminal organization at the same time..." He rubbed his mouth, frowning.

A vague flicker of memory returned to me. "He's got some new bill he's been pushing, doesn't he?"

Blaze nodded. "He's advocating for more severe

sentencing across the board as well as increasing the usage of convicted criminals in forced labor."

"Maybe Noelle and whoever else she's worked with saw him as an enemy, then." I suggested. "They could have simply been keeping an eye on him."

"Possibly. I'm not sure why she'd have felt the need to travel around going to his rallies in person for that. His activities are pretty well-publicized. She'd have found out more reading articles on the internet. So, maybe his supposed political stance is a really thorough cover-up for his real interests. Stranger things have happened." He let out a huff of breath. "Well, I'll download everything on here so I can do a more intensive search when we've got the time."

He plugged a hard drive a little bigger than his hand into the side of the laptop and clicked a few more times. A progress bar appeared on the screen.

The bar was nearly full when footsteps reached my ears on the other side of the door, shuffling along the carpeted hallway. I would have assumed it was another hotel patron heading to a different room if not for the voices I heard a moment later.

"Did he say where in the room we'd find it?"

"Of course. You know Damien—everything in its place. He left the notepad on the table at the left side of the bed."

Damien. My nerves jittered, and I leapt away from the door. "We have to go *now*," I hissed under my breath.

Blaze's eyes widened, but he didn't let panic throw him off. The progress bar had just topped out. He tugged the hard drive free without a sound, closed the laptop, and sprinted across the room toward the balcony.

I ran after him, jerking the doors shut behind us. The curtain would hide us—but who knew if Malik's staff would find some reason to come out here?

I yanked my rope taut in an instant. Blaze fumbled with his. Acting on instinct, I whipped myself into his arms.

"Hold me," I whispered as the door at the other end of the room squeaked open. Blaze hesitated for a split-second but wrapped his arms around me before I had to repeat my command. I grasped the rope and hauled both of us up there with the strength of my arms.

A burn spread through my muscles—and through my torso where I was pressed tightly against Blaze's lean body. It wasn't exactly an unpleasant sensation. When we reached the level of our own balcony, Blaze immediately rolled over the railing so he could release me, and some part of me regretted the loss of contact.

I leapt over the railing after him and hauled any remaining rope up out of view. I couldn't hear anything from the balcony below. It didn't sound like we'd been spotted.

Exhaling in relief, I glanced at Blaze. He gave no sign of having noticed how our closeness had affected me, though his own cheeks looked a bit flushed from the hasty escape.

"A tight one, but we made it," he said, offering a fist for me to bump.

I couldn't help smiling as I returned the gesture. "We make a good team."

When we hurried into our own room, Garrison was pacing by the front door. "Nothing from Julius or Talon yet?" I asked him.

He shook his head, only catching my eyes briefly before diverting his attention. I braced for some of his usual snark, but nothing came. The exhilaration that'd rushed through me with our escape dulled.

I *wished* he'd start snarking at me like he used to. At least then I'd know things were normal between us. Something about our passionate interlude on the deck had thrown off the dynamic between us, and I didn't know what to say to fix it. Especially when he seemed determined to interact with me as little as he could get away with while fulfilling our missions.

I might have tried to rile him up, but just then, Talon strode into the room. The urgency of his entrance hummed through the air.

"Malik's talk got bumped to an earlier slot," he said. "He's going on in fifteen minutes. Dess, Julius wants you to come and see if you can spot anyone in the crowd or his staff you recognize."

"Of course." My pulse hitched. That'd always been part of the plan, but we hadn't thought Malik would be giving his main speech until later today.

I hustled out of the room at Talon's heels. He walked on swiftly and silently like the predator he was, but his lack of conversation didn't niggle at me the way Garrison's did. Talon was quiet most of the time—it was just how he was, nothing to do with me. He didn't hesitate to meet my eyes, and once we were inside the convention center, he guided me through a staff-only doorway with a brief touch to my waist that showed no signs of discomfort.

I wasn't sure if *he* was going to want any more passionate interludes, but his steady demeanor put me at ease.

He led me to a maintenance area and then a ladder that brought us high over the auditorium, near the lights. I peered down from the metal catwalk, letting my eyes adjust. We were far enough up that I didn't think anyone would notice us through the thin slats in the walkway floor. Of course, it was hard for me to make out the faces below in much detail either.

Talon was prepared for that. He handed me a pair of binoculars. I shot him a smile in thanks and sprawled out on my stomach for the most comfortable viewing position from this angle.

"Where's Julius?" I murmured.

"He's keeping watch from below, just in case we're made. Do you have a good enough view?"

"With the binoculars, no problem."

I swept my amplified gaze over the audience, from the back to the stage and then in reverse, pausing just long enough here and there to fully absorb each group of figures. People sat in their seats, chatting amongst themselves and waiting for Malik, who I knew would be out soon.

I squirmed forward on my belly to lean my elbows over the edge, and Talon set a hand on my back as if to confirm my balance. There was nothing provocative about the touch, but it sent a pulse of warmth over my skin all the same. I glanced back at him. "Thanks. I'm okay."

He nodded at me with the briefest hint of a smile, which was practically a manic grin where Talon was concerned. "Of course you are." And all at once I was sure that even if he wasn't the type to want to hash out his intimate encounters after the fact, he didn't feel any regrets about what we'd shared either.

I couldn't dwell on that enjoyable realization. From the growing enthusiasm in the voices traveling up to us, Malik should be arriving at any moment. He might simply be waiting for whatever notes he'd asked his aides to go back to his room to grab for him. When he showed up, the lights would probably dim over everything but the stage, and I'd hardly be able to make out anyone.

I continued my scan as quickly as I reasonably could. The seconds ticked by. Then, just before I tilted the binoculars onward, my attention snagged on a face that'd turned to the side, on the far side of the auditorium near the back. I zoomed in with the binoculars as far as I could go, and certainty reverberated through my chest.

"Talon," I whispered. "There's a man here who was talking with Noelle in one of the other photographs Blaze found with his search."

At the same moment, the lights near us blinked out. Only a spotlight on the stage remained. The spot where the man had sat was swallowed in darkness.

Talon grunted and motioned to me. "We'd better get

out of here. You'll be able to point the guy you saw out in that picture?"

"Definitely." I could already see the image in my mind's eye, with the man walking just ahead of Noelle in a city park.

A cheer rose up, drowning out any other answer I might have given. Damien Malik had just walked on stage, his arm raised and his face beaming with a smile that could have lit the room all over again. My heart skipped a beat.

Was I looking at another of the household's targets... or the very man who'd orchestrated my kidnapping for a secret dark agenda of his own?

———

To be more discreet, we left the convention in two cars, me with Julius and Talon, and Garrison and Blaze on their own. I hoped they wouldn't end up biting each other's heads off before they made it home, but at least Blaze had the search for the new mystery man to keep him busy. He was already analyzing the convention records when we left.

Julius turned on a classic rock station at a low volume, and those tunes filled the car as he drove. I leaned my head against the window and tried not to wonder too much about the politician I'd just watched greet his audience. Speculation wasn't going to lead me anywhere. If there was evidence to tie Malik to the household or to me, Blaze would find it.

We'd been on the road only half an hour or so when

Talon's phone rang. He answered it on speaker. "What's up, Garrison?"

"We have a problem," he replied in a flat, terse tone that had my spine jerking straight. Whatever the issue was, it was serious.

"Are you and Blaze okay?" Julius asked.

"For now. But I just got a call from our client from the household job. I think it's best if I just play it for you."

"We're ready."

I wasn't sure if I was, but I braced myself in my seat. It took a moment and a few clicks before a rough voice spilled through the phone, taut with anger.

"You might think you can play us for fools, but this isn't a fucking game of Candyland, no matter what you seem to think. We know you have a young woman from the job site in your possession, and you need to turn her in before you're in even worse violation of your contract. Otherwise, expect that she'll be retrieved by whatever means necessary."

TWELVE

Decima

THE LAST WORDS in the voicemail message rang in my ears long after the call had ended. *In your possession. Retrieved by whatever means necessary.* Like I was a fucking *bauble* the crew had stolen that should be returned to its rightful owners. I had the urge to claw the tattoo with their awful mark right off the back of my neck.

Then the image filled my mind of the shadowy figures from the other end of the phone call storming in on the crew and slaughtering them to get to me. For them to have run the kind of assignments they'd sent me on, the people behind the household must have enormous resources. Now that they knew where I was, how the hell could we escape them?

I wouldn't be a prisoner again. I simply *wouldn't*.

My ribs felt as if they'd closed in around my lungs. Dragging air into my chest was a struggle. I squeezed my hands into fists against the back seat of the car and willed myself to calm down, but it didn't work. A faint wheeze crept into my breath.

I needed more oxygen. Somehow I couldn't get enough.

"Dess?" Julius said. I couldn't answer when it was taking all my concentration holding in the panic bubbling inside me.

He didn't say my name again, only jerked the wheel to pull us over onto the shoulder. The car slammed to a halt. He and Talon burst out, both coming around to the door next to me.

"Come out," Julius said firmly. "Get some air. Walk it off."

I fumbled with the seatbelt and pushed myself into the open terrain. We'd stopped in a desolate strip of countryside, only patchy fields around us and forest up ahead, no buildings or other vehicles in sight. For some reason, that reassured me just a smidge.

I started walking, pacing away from the car into the tufts of grass and back again. Frantic thoughts kept whirling through my mind.

The crew went to great lengths to keep the location of their home base secret, but they weren't completely infallible. And we couldn't live shut away in there for the rest of our lives anyway.

What would I do if the client found us and managed to capture me again? There was no reason for Julius to risk his whole crew for a woman he'd just met. But I couldn't let the people who'd run the household take me back. I'd *die* before I let those bastards touch me again.

I closed my eyes, retracing the steps my feet had already found without needing sight. *Get a grip on yourself, Dess.*

"He was bluffing," Julius said with deadly certainty. "Empty threats. No one would risk coming at us head-on, if they even knew how to find us. And if they tried, we'd destroy them. We fulfilled our obligations. You were never part of the deal."

"And now you're part of our crew," Talon said, simply but steadily.

Julius didn't argue with him.

Was I? Was I really one of them now, just like that? It was hard to wrap my head around the idea. But they'd both spoken with so much confidence that the quivers of panic inside me started to subside. I dragged a deeper breath into my lungs.

"That's right," Julius said, somehow commanding and gentle at once. "Let yourself come through it. You're still every bit as powerful as you were before. *You* won't let those fuckers take you down. I know that."

His words settled my nerves even more. He was right. I didn't have to let anyone control me ever again. I decided how I lived now—or how I died, if it came to that.

I stopped a couple of feet away from the car and the two men, a shamed flush creeping over my cheeks as I met Talon's and then Julius's gaze. "Sorry. I don't— I usually have more control over my emotions than that."

"You've got a good reason to be particularly emotional

on this subject," Julius said. "But what I said stands. Anyone who thinks they're going to come at you will have to get through us first, and they'll find that a losing game."

Could he really be so sure? He had no more idea exactly who we were up against than I did. My throat tightened, thinking of how much the crew had helped me —and what a horrible way of repaying them it would be if I got them slaughtered for their trouble.

"I wouldn't expect you to stand up for me," I said, keeping my own voice even so they'd know I meant it. "This is my battle, and you don't owe me your support. If anything, I owe it to you to keep you out of it. You'd be risking your careers, even your lives."

Julius stepped forward and gripped my hands, his gaze holding mine with a fiery fierceness searing through his deep blue eyes. "No one will ever get their hands on you again. You won't be torn from us as easily as they seem to think. You're a part of the crew now, and we protect our own. We *kill* for our own. And I say that without the slightest hesitation."

Those words held more loyalty and devotion than anyone had ever offered me before. The heat in Julius's eyes sent a different sort of flush over me. A connection hummed between us, electric enough to send a tingle over my skin. I wanted to sink right into it, to wrap myself in his strength and assurance.

If I leaned in and kissed him right now, how would he react?

He'd never given any clear sign that he was interested

in me that way. I didn't want to ruin the moment by asking for too much.

My gaze slid to the other man, the man who I knew could match my hunger even if he'd kept his own under wraps lately. Talon gazed back at me without retreating.

"How about you?" I asked. "Are you ready to put your life on the line so I can keep my freedom?"

Talon inclined his head as if he didn't even need to think about it. Which maybe he didn't. "You're one of us now," he said. "And no one threatens the crew and gets away with it."

If there was one thing I was sure about when it came to Talon, he didn't lie—not when he didn't need to. He was being totally honest in his dedication to me. But in that moment, with the remnants of my fears still racing through my veins, I needed to absorb his commitment with every part of my being. Words didn't feel like enough.

Without letting myself rethink the impulse, I moved toward him and gripped his shirt to tug him into a kiss. The moment I pressed my lips to his, his body reacted, his arms coming around me, his chest molding against mine. He loomed over me and surrounded me all at once. The confirmation in that kiss resonated through me.

It was brief, though, and then Talon shifted, starting to draw back. As he released my mouth, his gaze slid to Julius where I knew the other man was standing behind me. Talon's hands came to rest on my waist.

I glanced over my shoulder, weighing my options. Desire wound through me, chasing away the last of my panic. Julius was watching us, his shoulders pushed back and his stance commanding in his usual way, his expression unreadable. I could only imagine the ways he could make me feel if he touched me with all his power and authority brought to bear. The way that huge, brawny build would move against me if he fucked me as hard as I'd like.

A small, wicked smile crossed my lips. "You could join in too." I reached toward him, trailing my fingers down his chest over his shirt.

Julius caught my hand before it'd made it halfway to his groin. Heat flashed in his eyes. "No," he said, his voice rougher than usual. "You were upset—maybe you're not thinking straight. I'm not going to take advantage."

The hunger in his expression told me he was holding himself back for *my* sake, not his. It seared through my skin and stirred a deeper longing inside me.

"I'm thinking perfectly straight," I said. "I've wanted this—I've wanted *you*—since long before today."

"That doesn't mean it's the best thing for you right now."

I met his gaze firmly. "I decide what's best for me. I'm not the little girl you saved all those years ago, Julius, and I wasn't all that innocent even then. You know how many people I've killed. You know how much I've survived. I don't need to be coddled. When I say I want something, I expect you to believe me."

The muscles in his arms flexed with the effort of keeping himself still. "This is a far cry from killing, Dess."

I flicked my fingers against his chest again, as much as

I could reach while he still gripped my hand. "They do call it the 'little death' sometimes, don't they? Anyway, I can't think of a better way to say 'Screw you' to the assholes who want to lock me away than by screwing both of you instead of freaking out."

With those last words, I pulled away from Talon's grasp to brush my lips against Julius's. A groan reverberated from his chest, but his mouth crushed against mine, his resistance shattering. His hand leapt up to tease into my hair.

He was just as fantastic a kisser as I'd imagined he'd be. His lips and tongue moved together to caress my mouth, until every sensitive part of me throbbed with lust. I moaned against his lips, and he tightened his hold, one arm across the small of my back and one around the back of my neck, bringing me to him until my body was flush against his.

I heard rather than saw Talon approaching. He returned his hands to my waist and stroked them down my thighs and around to my ass. I ground back into him instinctively and then against Julius's hips to show him just how ready I was.

This time, both men groaned. Julius nudged me against the side of the car and kissed me harder. Talon leaned in beside us to slide his hands up under my shirt. As Julius worked over my mouth, his friend yanked my bra off with the same force that'd gotten me so wet for him in the workout room before.

These weren't tender, gentle men, but tenderness

wasn't what I was after. I wanted them to fuck the living daylights out of me.

I swiveled my head from Julius to seek out Talon's mouth. The other man kissed me with the brutal force I craved, his hand slipping farther down to cup my pussy. As I whimpered, Julius tugged up my shirt and closed his lips over my bared breast.

The rush of sensations was nothing short of heaven. I was starting to get the impression this might not be the first time they'd shared a woman. They seemed to have the whole coordination thing down pat.

I was definitely not complaining.

The searing heat between my thighs was becoming torturous. I rocked into Talon's hand and groped down his chest to the fly of his jeans. When my fingers closed around his bulging cock through the coarse material, his breath stuttered against my lips. I grinned.

It was such a thrill knowing that I had some kind of power over these powerful men. That I could conjure just as much desire in them as they did in me.

Talon stopped fondling me and tugged at my sweatpants so they pooled at my feet. When he teased his fingers over me with just the thin fabric of my now-soaked panties between us, a very undignified sound escaped me. I nipped his lip and hauled Julius up from my breasts for another kiss.

The two men ravished every part of my body with an unshakeable assurance that didn't trigger any of my horrible memories. They knew what *they* wanted, and now they were taking it, much to my delight.

I popped the button on Julius's jeans and delved my hand inside his boxers. He thrust his cock into my eager hand. "Fuck," he muttered, his lips scorching against the crook of my jaw. "You've got me close to bursting already. But I'm not coming until I hear you scream."

A giddy shiver passed through me. "Yes, please."

He cut his eyes toward Talon. "The emergency blanket from the back."

Talon didn't need any further instructions. He flung open the trunk and grabbed the blanket. In a matter of seconds, he'd spread it out on the ground next to the car.

Julius spun me around so my back was to him, tucking his hand beneath my panties between my legs. As he plunged his thick, skillful fingers right inside me, he lowered me onto my knees on the blanket. Talon sank down in front of me, tugging up my chin to claim another kiss. His mouth was pure fire. Every part of me was awash with flames of pleasure now.

With a jerk of his hand, Julius snapped the panties right off me. There was a crinkling of foil and the hiss of his jeans dropping, and then he gripped my hips. The head of his rigid cock rubbed against my opening.

As I moaned for it, he thrust into me. He was even bigger than Talon, stretching me with a blissful burn that radiated through my whole body. Seeking out even more of that incredible sensation, I pressed into him as he eased back and plunged even deeper.

But I couldn't leave the other man neglected. I made short work of Talon's fly and freed his cock with one hand as my body swayed to match Julius's rhythm. Another gasp tumbled out of me, and then I was closing my mouth around Talon's jutting dick, taking both men at the same time.

I'd witnessed this act, the sucking of a cock, in the middle of missions before, but this was my first chance to try it out. It hadn't always looked that enjoyable for the woman, but I found the feel of Talon's silky, pulsing shaft against my lips and tongue was an entirely new kind of thrill. Especially when he groaned and wound his fingers into my hair with the perfect sharp tug to make me hum with pleasure around him.

My hands dug into the blanket as I swiveled my tongue around his cock and bucked into Julius's thrusts. I had the two strongest men I'd ever met on their knees around me, and I could handle them both without missing a beat. A heady jolt of exhilaration raced through me.

As I swallowed Talon's shaft deeper into my mouth, Julius hit the spot that could send me screaming into release, just like he'd asked for. I could only moan around the other man's dick. He hit that spot again and again, clutching my hips tighter as he must have felt the shudders starting to race through my limbs.

Then all at once the pleasure of it completely burst inside me. I cried out, gasping against Talon's cock before sucking it back down, my body shaking with the force of my orgasm.

Julius finished next, thrusting deeply and erratically before he bowed over me with a grunt. As he tipped back, ragged breaths spilling out of him, Talon withdrew from my lips and pumped himself twice more before spilling his seed across the blanket before me.

I flopped down on the coarse fabric between the two men and grinned dazedly up at the blue sky that now seemed to beam back at me. Julius rubbed his hand over my thigh, and Talon brushed my sweat-damp hair back from my face. Sprawled there with them poised on either side of me, a realization struck me harder than ever before.

"No one owns me," I said with total conviction. "Nobody except myself."

Julius's lips curved with an approving smile. "And that's how it's going to stay as long as we have anything to say about it."

THIRTEEN

Talon

JULIUS AND DESS took the lead as we approached the old factory that Blaze had pulled up the address to. The symbol that marked the wall and bookcase in the mansion where Dess had lived—and the back of her scalp—had turned up in a photo on what Blaze called an "urban explorer blog." From the looks of the worn brick building, no one other than particularly bold and determined explorers had been inside here in a while.

Possibly they'd entered through the same loose window we found. The main door was locked.

As Julius shoved the pane high enough for us to squeeze inside, the stench nearly made me stop in my tracks. Garrison made a gagging sound.

"I *told* you it used to be a meat factory," Blaze said, but he pulled a face too as he slipped inside. Dess waved her hand in front of her nose.

Inside, hooks hung from the ceiling where carcasses must have once dangled. It was hard to tell how much of the ruddy marks on them and their chains were rust and how much old blood. The coppery tang to the stink suggested there was plenty of the latter still around. The owners hadn't done much of a cleanup when they'd cleared out.

I'd smelled blood, and I'd seen houses that had been covered in it, but in the middle of our jobs, it was fresh. The factory smelled of old, rotten blood.

"Whoever left this place like this should be drowned in raw sewage," Garrison grumbled, pinching his nose as he looked around.

I had to agree. And maybe we could burn the building down for good measure too. No one should be subjected to this ever again.

"Why are we here instead of tracking down that guy from the rally again?" Garrison added, shooting Blaze a baleful glance that the hacker returned.

"Because this is a way better lead than anything my searches for him have turned up."

A cockroach the size of my thumb scampered across the floor in front of Dess's feet. She stomped on it faster than I could blink, but the crunch of its shell made me grimace. "Let's search the place and then get out of here," she said.

"No argument here," Blaze piped up.

"Which part of the building was the photo taken in?" Julius asked him.

The hacker spread his hands. "I'm not totally sure.

This particular blogger went for flowery descriptions of his exploits over concrete details. The geotags indicate it should be in the back end of the building on the western side. We should check the whole place over to be sure we catch all the evidence that might be useful, though."

"We'll find it." Dess marched ahead with her chin held high, and an unexpected flare of admiration and desire washed through me. My mind flickered briefly back to the amazing fuck the two of us and Julius had shared by the side of the road, of all places.

I generally preferred to have four walls around me if I was going to get down and dirty, but Dess had an effect on me that I couldn't explain. She was some woman, that was for sure, striding through the wide room all cool and collected like she owned the place.

She skirted the thickest patches of reddish-brown on the floor beneath the hooks. "I wonder what exactly they killed in here."

"At this rate, it'll be me next," Garrison muttered. "Suffocated by the stink."

"Pigs," Blaze said. "The blog did mention that. Apparently there are rumors of hauntings in here. According to the guy—if he didn't just make this up for views—when the factory was operational, an occasional human body was tortured alongside the hanging pigs. I guess that's one way to cover up murder."

"Sounds like a myth to me," Julius remarked, but he eyed the hooks pensively.

Dess marched onward to the door at the far end of the room. "I don't know why this place would be connected to the household. Let's grab what we came for and get out of here. I don't have a great feeling about this."

Neither did I. Apprehension prickled over me as I moved through the room. I headed to the front hall and unlocked the heavy deadbolt from the inside. "So we can make a quick getaway if we need to," I told Julius when I saw him watching me.

He nodded in acceptance.

When I returned to the others, they'd split up between the side rooms. Dess was searching a smaller area with a few long metal tables and shelves built into the walls. The shelves were empty.

"It looks like a... filleting room—is that what it's called?" she asked. "You know, the place where the pigs were skinned and cut up."

I shrugged. "The butchering room, maybe? I don't know."

She peered under the table and nudged the shelves to see if they'd move. "At least they cleaned up a little better in here. The smell isn't quite so bad."

I checked a cupboard at the far end of the room and found only a couple of old butcher knives. Dess came up beside me and reached past me to snatch one up with a low whistle. Her arm brushed mine, sparking another rush of heat where our bodies touched.

"I bet you could make good use of these," she said, and spun the one she'd grabbed in her hand without moving away from me. "Do you think the ghosts would mind if I pilfered one just for our explorations here?"

A tickle of amusement rose in my chest. "I'm sure they'd forgive you."

Even twirling it casually, I could see the skill in the way she handled the blade. "Guns are more direct, but knives let you stay connected to the act, don't you think?" she remarked.

I couldn't restrain a chuckle. "I think I wouldn't want to go hand-to-hand with you with any kind of weapon, but especially not that."

She peeked through her eyelashes at me with an abruptly flirty expression. "Oh, I'd go easy on *you*. It'd be more fun that way."

She flipped the knife in her hand again and drifted toward the doorway, not even waiting or pushing for a response. No demands. No expectations.

That might be the most miraculous thing about her. Despite the physical intimacy we'd shared twice now and the fact that we were still around each other regularly, Dess didn't seem to need or even want me to fawn over her, to treat her like more than a colleague. I knew she appreciated our physical connection, but she wasn't insisting on it becoming anything fraught and romantic.

I knew how unusual her attitude was. Because of that problem, I'd stopped sleeping with women except an occasional one night stands when the itch got strong enough. If I'd hooked up with the same woman more than once, it would inevitably turn into long text chains, hopeful phone calls, and teasing pet names fishing for one in return. No matter how clear I tried to be about only looking for something casual, that never stuck.

Until Dess. She knew how to take the good and not worry about the depth of emotion I couldn't offer her. Strangely, that fact stirred more actual affection in me than I could remember feeling for anyone… in a very long time.

I wasn't totally sure what to make of it, but since she wasn't nudging me for passionate declarations, I didn't have to make anything of it at all.

I trailed after Dess into the next room. Just as I made it through the doorway, she called out, "Hey, I got something. Is this the wall from the photo?"

I hustled the rest of the way inside, the other guys converging around us. Dess was standing by a sagging metal desk in what appeared to be the factory's office room. On the wall across from her, up near the ceiling, a spiderweb of cracks stretched through the plaster. They crossed through the deeper groves of a carved symbol that matched the one in the mansion.

"That's it," Blaze confirmed, snapping his own picture of it.

"It's obviously been there for a long time," Julius said. "We need to figure out why. Spread out—maybe there's been some kind of record left behind. Even a scrap of torn paper on the floor might give us the link we need."

Garrison moved to a creaky filing cabinet in the corner. The drawers appeared to be mostly empty, but he fished out the few papers he found inside, glanced at them, and stuffed them into the satchel he'd brought. Dess started paging through the few decrepit binders left on a shelving unit next to it. Julius checked the desk drawers, and Blaze and I knelt down to paw through the stray documents that had fallen to the floor.

They were grimy with the grit that scattered the linoleum, a coating of dust—and an occasional footprint. Those were probably from the "urban explorers" who'd passed through, but they could be more relevant than that. I passed them to Garrison to add to his stash.

"Hold up," Blaze said suddenly, freezing in his hunched stance next to the desk.

The rest of us stiffened automatically, even Dess. She'd been around us long enough to recognize that if any of us sounded a warning, it should be heeded.

"What's the matter?" Julius asked.

"There's a fixture on the ceiling in the corner," Blaze said without looking directly at it. "I didn't notice it before because the shelving unit blocked it from my line of sight near the doorway. I don't know *for sure* what's inside it, or if there's anything at all, and if it's what I think it is, there's a strong possibility it isn't even active—"

"*What* do you think it is?" Garrison demanded through gritted teeth.

Blaze shot a glower at him. "A camera. If I were going to bet on it, I'd say there at least *used* to be a security camera in there."

Dess frowned, but her stance stayed tensed. "Why would anyone still be monitoring security feeds in this place? It's obviously been abandoned for years."

"Exactly," Blaze said. "That's why I said it probably isn't even active. If it even is a camera. But still… if it *is* active and monitored, it's too late now. We've already been caught on it." He paused. "And if I missed that one at first, it's possible there are others I missed too." He muttered a curse at himself.

A deeper chill prickled down my spine. Was *that* why I hadn't liked the feeling of this place—some part of me had sensed that we could be being watched? Of course, the stink explained my uneasiness perfectly well on its own.

"They apparently didn't mind the urban explorers before us," Garrison pointed out. "No reason to think they'll have a problem with us. If someone is watching."

Julius's expression had turned even more stern than usual. "We shouldn't take the chance, especially since we don't know how long we might already have been under surveillance. Grab all the loose material in here that you can quickly, and let's move out."

Dess swept the binders into a bag of her own and opened it wider for Julius to shove handfuls of crumpled papers into. Blaze and I scooped everything we could off the floor into a heap that we crammed into Garrison's satchel. We might have missed a few bits and pieces, but I agreed with Julius that it was best not to tempt fate by thumbing our noses at the risks any longer.

Tramping back into the thicker stink of the front room with the hooks, my stomach lurched despite myself. I hesitated, wondering whether we should squeeze back through the window or walk out the front door.

And then that question didn't matter anymore.

The front door burst open, and at least a dozen men charged in through it. More leapt through the window we'd opened and smashed others besides. In an instant, we were all but surrounded.

My hand shot to my ever-present weapons, a gun at one hip and my knife at the other. Garrison dropped his satchel and brandished his own pistol. Blaze and Julius whipped out their weapons. Dess waggled the butcher knife she was still carrying, her free hand dipping toward the gun strapped to her calf.

We might have retreated into the rooms we'd just left, but the incoming attackers charged at us without giving us a second to prepare. As they opened fire on us, I leapt toward the cabinets along one wall for some kind of shelter, dragging Dess with me and shooting as I went. Weirdly, the second I had my arm around her, the bullets flying my way seemed to falter. But bangs were still echoing all around me.

My comrades had all dived for whatever other cover they could find. Our attackers kept shooting in their general directions, but they all marched toward the spot where I'd ducked down with Dess next to me.

An icy sense of understanding snapped into place in my head.

They were here for her. They'd kill us to get to her, but they didn't want *her* dead. They were aiming to take her back, just like Garrison's contact had threatened.

Fury unfurled in my chest, searing hot. They'd only capture her over my dead body, and I didn't intend to give them that.

I fired off a few more shots, and the advancing men fell back to the side where I couldn't reach them without leaning out of the minor shelter I'd found. My gaze caught Julius's, and then Blaze's, and then Garrison's around the room. A matching rage shone in all their gazes.

All of us were ready to fight to the death to protect this woman. I had no doubt about that. She was one of us now, and we protected our own.

Bullets started rattling the side of the cabinet, some puncturing one or two layers of metal. It wouldn't be long before they passed right through the side where we were crouched. Dess sucked a breath through her teeth with a hiss, and I knew what I needed to do.

Yanking the cabinet door in front of me like a shield, I lunged out and squeezed the trigger.

FOURTEEN

Decima

AT THE SAME moment as Talon sprang forward, blasting shots at our attackers from behind the cabinet door, I leapt past him toward a small cluster of men who'd been closing in on us from the other direction. I yanked my pistol from my calf holster as I rolled across the floor, shot three of them in the head in quick succession, and had my butcher knife ready to plunge into the chest of the fourth the second I reached him.

More bodies swarmed around me. I kept low to give the crew clear aim at our attackers and dashed for the shelter of a meat processing machine. From that vantage point, I surveyed the room.

Two things became clear very quickly. The first was that this room offered lots of advantages I could put to use. All those hanging chains would allow for swift movement over the heads of our attackers, and the hooks on their ends could serve as makeshift weapons.

The other was that the horde of fighters appeared to be mostly focused on me. They spewed bullets at the men in the crew as they charged forward, but they were barreling toward me again, even though Talon was still by the cabinet where I'd left him.

A chill trickled through me. I didn't need to see any more than that to understand. This building belonged to the people associated with that teardrop symbol, and those were the same people who thought they owned me. They'd come to collect.

The crew were doing their best to defend me, as Julius had sworn they would. Talon kept firing on the incoming attackers, and Julius sprayed bullets from the other side of the room. Blaze and Garrison were getting in as many shots as they could too, but we were vastly overwhelmed. There had to be at least twenty men still rushing through the room. They shot at the guys the second any of them tried to take even a step from cover, and the vests they wore absorbed any shots that caught them in the torso.

"Aim for their heads!" I hollered out, although I suspected the crew had already figured that out for themselves, and scrambled onto the top of the sprawling machine. With a swift jump, I grasped one of the chains and swung out over the men who'd nearly reached me.

I had to keep one hand around the rust-speckled chain, but with the other, I hailed bullets on the men below. They scattered in an instant, but I caught two in the skull, splattering brains and blood across the already gruesome floor in a mess the crew might have appreciated if we hadn't all been fighting for our lives.

Unfortunately, the chain chose that moment to give out. It unraveled abruptly from the fixtures on the ceiling, and I thumped to the ground, managing to brace my feet beneath me in time to save me from landing on my ass.

I whirled around, finding myself in the midst of the attackers I'd just been harassing from overhead. As they converged on me again, the crew burst from the shelter they'd taken, Talon and Julius whipping out knives to take on our opponents in ways that wouldn't risk me taking one of their bullets. I shot one man who loomed over me in the throat, wishing I hadn't needed to leave behind my own knife.

When I ducked and swiveled, arms wrapped around my waist from behind. I slammed my foot down on my attacker's and heaved him over my back. With a well-timed shove, I rammed him into one of the dangling hooks with a sickening crunch as it penetrated his spine at the base of his skull. His body jerked and went still.

More of the men were grabbing at my limbs. I kicked, punched, and aimed careful bullets to avoid my allies, opening a path through the menacing swarm. I hurtled out of the worst of the crowd in time to see Garrison dueling another attacker who'd lost his gun. As he aimed a punch at the guy's face, another man lunged at him from behind, right near me.

I didn't think, only moved. Flinging myself at the man, I knocked him to the ground just inches from where

Garrison stood. I snapped the attacker's wrist, yanked the knife he'd been wielding from his loosening fingers, and plunged it into his back right through the vest. Bulletproof didn't mean blade-proof.

Garrison had just managed to get a clear enough opening to shoot his opponent in the forehead. He spun around and saw me on the floor behind him, wrenching the knife free from the dead man who'd meant to do the same to him. I glanced up, and his hazel eyes locked with mine.

His jaw twitched. "Thanks," he muttered, not sounding particularly grateful despite the word.

I didn't have time to lecture him on his tone, because another bunch of men launched themselves at us—mostly at me—in the same moment. I hurled myself away behind another machine, but they pounded after me.

My breath was coming ragged from the intense pace I'd been keeping up. More gunshots reverberated through the large room.

I had to give the crew more of an opening. Get our attackers into a tighter space where they'd have less room to maneuver, and then we could surround *them* despite having smaller numbers.

The pricks were after me, obviously. So I'd just have to lead the way.

I dodged the closest attackers and sprinted toward the hall. The slaughtering room where I'd found the knife seemed like my best bet. I could grab another blade there if I needed to. I veered toward it—and realized I'd failed to take one factor into account.

A few more men had broken into the factory through other windows at that end of the building—maybe backup that'd just arrived. I dashed into the room I'd been aiming for, several other attackers right on my heels, and nearly ran straight into three others. Suddenly, I was the one surrounded.

I fired off two quick shots, managing to take down one man and wound another in the leg before someone behind me closed in enough to wrench my wrist and disarm me. When I swung around, snatching up the abandoned butcher knife in my other hand, the men behind me leapt at me. I caught one in the gut with a backward kick, slicing at the ones coming at me through the doorway, but there were too many. If the crew were following, they hadn't reached me yet.

A bulging arm slammed around my throat. I went still, knowing that thrashing could force him to crush my windpipe, willing my body to relax so I could move swiftly as soon as I saw my opening.

"The boss wants us to take you in alive," my captor snarled by my ear. "But we're authorized to kill you if we can't accomplish that. It's up to you whether you walk out of this shithole with your life."

A sudden chill washed over my mind as I stared at the mass of attackers closing in around me. The crew might not make it to me in time. I could take down another three, maybe four of these assholes… more if I was lucky, but I didn't like relying on luck.

The odds were against me. If I kept fighting, I might very well die here at these pricks' hands.

A flicker of panic shot through me—and then faded away. In its place, my nerves went totally still with a weird sense of calm.

I didn't care. If I died, I died. I'd rather become a corpse than end up locked away and essentially a slave all over again. This was *my* choice.

"When you bring back my dead body, I hope they kill you out of spite," I said. In the same instant, I jerked my body to snap his hold.

My knife caught another guy who leapt at me in the neck. I kicked the one behind me into the edge of one of the tables and dropped to the floor both to avoid the groping hands and to snatch up the gun I'd lost.

I flipped onto my back and fired at the faces looming over me. Someone dove in with a knife that raked across my shoulder when I deflected it from my throat at the last second. Hissing at the sting of pain, I clamped my free hand around his wrist and wrenched to plunge the blade into his own chest.

I tripped another attacker with a slam of my heel, rolled under the table and shot a few legs before someone slammed a steel-toed boot into my ribs from the other side. With another wince, I whirled around and shot the kneecap on the offending leg. The man toppled over, and I added another bullet to his head.

More attackers swarmed on me, but other shouts joined the fray—voices I was much happier to hear.

"Take this, fuckers!" Blaze called out with fierce exuberance.

Julius's growl followed. "This is what happens to anyone who messes with the Chaos Crew."

What followed was a blur of adrenaline, movement, and gunfire. I snatched my last cartridge from my pocket and shoved it into my gun as the guys did their work and then added more of my own bullets to the deluge from beneath the table. Bodies swayed and crumpled around me.

One final attacker sprang at me with a knife in both hands, but my kick to his belly sent him sprawling—right beneath the swing of Talon's knife.

In the sudden quiet, I scrambled out from under the table. Our dead opponents littered the room around me, and I could see others sprawled in the hallway outside. Julius looked the scene over with a grim smile.

Blaze's gaze snagged on me—and the cut carved into my shoulder. "You're hurt."

I pressed my hand to the wound. "I'll be fine. It's not that deep." The stinging had already dulled to a faint ache.

Garrison looked up from where he was crouched in the corner, checking the attackers' pockets. "I'm not finding any ID, but this prick is still alive," he said, motioning to a man who was bleeding from his thigh and stomach. "Maybe he can cough up some details for us?"

A hard glint came into Julius's eyes. "I'll bet he can. But we shouldn't wait around here for more of these assholes to come at us. Bring him. With a little convincing, I'm sure we can find out everything he knows."

Talon went over to haul the guy into his hold. The

injured man flailed ineffectually as we strode back through the factory.

Blaze glanced at me, managing a wry smile. "Not such a bad lead after all, in the end."

I nodded to the man. "Let's see if he gives anything up before we make a final judgment on that."

FIFTEEN

Garrison

I KNEW my time to interrogate was coming when the screaming had faded into an occasional dull whimper of pain. A few minutes later, Talon came striding out of the basement room in the old warehouse we'd stopped by, wiping his hands across a tan towel that had been stained red.

This was how we did interrogations. Talon broke the fuckers apart, and I pieced them back together just enough and in just the right way to get the answers we needed. If they hadn't already spilled their guts to get Talon to stop. The odds were about fifty-fifty.

This guy was one of the more resilient ones.

Talon nodded to me. "He's ready for you."

I glanced behind me to where Dess sat beside Julius, leaning back in her chair and appearing unfazed by the entire situation as he finished bandaging her shoulder.

Blaze eyed his laptop, trying and failing to find out exactly who had access to the camera within the factory. He swore at the computer under his breath.

"Gave you a tough time, did he?" I asked Talon with purposeful bravado. The man was fucking good at what he did, but that gave me an extra ego boost when it turned out my skills were the ones that'd get us what we needed.

"He's stubborn, but he's weak and out of it now," the other man replied. "Threatening him only made him clam up more."

That was useful to know. Some people coughed up the information we needed in the face of someone physically intimidating. Some responded better to psychological threats. Others needed a more nuanced approach. It sounded like this guy belonged to the last group.

As I stepped into the room, I was already formulating a strategy in my mind. I walked in with a slight slouch and a hesitant expression on my face, watching our captive's reaction from the corner of my eyes. Sometimes after a battering, what an opponent responded best to was the chance to exert some kind of power over another person. That meant looking meek and nervous, but not so much that he couldn't get any satisfaction out of lording it over me.

The man was slumped in the chair we'd tied him to. We'd bandaged the wound on his stomach, because we didn't want him bleeding out before we were done with him, but little rivulets oozed from the shallower wound on his leg and other minor cuts that Talon had added to his collection, in between the mottling of bruises. A few fingers dangled limply, broken, and the guy's lip was split.

He raised his head slowly, swaying, at the sight of me. When I let myself make eye contact, it was only for an instant before jerking my gaze away. At that show of uncertainty, he managed to draw his posture up a little straighter.

Ah ha. He thought I was someone he might be able to gain an advantage over, and he liked that idea. I'd just keep playing to that tune.

I wandered over to the torture table laid out with Talon's instruments—mostly various types of blades, his favorite tools. "Always on clean-up duty," I muttered to myself. "As if I want to be around all this blood and crap."

I sighed and turned to look at the man again, as if I were sizing him up. At the same time, I shrank in on myself a little. But I spoke, making it sound like I was forcing out the offer despite my nerves. "It doesn't have to be that way, you know. We could both get something out of this."

The man studied me warily. "What do you mean?" he asked, his voice rasping.

I twisted my mouth at an uncertain angle. "This doesn't have to end with them killing you. If I could show I got something out of you—something they want to know—then they'd see that I can be more of a part of their stupid crew. And I'd make sure you get the chance to escape."

The man scoffed weakly, but a glimmer of hope lit in his face at the same time. I'd presented him with a picture of a man who didn't like killing and hungered for more recognition, and he'd lapped it up. "I'm supposed to believe that?" he asked anyway.

I shrugged, walking around him but careful to move closer to the weapons than to him—to show that I didn't want to be near him and risk myself. I didn't want him to think I was outright afraid, but I certainly didn't want him to believe I was fully comfortable, either.

"I don't have any interest in cleaning up another corpse," I said, with a shudder I didn't have to fake. The gore of our killings did actually make me a little queasy, even if I stomached it for the sake of the job. "So really, it's all a favor to me. But I can't let you go if you don't give me anything. Then they'll kill *me*."

The man blinked at me, his eyes going momentarily bleary. Talon had left him in quite a state. He couldn't focus or think clearly, and I knew that if I pushed the right buttons, he'd slip up and give something away.

He shifted against his restraints. "I can't tell you anything, man. I'm at the bottom of the information chain. No one even told me why we were going after you and the girl."

"I guess you could start by telling me who this 'we' is? What group are you with? Who sent you on the job?"

When he hesitated, I grabbed one of the short, serrated blades off the table and walked toward him. His mouth flattened and his nose flared, and I could tell Talon was right. He wouldn't say a word if I was threatening him with a weapon.

That was fine. I hadn't picked it up to do that.

"I can show you I mean what I'm offering," I said, coaxing just a hint of a quaver into my voice. Bending down, I sawed through the rope that bound his left wrist. With a few quick jerks, the cord fell away. I jumped back, out of range of his reach.

The man turned his hand over, staring at it in disbelief. He swayed again and sucked in a ragged breath.

"I told you I don't want you dead," I said in a pleading tone. "Just tell me what you know."

I set the knife back on the table, but at the edge as if I anticipated needing it soon to finish releasing him. The man considered it and then me. His jaw worked.

"This won't do you any good, you know," he said. "No matter what you hear from me, you're all going down. We were just the first, because we've got the direct connection. A call went out, wide, with quite the bounty on your heads. Every mercenary group in the country will be eager to bring in your heads."

A gleam had sparked in his eyes. He was relishing the idea of intimidating me.

I let him have a minor victory, wincing and hunching my shoulders a little more. "Why would they care so much about us?"

He shook his head, a hint of a grin crossing his lips, weary though it was. "Like I said, I don't know. I just know you're dead meat."

Big talk for a man who didn't currently look like much more than meat himself. I kept that observation silent and prodded in a different direction, letting a hint of panic color my words. "Fuck, I knew we were screwed. *Who* put out the call? Who's got it in for us?"

"A man you're going to regret you ever crossed," our captive said darkly, and then sputtered several wet-sounding coughs. I suspected there was some internal bleeding going on.

I switched tactics just a tad to prompt him to spill more. "The guys I work for are the most powerful crew out there. That isn't possible."

The man managed a feeble-sounding snort. "They might like to think so, but they're nothing compared to the real kings of the criminal world."

I honestly had no idea what he was talking about. Maybe the Chaos Crew wasn't anywhere near as big as various mafia-style organizations, and we didn't have as wide a reach as those, but we weren't aiming to be some kind of syndicate. We could have taken down any of those trumped-up pricks any time we wanted. But I guessed they liked to think that wasn't true.

"Some kind of mafioso, huh?" I said doubtfully. "We've tangled with the Russian mob and the Italians, even the Chinese. Sounds like you're just bluffing."

The man just sneered at me with so much confidence that I found my own was shaken. Was there someone higher up than the mafias who had it out for us? Just how well connected were the people who'd run Dess's household?

They *had* managed to nearly get the better of us at the old meat factory. That didn't bode well.

"Please," I said, going back into meek mode. "If we can't get out of this shit situation, at least give me something so I can protect myself. I'll make a run for it after I cut you loose and let the others deal with this fucking problem."

He shook his head again. "*I* don't even know his name. Just that when he says jump, you'd better jump. And a whole lot of mercs are doing that right now."

I sensed that I'd gotten everything I could out of that line of questioning, as much as it frustrated me. But now that I had him feeling superior to me, it was the perfect time to throw a spanner into the works and see what came out of him when I took him by surprise.

I sucked in a breath and frowned at him. "How does this all connect to Damien Malik?"

The guy stiffened too quickly for him to hide his reaction. He forced his body to relax a moment later, but I'd already marked his response. He knew *something* about Malik—something that related to this powerful criminal figure he'd been taunting me with.

Was Malik on this master criminal's payroll too? Had the guy been lying and he happened to know that Malik *was* the master criminal?

I stepped toward him. "We know he's mixed up in this somehow. You obviously do too. Do we have to watch out for him?"

The guy's eyes narrowed. His walls were going up again. "I'd say we all have to watch out for that fucker."

"What do you mean? What's he been doing?"

The anxiety I showed didn't get me anywhere this

time. The man had turned even cagier. He simply shot me a tight smirk and sat in silence.

This information could be the key to everything—to the attack on us, to Dess's kidnapping and training—all the mysteries we'd been working so hard to unravel. I released my cautious demeanor just a little, framing my eagerness as desperation. "Come on, man. Just give me this one thing, and I'll cut you loose right now."

The man just kept giving me a crooked but mocking smile even as his head started to droop again, and a prickle of real frustration shot through my chest. I was *so* close, and this asshole decided to balk now?

"Look at you," I said, moving close enough to give his chair a little shove. "You're halfway free already. Help *yourself*, you idiot!"

He chuckled, but it was a hopeless sound that knotted my stomach. If a person started feeling they had nothing left to lose, you had no more leverage.

"Your boys will kill me anyway," he said in an even raspier voice than before. His eyelids quivered as a swell of pain must have washed over him. "And if somehow you got me out of here, *he'd* kill me because he'd assume I'd talked. There's no fucking way out. Just give it up."

No. I didn't give in that easily, and neither should this halfwit. I shoved his chair again, distantly aware that my cringing front was falling away and not particularly caring. I had to shock something out of this asshole before he slipped from my grasp completely. Julius was counting on me—Dess was counting on me—

The chair skidded a few inches to the side, its legs

grating against the concrete floor. I recognized my mistake a split-second too late.

I'd jostled the guy toward the torture table. His free arm whipped out, and his fingers closed around the handle of the knife I'd left on the edge.

If he'd slashed it at me, it wouldn't have been so bad. I'd have dodged with maybe some split skin for Julius to stitch up. But instead the captive let out one last, hollow laugh and plunged the blade into his own throat.

Blood gushed forth, soaking him and spraying me in an instant. I jerked back with a noise of strangled horror—both at the sudden, stinking mess and the fact that I'd allowed it to happen.

Our victim had found an escape route after all, and it was one where I couldn't chase after him. His body was already crumpling in the chair, the life draining out of it. I knew without feeling for a pulse that he was a goner. He sure as hell wasn't talking any more with a knife in his throat.

Shit. *Shit.*

I paced from one end of the room to the other as the blood formed a thick puddle beneath the chair. My hands balled into fists at my sides. I had to go up and tell Julius about my fuck-up. I'd found out a few things, but it was all too vague to be really useful—and I'd screwed up when I could have gotten so much more.

How could I have let myself get so impatient? For fuck's sake, I knew better.

I dragged a breath through my clenched teeth, and the door eased open. The most likely source of my frayed control peered inside. My jaw tightened even more.

"What happened?" Dess asked, staring at the scene.

"What does it look like?" I snapped. "I pushed him too far, and he found a way to jump right over the edge."

Her gaze slid to me, and something softened in her expression. Somehow that made me even more pissed off. How dare she *sympathize* when half the reason I'd screwed up was that I hadn't felt totally like myself since she'd come barging into our lives?

"I'm sure you were doing your best," she said. "It's not like torture is an exact science."

"I still should have done better than letting him off himself. Why don't you get out of here and let me clean up my own mess?"

Dess knit her brow. Her voice came out terser. "I'm trying to help. It's not like there's anyone in the world who doesn't make mistakes."

I sputtered a laugh. "This is more than just a mistake. I don't need you sugar-coating it. I can face my fuckups like a man."

She folded her arms over her chest. "Then maybe you should act like a man now and stop bitching about this. Stop acting like *I'm* the enemy. I don't know what the hell your problem with me is, but I'm getting sick of you treating me like I either don't exist or like I'm garbage."

I winced inwardly but contained my reaction. I couldn't afford to let her see how much she affected me. No fucking way.

"I'm not going to cater to your every whim just

because—" I started, and just then, Julius stormed into view behind her.

"What the hell is this all about?" he demanded.

Part of me wanted to shrink back like I'd been pretending to do around our captive. I forced my chin up and my shoulders back. "I screwed up. He got too close to a knife and offed himself."

Julius swept his hand through the air. "I'm not talking about the interrogation. We were going to kill him anyway. I'm asking why the hell you two are fighting after all the shit we've just been through?"

Dess stiffened. "I was just telling Garrison to stop acting like such an ass all the time."

Julius gave her a stern look. "Garrison is how he is. But he can learn to watch his mouth when the situation calls for it." He glowered at me next. "We've got enough people attacking us without going at each other."

Annoyance started to flare in me again, but Dess lowered her head. The slant of her mouth and the slight deflating of her posture gave more of an answer than any words could have.

She wasn't *angry* with me. She was hurt. I'd been pushing her away ever since we'd hooked up, and… and it genuinely bothered her.

She wanted more of a connection with me, more comradery and warmth, and I'd been shutting her out. Even though if I let myself think about it instead of giving in to my kneejerk reaction to push her away, I knew I wanted the same thing.

Julius kept studying both of us. "I was hoping the two

of you could collaborate on the next steps we need to take from here. Is that going to be a problem?"

I shook my head quickly. "No. We can work together. It wasn't Dess's fault. I was frustrated with the interrogation, and I shouldn't have taken it out on her."

Julius nodded and turned to Dess. She tipped her head in acknowledgment of what I'd said, but her expression was a little more skeptical than his was.

I guessed I couldn't blame her. Whatever connection had already formed between us, I must have hammered a lot of cracks into it over the past few days.

This wasn't how I wanted things to go, not really. I'd better figure out my bullshit before it got in my way again.

SIXTEEN

Decima

GARRISON CLEANED UP *NICE.*

Seeing him in his new tailored tuxedo, I couldn't seem to peel my eyes away from him. He strutted up the sidewalk toward the hotel that was the site of our current mission with a confidence that shouted, "I'm rich, and you're below me." A mask, I had no doubt, but one that would fit the fundraiser we were crashing perfectly.

His hair had been arranged elegantly atop his head—all the shaggy dirty blond strands falling in a way that looked both styled and messy simultaneously. His well-built frame might not have been quite as massively brawny as Julius's or as dangerously toned as Talon's, but it filled out the suit to impressive effect, one I suspected the other men around us had to envy. He moved with a sense of power that practically radiated through the air.

Which was good, because our fellow attendees were

among the most powerful figures in business and politics in this part of the country. I only hoped that I could give off half as convincing a vibe.

I was more used to slinking through the shadows than being on display. Noelle had taught me how to handle myself among the wealthy and pompous, of course, but it'd always taken more energy than the stealthier parts of my missions.

After he flashed the fake IDs at the door and we'd been ushered in thanks to Blaze's prep work, Garrison tsked his tongue at me teasingly. "You're staring… again."

"Just making sure you're not giving off any red flags," I said, which was a total lie, but he didn't need to know that. His ego was big enough as it was.

Anyway, I should be focused on the job, not my co-conspirator. I tugged my gaze away to take in the mass of people circulating the room.

Champagne was flowing, its crisp scent tickling into my nose, and rich patrons in designer clothes tittered in that way that passes for laughter when you need to keep up appearances. I resisted the urge to tug at my own sleek silk evening gown.

This was a fundraising event for Damien Malik, and we intended to use it to find out exactly what intel the guests had on him and his activities. Rich people *always* had information that didn't belong to them. I'd learned that through my years of infiltrating similar parties.

It only took a bit of manipulation to get people like this talking, but that was Garrison's specialty. I was going to practice my pickpocketing skills.

I caught Garrison's eye with a subtle nod to indicate I was going to get started, and he returned it with a flash of a smile that was warmer than anything he'd aimed at me recently. I couldn't tell whether it was part of his act or whether he'd actually gotten his head on straighter since Julius had chided us for our argument the other day. For now, either was fine.

Leaving him behind to work his verbal magic, I roamed through the crowd. Some thieves relied on distraction to get the job done, but that meant drawing the target's attention to you first. I didn't want anyone even thinking about me when they noticed their phones were missing.

I dipped my hand into one woman's sparkly purse and tugged another phone from a posh gentleman's back pocket. Discreetly tucking them into my own purse, which was the largest I could get away with wearing this outfit and doctored with special lining to block the signal, I stalked onward. I'd take as many as I could get, as many devices as offered themselves in easy reach. There was no telling who might have passed on a stray observation or bit of gossip about the man we were most interested in.

A couple of guys I recognized from Blaze's research into Malik's security detail stepped into view. I handily dodged them, weaving my way toward the other end of the room. Spotting a man who looked particularly well-connected based on the numbers of hangers-on gathered around him, I managed to trip one of the women next to him without her even realizing what'd knocked her off balance, brushed past the man as he leaned in to steady her, and scored his phone from the inside pocket of his jacket quick as lightning. No one suspected a thing.

My purse was starting to feel pretty full. It weighed on my elbow, where I'd left it dangling. I grabbed a glass of champagne to give myself the extra cover of alcohol if anyone noticed any odd movements and circulated through the crowd some more, keeping my ears pricked for interesting conversation rather than my fingers slippery.

I was right in the middle of the vast ballroom when my gaze caught on Damien Malik himself. At the sight of his neatly slicked silvery hair and polished smile, my stomach dipped. I sidled out of his line of sight, monitoring him from the edge of my vision. My pulse thumped harder.

The man the crew had interrogated had all but confirmed that Malik was involved in the organization that ran the household. I had no idea whether he knew anything about my kidnapping and training or if his connection was in some other area, but a thread of tension ran through my chest all the same.

How big a menace was this man who pretended to be trying to make the country a more peaceful place?

My fingers itched, and I couldn't help wondering whether it'd be better just to kill him now. I could wait until he strayed away from the crowd and accomplish it so quickly no one would realize what'd happened until I was well away. Or slip into the kitchen and quickly concoct one of the basic poisons I'd learned and slip that into a drink or hors d'oeuvres.

I reined that impulse in. All of my missions before I'd met the crew had been with the intention to kill, but that wouldn't actually help me now. Malik was our main lead to the rest of the surviving organization, now that Noelle and everyone else from the household was dead. He'd lead us to the people responsible for my imprisonment one way or another.

Besides, we didn't know for sure that his association with those people was as an ally and not a victim of some sort. It was possible that the man we'd interrogated had refused to talk because he didn't want to reveal other plans his employer had in the works that would target the politician.

I might have gone for one last phone—Malik's—but I doubted there was anything on there that Blaze hadn't already found on his computer, which didn't amount to much. No, right now we wanted to know what people who didn't necessarily have his best interests at heart were saying to or about him.

After a few more minutes, I spotted Garrison, and then I stopped in my tracks. I couldn't approach him, because he was obviously still doing his own work—which at the moment involved leaning close to a middle-aged woman with a sculpted updo as she giggled at something he'd said. She tapped the lapel of his suit, and he responded with a reserved grin I suspected was designed to give her hope while not promising his continued attention. He let his fingers trail over her wrist.

My teeth set on edge. A different urge gripped me, one to march right over there and tear them apart. Which was ridiculous, because he was only doing his job getting her to open up, and besides, we weren't really anything to each other than colleagues. He'd made it very clear that one hookup on the rooftop hadn't changed that.

Still, seeing her fingers caress his sleeve provoked another flare of jealousy. I distracted myself by turning away and searching out one of the attendants carrying their trays of little treats. I ate the bit of toast and caviar I selected slowly, trying to make even my bites look elegant. Then I meandered over to a table in the corner.

To my surprise, Garrison sauntered over not long after. He stopped beside me, taking a sip from his glass of champagne, and tipped his head casually toward my purse. "Good haul?" he asked quietly.

"Nothing to scoff at," I replied. "How about you?"

"A couple of interesting tidbits that will lead Blaze down a rabbit hole, I'm sure, but nothing definitely useful. I'm just taking a breather before I hit up a few more of these idiots."

He didn't look or sound tired, but I studied him more carefully. A question I probably shouldn't have been asking tumbled out. "Is it hard? Not just talking with people but, like, getting flirty with them and all that?"

Garrison raised an eyebrow at me. "Still having trouble keeping your eyes off me, huh?" He gazed out at the horde again, and his voice sobered. "It's totally easy when I don't mean it. Everything's easy when I don't mean it."

Suddenly I felt as if he'd just said something more honest than even he had realized in the moment. A brief glimpse of the man behind the many masks. Maybe that was why I found the courage to venture, even as my throat constricted a little at getting this personal, "Is that why it seems to be so hard for you to even stay friendly with me? Because you would mean it?"

Garrison's eyes jerked back to me, startled and wary. I found myself wishing I could take the question back. But I still wanted to know the answer.

I thought he'd meant at least some of the friendly overtures he'd made, as seldom as they were. I didn't think I'd imagined the momentary tenderness after we'd had sex. I'd assumed his hot-and-cold routine had something to do with my own behavior, but maybe it was only about him. About not wanting to let those masks down once he realized he'd started to.

The personas I put on for my jobs had always felt just like that—like a job. I couldn't wait to strip off the posh demeanor I'd put on for this mission the second we were out of here. For Garrison, though, I was getting the impression that his masks were a way of life.

His mouth tensed, and he let his attention drift away again. I thought he was going to pretend I hadn't spoken. But then he said, with his eyes on the crowd, "Maybe that's some of it. I don't hate you, that's for sure."

"Well, that's reassuring," I grumbled.

"If you were looking for reassurance, I'm not the guy to come to."

"Yes, that's been abundantly clear." I paused and shook my head. "I'm sorry. I didn't mean to make things awkward. I'm just trying to understand. I realize I haven't always been completely upfront with you, but when I was playing those roles before, it was a matter of survival. I didn't know if I could trust any of you at all. Since you found out the truth, I've been trying to be the most *myself* I can, even if I'm still figuring out who exactly that is."

Garrison was silent for a moment. Then the corner of his mouth curled upward. "I have a pretty good idea of who Dess is. And I—I appreciate that you're honest, even if I haven't been the best at showing it."

At that admission, I couldn't resist prying a little more. "Then why is it hard to act like you do?"

Garrison swiveled the champagne flute between his fingers. He stared down at it, and his shoulders squared as if he'd gathered some sort of resolve.

"It's really just been me for a long time," he said in a low voice I could barely hear over the chatter of the crowd. "When I was a kid, my family was in a car accident—my parents and my brother were killed. It was *my* fault. I started a stupid argument with my brother, distracted my dad at the wheel... Since then, I've always had this idea in my head that I deserve to be on my own. That it's fair punishment for what I did."

The tightness in my throat became an ache. The memory came back to me of the pain and grief I'd thought I'd glimpsed in him briefly weeks ago. No wonder he'd buried it down deep.

"Of course it isn't," I had to say. "It sounds like it was just an accident. Don't kids squabble all the time?"

He shrugged. "Not to the point it gets their whole family killed. Anyway, I've never been worth anything as myself. When I become someone else, I can offer something of value—I can con things out of people, open doors that need opening… So that's all I've been doing for ages now. That's all I'm used to."

"I bet there's a lot you could offer as yourself," I said stubbornly.

A dry chuckle fell from his lips. "I'm not sure how you can say that when I don't even know what it'd be. But that's *your* talent, huh? You always see right through my bullshit. I guess I don't really know how to deal with that, so I deal with it badly." He lifted his gaze to meet my eyes again. "I'm sorry about that. I got my head up my ass and was too chickenshit to pull it out again and admit I'd screwed up with you. But I'm trying to get my act together now. Or my not-an-act."

A smile tugged at my own lips. A giddy sense of light spread through my chest. "Well, good. I'm looking forward to getting to know the real Garrison more."

He eased a little closer, his arm coming to rest against mine. "The real Garrison can also admit that I haven't been able to take my eyes off *you* all evening. I usually go for the red dresses, but damn, do you make purple look sexy as hell."

I looked down at myself, having some trouble wrapping my head around the idea of me as "sexy." But I could see the heat in his eyes when I glanced back up at him. He meant it.

"I wanted to kill the woman I saw you flirting with," I offered up as my own truth.

Garrison grinned—a broad, open grin, not the studied ones he'd flashed at the people in the crowd. "And I'm sure you could have in two seconds flat. But let's not slaughter these obnoxious people while they still might be at least a little useful to us."

I had to laugh. "Deal."

He slipped his arm right around me, his hand coming to rest on my waist with a stroke of his thumb that lit up every inch of my skin. "Also, for the record, I wouldn't mind a repeat of our time on the deck. Maybe even several."

A flush washed over my face, but I kept smiling. So nothing about our hookup had messed things up at all. And I couldn't say I didn't share the sentiment.

I let myself lean into his solid frame just slightly. "Same here."

I was just wondering if there was some alcove we could duck into and celebrate our new honesty in passionate fashion when Garrison's watch vibrated on the small of my back. He let me go so he could check the message that'd appeared on its digital face. His forehead furrowed, and he tilted it toward me.

It was a text from Blaze. *Pull out of there ASAP. I'm seeing activity I don't like. I think we could be in for some more trouble.*

SEVENTEEN

Julius

DESS AND GARRISON were the last to arrive, and I had to do a double take. I'd seen Garrison in his finery while he was getting ready, but I hadn't been here when Dess had come out of her room, dressed in that resplendent purple gown. Striding through the room in that get-up, she looked like something out of a dream.

She nodded greetings to the rest of us and ducked into her bedroom to change. Garrison stayed behind, shrugging off his tuxedo jacket and loosening his tie. He took off the vest of his tuxedo and hung it on the back of Blaze's chair before pulling both of his white undershirt sleeves to his elbows. Then he leaned across the counter of the kitchen island where Blaze was tilted toward the screen of the laptop. "What was so important that you pulled us out of the mission?"

Blaze frowned, his gaze still flicking back and forth as he took in the data streaming by him. "There's a lot of activity in the criminal underbelly of the city, and throughout the night, it's been spreading."

Garrison shook his head. "And? Forgive me, but that's not exactly a new pattern."

Blaze nodded and opened his mouth, but then he closed it again. "I'm going to wait for Dess to get into the details. In the meantime, did you get any information at the fundraiser?"

"Would have gotten more if we hadn't been pulled out," Garrison muttered, and tipped his head toward Dess's room. "You'll have to go through all the phones she pilfered. I have a couple of notes for you to follow up on, but nothing that seems all that promising."

I held myself back from clenching my jaw in frustration. I'd hoped the fundraiser would get us more of the answers we needed—and it might have if we hadn't needed to end the mission halfway through. But the activity Blaze had picked up on had felt too ominous to risk leaving our people in the field. Their safety came before anything else.

"Here you go." Dess strode into the room in her usual T-shirt and sweats and tossed her purse onto the counter. It landed with a heavy metallic thump.

Blaze's eyes lit up as he unzipped the purse. He started pawing out phones onto the countertop until Garrison cleared his throat. "Are you going to get to the point now?"

"Tell them," I said. Dess moved to stand between

Talon and Garrison, a shadow of worry crossing her expression as she watched Blaze.

The hacker motioned to his laptop. "I'm seeing activity that specifically suggests that several other groups of mercenaries have arrived in this area and are trying to track down our location with the intention of attacking us. A few of them stopped by the meat factory, looking like they were attempting to pick up our trail there. Another two groups found the safe house that was compromised by that idiotic attack by the Cutthroats."

"We still have to pay *them* back," Talon muttered.

"This is what the guy we interrogated warned us about," Dess said, rubbing her hand along her jaw.

"Exactly." Blaze exhaled in a rush. "These are crews from all across this part of the country. I wouldn't be surprised if we start seeing some from farther abroad once word gets out that there's a huge bounty and no one has cashed in yet."

Dess's arms went rigid where she'd braced them against the counter. "It's because of me," she said.

My head jerked toward her. "What?"

She met my gaze steadily but with unmistakable horror in hers. "They're all trying to track you down because they know I'm with you. That's why the men at the factory attacked us too. If I wasn't here, they wouldn't bother you at all."

A growl formed in my throat so swiftly I had to swallow it down before I spoke. "It isn't your fault. You can't blame yourself."

She tilted her chin a little defiantly. "Why not? I'm just

pointing out the facts. You wouldn't be in this situation if it wasn't for me."

Damn, did that woman have an effect, even when she was just standing there in plain clothes. She gave off such an assured air even now that I had no doubt she was capable of meeting this threat on her own if she had to. Just as capably as she'd moved those skilled hands over my body days ago. A flicker of heat coursed through me at the memory of her leaning back into me, taking my cock with abandon as she sucked off Talon at the same time.

But she didn't need to be alone to face the threat, any more than she'd needed to satisfy her physical desires alone. As strong as I knew she was, I *wanted* to protect her. She sure as hell didn't deserve to go through even more shit than she already had in the past two decades. I wanted to defend her from the pricks who were determined to stick her back in a cage... and I wanted to defend her from her own self-recriminations.

Blaze piped up first. "Technically, *we* kidnapped you, so even as far as you being in our company goes, that's our fault."

I could already see Dess gearing up to argue his point. I stepped in firmly. "And ignoring all that, it's not your fault that a lunatic has decided he owns you and pulled out all the stops to get you back. You *don't* belong to him, and nothing's going to stop us from helping you drive that fact home to him, no matter what he throws at you."

She stared back at me, but then she nodded just slightly in acknowledgment. Accepting the help while not compromising her pride. I had to admire her even more for her grit.

"We also need to give you more freedom even from us," I admitted. "When we're done talking here, I'll take you through the tunnels and show you the exact route to and from the street and this building. No blindfolds, no tricky turns. I should have done that earlier. You've earned your spot with us, and you should be able to come and go if you need to by that secure route without having one of us escort you."

A more eager light came into Dess's cool gray eyes, one that warmed me to the core. "Thank you," she said quietly, but I could tell she understood what a show of trust the gesture was. She was going to be the first person who knew the hidden route to our main apartment outside of the four of us and Steffie.

I braced myself for Garrison to bicker the point like he seemed to so often when it came to Dess, but he actually relaxed at my offer. "About time," I thought he muttered under his breath.

A twinge of surprise shot through me. Had something happened to make him suddenly willing to support Dess without complaint? Maybe even *he* had finally gotten tired of all his grousing, however much it'd always been an act.

Talon folded his arms over his chest, his expression grim. "How are we going to deal with all these opportunists? Assuming we aren't going to try to simply mow them all down."

"I think that might be a tad beyond even our ample

abilities," Blaze said. "At least with so many all at once. They're only following the money like we do most of the time anyway. Hard to blame them for that."

Well, I certainly could. There were lines I wouldn't have crossed when it came to those who were our closest colleagues. But then, I know our standards weren't necessarily typical.

"How secure are we as long as we stay in the apartment?" I asked. We had enough food stockpiled for at least a week in case of emergency, and Steffie could potentially get more to us without being detected.

Blaze's mouth twisted. "Well, we definitely run a significant risk any time we step outside it, now that so many people are searching for us. I don't think anyone has software on the level of my facial recognition app, but even if we rely on disguises, I wouldn't want to be taking many casual strolls." He paused. "The apartment itself is definitely our most secure location, but I can't say that it's impossible that one of these mercenaries could eventually connect us to it. Especially if they start cooperating and putting their minds together."

"And if we just hide away in here, then we have no chance of finding the prick responsible and putting an end to the whole bounty," Garrison pointed out.

Yes, that was the problem. I didn't love the idea of holing up in hiding regardless, but it was a losing game any way you sliced it. We had to cut to the heart of the problem.

We couldn't track down this criminal kingpin while we had dozens of mercenary groups on the hunt for us, and we couldn't get them off our tails without ending the bounty. Unless…

Unless we made it clear what the consequences of coming at us would be, in a way so emphatic that no one would think it was worth the risk of tangling with us. We might not be able to take down *every* crew out there, but if we made it obvious how easily we could take down at least a few of them before we fell ourselves, no one was going to want to be first in line.

I glanced around at my crew. "We have one other option, and I think it's our best one. We're going to take a trip to the Funhouse and make a statement."

Talon took the news in stride as I'd known he would. The trust we shared went back nearly twenty years and across continents. I wasn't surprised, though, that Blaze blinked, his eyebrows leaping up, and Garrison stared at me as if I'd announced we were going to take the crew to the moon.

They knew exactly what I meant by a *statement*. It wouldn't be pretty, and it would certainly be bloody, in expected Chaos Crew style.

Dess took in the guys' expressions with her penetrating gaze. She turned back to me. "What's the Funhouse?"

Blaze's mouth formed a smile that was tight with nerves. "The Funhouse is a sort-of nightclub in Pittsburgh. Very exclusive. Only the best-connected criminal outfits in the northeast know about it and can arrange to get in. People go there to hang out and make deals with each other."

Garrison was still eyeing me. "And it's understood that

getting into any conflicts there is risky for a whole lot of reasons. But I'm assuming our fearless leader is about to explain how he's figured out ways around all that."

"Do you think the hit placed on us came from the Funhouse?" Dess asked.

I shook my head. "Someone this secretive and high up probably doesn't bother even with venues like that. But most of the crews who'd dare to come after us are part of it. The people there will know about the bounty, and they'll spread the word about any message we end up sending."

"Still going to be fucking crazy," Garrison said.

I gave him an even smile. "Sometimes setting expectations requires a little risk. We lay down the law, show what we're capable of, and then we'll be able to continue our investigations without interruption."

Frankly, I was tired of being on edge and reacting instinctively. The Chaos Crew orchestrated jobs, and we *never* tackled a problem without my diligent planning. It was why we'd always been so successful and why we'd remained on top for so long. Nothing good came from flailing around without a concrete strategy.

It was time that we took back control and showed our dominance to the underworld. I needed to protect my people, and this was how I could do it.

"If this is what needs to be done, I'm in," Dess said angling herself to fully face me. "Let's get started."

I felt my smile soften as I aimed it at her instead. Funny to think that a couple of weeks ago, she'd kept us at arm's length, and now she trusted me so fully that she'd stride into any kind of danger as long as I was leading the way.

This was how I liked seeing her most: rising to a challenge, fearless and confident in her abilities—and mine. The longer she was with us, the more certain I became in my assessment: She would make an irreplaceable addition to the crew if we could convince her to stay once all the trouble and mystery around her past was resolved.

My mind darted back to our encounter on the side of the road again, with a deeper wash of heat. Maybe if I could convince her to stay, she could be more than just a colleague.

I'd never expected to find someone I thought it'd be worth trying to navigate an ongoing relationship with, not in my line of work. Not with the bloodlust and yearning for justice that ran through my veins. But Dess understood all of that.

I also hadn't thought that if I did find a woman who could match me, I might have to share her with Talon. We'd had threesomes with the same partner in the past, but only as one-offs.

Somehow, looking at the woman in front of me, none of that seemed to matter. I was starting to feel like I'd be an idiot *not* to work her into my plans for my own life.

She was *my* woman now. She had been since she'd shuddered against me with my cock impaled inside her, and I wasn't going to let anyone tear her down or rip her away from me.

Which meant it was time to take care of business.

I let a slow grin unfurl across my face. "First, we're going to need some better guns."

EIGHTEEN

Decima

AS THE ELEVATOR careened up through what had looked like a bland office building from the outside, I was overly aware of the weight across my shoulders, belt, and abdomen. Two incredibly precise guns were strapped to my body, one now visible at my hip and the other hidden in my boot. My hoodie and jeans concealed various blades and a set of compact rappelling gear. Each of the guys in formation around me was carrying at least as much if not more.

I threw my hood back, revealing my face in the way Julius had planned. The guys did the same, pulling back the fabric that had been used to conceal our identities as we made our way here—as we waited for what we'd spent two days meticulously planning.

Anticipation hummed through the air. Nothing about the space around me told me this was anything other than an office building, but I had to assume that the men knew what they were doing. It wasn't the kind of mistake they were likely to make.

And where better to hide a top-secret criminal nightclub than in a spot so innocuous-looking?

"We're clear on the plan?" Julius asked, really a formality at this point.

We all nodded. My fingers tingled with excitement, ready to try out those immaculately sighted pistols. I held my hands still, keeping my calm with careful focus. I wasn't about to forget all my training and experience over a trip to Pittsburgh.

The elevator reached the third floor from the top and dinged. The crew had said that the Funhouse encompassed all three of the uppermost floors in the building. I straightened my back and threw back my shoulders, standing behind Julius and Garrison who did the same. I imagined that Blaze and Talon—sandwiching me between them—prepared themselves, too.

The elevator door swung open, and it took every effort for me not to drop my jaw at what lay ahead in the wide-open room before us. The men had described it to me, but somehow I still hadn't been prepared.

Julius strode out onto the entrance platform outside and paused there as we gathered around him. It was both a power move, showing he wasn't in any hurry, and an opportunity for me to adjust to my surroundings. I couldn't be more grateful for the kindness, because this place was unlike any nightclub I'd ever seen. Despite what the guys told me, I couldn't have ever imagined... *this.*

I understood where the place got its name now.

The Funhouse had windowless outer walls, but every surface between here and the roof—walls, floors, and ceilings—was made of glass. Some of it was transparent and the rest of it mirrors that bounced the artificial light back and forth and reflected it at unnerving angles. Even the elevator shaft this far up was glass. I suspected that from any point within the club, you could see every other corner of the place. You'd also see at least a few different views of yourself in those eerie mirrors.

In other words, there was no hiding up here.

Only sparse furniture scattered the glass rooms, but the pieces looked opulent—all silks and velvets, fine leather and mahogany. It was mostly placed around the far ends of the private booths so as not to interrupt the flow of light. I could see right into all those booths, of course, and about half of them were occupied right now. Some of the inhabitants had posh suits and carefully trimmed hair, others more urban clothes like us, but they all gave off a potent vibe of menace and power.

I had no doubt that these were among the upper echelon of criminals. And now an awful lot of them were watching our arrival with gazes I couldn't read.

"Our usual booth is free," Blaze remarked. As one, the crew began marching toward the place that they claimed with only their glances.

As I walked with them, my gaze flitted through the space like the light bouncing off the mirrors, taking in even more details. A handful of aerial artists dangled from knotted silks hung in various hollow columns of glass, twisting, posing, and swaying in a weird sort of dance to match the bass-heavy music that pulsed through the club. They all wore skimpy clothing that bared most of their bodies. Not just women, though—I spotted a couple of men wearing only thongs as well.

I traced the ropes up toward the ceiling high above us on the uppermost floor, and my jaw went slack a second time. There on the top floor, in an enclosure made of— what else?—solid glass, a fully grown *tiger* was prowling from side to side. Not just a nightclub but a zoo too, apparently.

We strode toward the mirrored staircase, and as I turned my head, I noticed the elevator descending, leaving a completely translucent glass case where it had been.

"It goes back to the bottom for appearances," Garrison explained with a smirk. "Can't have anything blocking the view."

My lips twitched with amusement, but I wasn't sure I wanted to show anything other than a solemn front with all these hardened criminals watching. I was an unknown quantity here, and I didn't want them pegging me for a silly girl. Other than the female dancers and some of the servers prancing through the levels from the bar at the very center of the club, I might have been the only woman in the place.

Oh, no, maybe there was one lady down there in the far corner with a couple of men, her hair cut short but her lips a stark ruby red. Still, we were clearly a rare breed.

We passed one of the female servers on our way to our booth, and she trailed her hand over Blaze's bicep and leaned in to whisper something quick in his ear. Huh. From the look on her face, she was aiming to hook up— with full knowledge of what to expect from him.

Had he slept with her before? From the playful wave one of the other servers aimed his way, he was pretty popular around here.

I'd known he was a flirt, but I hadn't realized he followed up on it with much action. Now, he tugged on a lock of the first woman's blond hair but said in a warm tone, "Not tonight. Tonight's all business."

But other nights? A spike of jealousy I hadn't been prepared for lanced through me and soured my mouth. I swallowed thickly and yanked my gaze back to our path through the club. It wasn't *my* business who he'd slept with before, especially when our relationship had never progressed to anything like that.

Julius marched first into the booth that was apparently the crew's regular one, the rest of us flanking him. A tan leather sofa stretched the length of one wall, impossibly buttery when I sank down onto it. Two matching armchairs sat at either end of it, and a glass coffee table with mahogany legs gleamed between them all.

Julius and Talon seated themselves on either side of me. Blaze flopped into one of the chairs, and Garrison stayed standing with a typically cocky air.

"Order me an Old Fashioned," he said. "I'm going to make the rounds." He arched an eyebrow at me. "Try not to get into trouble while I'm gone."

I had the urge to stick my tongue out at him, which

really wouldn't have given the right impression at all. Instead, I wrinkled my nose, and he laughed.

He sauntered out of our booth and wandered to our nearest neighbors, and then the next occupied booth, and the next. From the nods and words exchanged, it looked like everyone was aware of who he was. His demeanor shifted slightly as he approached each group, subtly reflecting their pre-existing energy. I watched his chameleon-like skills with a flicker of admiration.

I'd never seen him so fully at work before. He was masterful.

Not all of his friendly overtures seemed to be met with equal enthusiasm. I noticed a couple of the men whose groups he approached tense up slightly as the others spoke to him, and made a mental note to remember them later.

A different server sashayed into our booth and asked for our drink orders. "A whiskey highball," I said, picking the low-alcohol cocktail I usually turned to on missions so I could sip it without being worried that it'd go too much to my head. "Extra ginger ale."

"Just club soda and lime for me," Julius said.

The server giggled. "Right, you're the teetotaler."

Talon asked for a beer and Blaze a marguerita, putting in Garrison's order as well. As the server headed out, I glanced at Julius. "You don't drink."

He lifted his shoulders slightly. "I have on occasion in the past, but only very rarely since I started the crew. You never know when you're going to need a totally clear head."

"And Julius is the one who makes sure we all keep *our* heads attached," Blaze said with a chuckle.

"Exactly," Julius said without any humor of his own. "I won't risk the crew's lives by being in any way mentally compromised."

It made sense, I supposed. Because he was the one who led most of the missions, he felt responsible for seeing them through entirely. And maybe even in between missions, he wanted to be on guard for unexpected problems. I didn't think drinking was an irresponsible decision, especially when we needed beverages in front of us to hold our cover, but I understood why Julius wouldn't do it.

The server came back in just a few minutes and set out our glasses in front of us. Remembering Julius's words, I only took the smallest sip from mine, rolling the tangy liquid around in my mouth.

As the woman left, Garrison strolled back in and plucked his Old Fashioned off the table before sinking into the free chair. I watched him take a small swallow. Was that really his drink of choice, or was it part of a persona he was putting on even now? I guessed any face you wanted to show to the criminal underworld, you had to keep it up every second you were in this place.

We relaxed back into our seats as if we were only there to enjoy the atmosphere. "Observations?" Julius asked Garrison.

Garrison cradled his drink against his chest and cocked his head. "I'd say there are four teams currently here who are aware of the bounty and seriously considering pursuing it, if not already working on finding our usual base of operations. The Chicago Turks, the Burning Whips, the Jackhammers, and the Angel's Fiends." He surreptitiously pointed out the groups as he spoke—one on the top floor near the tiger's enclosure, two on the second floor with us, and one down by the elevator platform. Among them were the groups I'd noticed getting edgy at his arrival.

"I thought we had pretty good relations with at least the Turks and the Fiends," he added. "It must be an awfully big pot for them to be jeopardizing that."

Talon hummed darkly. "They aren't friends if they're willing to betray us."

"How can you be sure?" I asked.

Garrison made a vague gesture and took another gulp of his drink. "I read it in the way they looked at me and talked to me. The tension was obvious, as much as they tried to hide it. They were startled to see us here, so between that lack of preparation and the nature of the Funhouse, I doubt they'll make any move on us."

I glanced at the glass floor beneath my feet and realized how impossible an attack would be in this place, at least one that hadn't been meticulously planned. One misplaced shot and you could easily damage the entire structure of this part of the building, shattering the floor beneath you or the ceiling over your head as well as destroying your target. Peace was enforced through a sense of mutually assured destruction.

But we were going to rise above that mutual assurance. Julius was the most meticulous man I'd ever met, and I knew he'd considered every possibility. The statement he meant to make would be a powerful one as long as we survived it.

"Just those four groups?" Julius asked.

Garrison shrugged. "As far as I can tell. The others might have hid it better, but that'd mean they've developed much better poker faces since the last time I met them."

"Four is plenty." The crew's commander scanned the club. I could practically see the final pieces lining up in his head. "Talon, you deal with the Turks up top. Dess, you take the Jackhammers down below. I'll handle the two on our level, although feel free to jump in if either of you finishes with your targets before I do. We need them all down ASAP, before they have a moment to *think* about striking back."

I nodded, enjoying the deeper thrum of authority that'd come into his voice. It was only the three of us doing the shooting for this operation—the three of us who were the most skilled. Blaze and Garrison were proficient enough to handle backup during a regular mission, but this one required too careful a touch.

They were contributing in their own ways, of course— Garrison with his rounds and Blaze now, glancing at his phone and watching the movements of the employees around the club. "Ready on your signal," Julius said to him.

"Just a few minutes," Blaze murmured.

We needed to time our attack perfectly. No servers or dancers could be in, but Blaze had said they followed obvious patterns. If we worked around their circuits of the room, we'd get a small opening to make our move without hurting any innocent bystanders.

I casually adjusted my visible gun, refamiliarizing myself with its exact position. We drank from our glasses and exchanged a few random remarks that passed through my mind without sticking. I was too focused on the task ahead, braced for the moment when Blaze would say—

"Now," the hacker murmured, standing.

Julius, Talon, and I leapt to our feet and sprang forward. Without looking back, I knew Blaze and Garrison would make their way to the elevator shaft while we did the dirty work.

Talon charged up the staircase, and I flew down it, dropping to grab my second gun from my boot as I went. My momentum whipped back my hair.

All my attention narrowed down to the squad of five men lounging in the booth Garrison had indicated. I noted the carefully sculpted scruff on their jaws, the leather jackets that hung off their bulky forms, the bottle of brandy someone had bought now empty on the table between their glasses. The twitch of their heads toward me as they registered the sudden action around them—

But all that was in fleeting seconds, the space of a heartbeat or two. Then I was diving into their midst, pulling the triggers with my two guns aiming in separate directions.

We'd picked the guns and ammunition for both accuracy and more moderate power. Bullets that tore straight through bodies with enough force to crack the glass behind them would have screwed us over too. These would embed themselves in our targets' flesh and lodge there as the blood flowed out around them.

But I still had to aim well. Hit the fleshy parts that offered plenty of blood flow while also proving instantly fatal. We still wanted impact, but we couldn't afford any flailing around as the life drained out of them. Not when these targets were such skilled criminals themselves, equally armed and dangerous.

I shot one man three times in the chest in quick succession—above and below his heart to puncture the aortas and then right into the heart itself. As his body keeled over, blood gushed over the table and across the floor. At the same time, I shot one of his colleagues in the throat. More blood spouted out of his mouth and neck as he tumbled over.

Their three companions were leaping up with noises of shock. Those noises died as I buried bullets in two of their throats too. The fifth guy, the one who'd be our survivor to return to his larger organization and everyone they knew to spread the word, I simply shot in both arms, rendering them temporarily useless. He wasn't going to be tossing back any more drinks—or aiming his own weapons at us.

I whirled and dashed back up the stairs without a second's hesitation. Julius had already taken down three of the four men in his first group. He was just shooting the second guy in the other booth. I blasted the third and fourth in the skull, one in the front and one in the back thanks to the way they were standing. The fifth cringed and spluttered on the floor as Julius kicked his gun out of his hand.

Exhilaration rushed through me. I'd never had a job quite like this, and it felt *good* to stretch my skills again, to test the limits of what I was capable of. Especially next to men who were equally capable.

We were a pretty fucking fantastic team.

Speaking of capable men—

My gaze leapt to Talon on the floor above us. He was just plunging his knife into the chest of one of the men among his targets, two already lying dead from gunshot wounds, another's throat slit.

Talon launched himself at the fifth, who was groping for a weapon, and sliced that hand neatly off through the forearm. He whipped the severed limb into the tiger's enclosure, where the predator pounced on it with a pleased growl. Then he hurtled down the stairs to join us.

As Talon and I moved to the elevator shaft where Blaze and Garrison were already waiting, Julius held up his hands.

"We're done here," he shouted, his voice ringing through the entire club. Some of the other patrons had frozen, flattening themselves against the furniture defensively; others were groping for their own weapons.

Julius continued quickly, wanting to get his message out before we faced any backlash—if anyone dared. "We don't want to kill anyone who doesn't deserve to die. Remember what'll happen if you fire a shot and it goes badly. Well, we won't be the only ones who fall." He gestured to the glass surfaces around us. "This was just a reminder of the consequences if you mess with the Chaos Crew. Leave us be, and we'll leave you be too."

That sentence was the signal to depart. I hooked my rappelling line onto the elevator cable in sync with the men. With a collective breath, we dove into the abyss below, soaring down the shaft out of the Funhouse.

Not a single shot rang out after us.

NINETEEN

Decima

EVERYONE'S SPIRITS lifted the next morning when Blaze said the magic words that made our entire risky gambit worth it. "Most of the concerning activity that I noticed in the city has stopped. It seems like the groups who were after the bounty have backed off. We're in the clear to keep up our search."

I knew that we needed to accept the wins where we found them, so I didn't bother dwelling on the lack of information that search had brought us so far. We'd found a few puzzle pieces, and they would lead us to more clues. They had to. With the crew at my side, I already had one major advantage.

I strode to the side of the kitchen where Garrison was cooking bacon and Talon pouring one of his bottles of… something into a frosted mug. I looked down at it, and the immediate revulsion that rose in my chest was unprecedented. "What even *is* that?" I asked, leaning closer to him.

"Kombucha," he said, swirling it around and taking a long gulp before pushing it toward me. "Do you want to try it?"

The offer came genuinely, and I reached for the mug that he extended, my fingers brushing across his as I took the mug. The contact of our hands sent a jolt of heat through my chest, and I ran my tongue over my teeth to keep the feelings at bay. His strong fingers brought back *plenty* of memories.

I lifted the glass mug to my lips and took a small sip, coughing and wrinkling my nose the moment the sour flavor registered.

"You like this?" I asked, scanning the counter for a less repulsive drink to wipe away the horrendous taste that plagued my tongue.

Talon shrugged, taking another gulp. "It's an acquired taste."

Garrison chipped in. "Don't let him fool you. Only he likes that battery acid."

"Thanks for the warning," I said, rolling my eyes and looking over Garrison's shoulder at the crispy bacon that he was now pulling from the pan. When he'd placed the last piece on his plate, I reached around him and grabbed one, plopping it in my mouth with a small smile before he could stop me.

Garrison didn't seem bothered as he looked over and met my eyes, his filled with just as much amusement as mine had been. I had the sense that reaction was genuine too. No masks or barriers, just Garrison and his genuine self. The realization sent an appreciative tingle over my skin.

I didn't think he could ever fathom how much that single look meant to me.

I poured my usual bowl of cereal and ambled over to the dining table. Talon had just sat down, and Julius was standing by one of the other chairs with his mug of coffee. As I slipped past him, I allowed my arm to brush his chest. His back straightened at my touch, and his hand came to rest on my hip just for a second to guide me past him.

Such a gentle gesture, but it sparked a flame of its own. I didn't look back at him as I took my seat, still chewing on my stolen piece of bacon.

"Do you want hot chocolate, Dess?" Garrison hollered across the kitchen.

I laughed. "Of course, I do."

A small, almost imperceptible smile pulled to Julius's face as he nodded at something in his own mind. I wondered what was on the agenda for the day, but before I could ask, Talon looked at Julius. "Are we still planning on haggling with that weapons supplier today?"

Julius exhaled slowly. "Well, it sounds as though sudden assassination should no longer be a major concern. And our stash does need a top-up after last night. I think it's better if it's just the two of us, though. Dess's former captor will still have his own people looking for her, and there's no reason for her to leave the apartment and risk being seen for this."

"*I* should come," Garrison pointed out. "You two can't

haggle properly to save your lives. I'll have this guy wrapped around my finger in no time."

"I can stay here with Dess," Blaze piped up from where he was perched on the sofa with his laptop. "Happy to stand guard and protect her... even though it'll probably be the other way around if someone does come crashing in here." He grinned at me, and I had to smile back.

"That's fine with me," I said. After last night, my nerves could use a little break from the action anyway.

Garrison gulped down his bacon at a speed that could have rivaled Blaze with a plate of pasta, and the three of them headed out. I polished off the last of my cereal and went over to join the hacker on the sofa. He seemed intent on his computer even though he'd said the threat was mostly gone.

Still carrying out his own search for information to unravel my mysteries, presumably. I admired the way his intense concentration honed the lines of his handsome face, but didn't he deserve a break too?

"I'm sorry," he said before I could speak. "I still haven't turned up anything else that seems like a solid lead. The image searches will keep running, though. It could take a few more days before they've combed the entire internet."

"The app doesn't need you watching it to run those, right?" I said, nudging his laptop away from him.

He set it down on the coffee table in front of us, playful curiosity lighting in his eyes. "Do you have something else in mind that you need me for?"

"Yep. I need you to queue up another one of those *Spy Times* episodes, if you don't mind."

He laughed, exactly the response I'd been looking for, and leaned over to tap on his laptop some more. "I'd be more than happy to. Maybe I'll even let you watch two."

I raised my eyebrows. "So generous of you."

I couldn't have said exactly what it was about this show that hooked me so much. I could tell that a lot of parts of it were pretty silly, and most of the missions would have been total failures if the spy and her husband had handled them like that in real life, speaking from experience. But maybe that was why right there. It had the same kinds of scenarios and problems I was facing right now—and had faced throughout my life—but through a breezy, fun-loving sort of lens as if none of it could be that horrible.

Wouldn't it be nice if the challenges I ran into from here on could be laughed off and conquered with a few clever tools?

When the credits for the episode rolled across the screen, I stretched my arms over my head, sinking deeper into the cozy sofa and feeling more relaxed than I had in at least a couple of days. I looked over at Blaze to check whether he'd enjoyed the break too.

He wasn't looking at the TV but at me, but he did look happy. A soft smile played on his lips, and there was a light in his bright brown eyes that wasn't quite like any I'd noticed before. It brought a flutter into my chest.

He was a striking man, after all.

"What are you so pleased about?" I asked, aiming for a teasing tone but really wanting to know underneath.

Blaze's smile widened slightly, the corners of his eyes crinkling to match it. "I like seeing you really relax. I know you haven't gotten to very often. And I'm glad that I can help you do that."

The previous flutter turned into a swell of affection. He'd spoken simply but honestly, and I wasn't used to having people care about my contentment that much. I knew the other men in the crew would fight for me, but Blaze was the one who'd gone out of his way to bring joy into my life.

"I appreciate it," I said, a husky note creeping into my voice without my meaning it to. I had the urge to reach over and stroke my fingers over the light red stubble that gave his otherwise boyish face a more rugged look that was undeniably appealing.

Before I could decide whether to follow that urge, Blaze's smile slanted. He glanced at his hands and then at me again. "I don't want you to take that the wrong way. I really am glad to help you just as a friend. I know when I came on too strong before, it made you really uncomfortable—I definitely wouldn't push for anything you're not into."

My pulse stuttered, remembering the moment when I'd rammed him against the safe house apartment's kitchen counter in what'd felt like self-defense. The memory made my throat constrict now, but mostly because I knew he hadn't deserved that level of aggression. "Blaze…"

He held up his hands. "Really, it's okay. I can see that you've got more of that kind of connection with the other guys, and maybe something's even happened with them already, and that's okay. It's great that you're getting what you need with someone. I'd never assume it has to be me. I just want you to know that I'm here for you too, in whatever ways you need me."

My throat closed up completely. I couldn't imagine ever voicing all of my feelings the way he had just laid them bare before me. It was hard to picture any of the other men expressing themselves so plainly either. He didn't hide like Garrison or avoid feeling like Talon.

Blaze knew himself, and he didn't hesitate to share who he was. But at the same time, he wasn't forceful, and he didn't blame me for anything. He took responsibility for how he felt without pressuring me for even an ounce more than I wanted to offer. As his words sank in, they dissolved any lingering hesitation I might have felt about his interest in me.

Did he really think I wasn't attracted to him at all? I guessed my reaction in the safe house had driven the idea home too forcefully for him to notice any indications I might have given off since.

I couldn't stand the thought of him going on thinking that I was somehow *repulsed* by him when it was so far from the truth.

I grappled with my words for a few seconds before I managed to speak. "You should know—it was never *you* I had a problem with. Not really. There's just... I have kind of an instinctive response to people getting flirty or acting sweet in a specific way. I had... a really bad experience with a seduction that started like that."

Even as I said the words, a realization clicked together

in my head as it never had before. I didn't like that my reactions were so off-kilter to what was normal, but it was useful at the same time. I'd never had to worry that I'd be led astray by a man putting the moves on me in the middle of an assignment.

Which was very convenient for my handlers too, wasn't it? And it was a pretty big coincidence that the man who'd warped his sweet words and caresses into something horrifying had just happened to approach me the very first time Noelle had given me a few hours of freedom to enjoy myself at that dance club. I'd been a clueless fourteen-year-old, and he'd homed right in on me... And Noelle hadn't even seemed *that* surprised when I'd told her afterward what had happened.

Had she set the whole thing up? Maybe even *paid* that man to treat me that way, to force himself on me—

Inwardly, I cringed away from the memory. But it made a sick kind of sense. I'd just been noticing my physical urges, starting to daydream about the romances and sexual encounters that managed to seep into the sidelines of the movies I was allowed to watch. Scarring me like that had been a surefire way to prevent those sorts of feelings from compromising me in the field.

My anger toward the household and whoever had brought me into it flared with an even sharper edge than before.

The insinuation of my words clearly hadn't been lost on Blaze. His own eyes flashed with fury. "Someone hurt you."

"It doesn't matter now," I said. "It was almost ten years ago."

"Ten years is nothing." He reached for his laptop. "Tell me everything you remember about him. I'll find him, and I'll burn his whole fucking life down."

The vehemence in his voice told me he meant it. He might be the kindest of the men in the crew, but that didn't mean he couldn't be fierce when he needed to be. That brutal protectiveness only increased the draw I felt toward him.

"You can't," I said. "I got free after it was over, and I killed him. He's gone." And the woman who might or might not have orchestrated the whole thing was dead too. It was all behind me except in the marks left on my soul. "I don't even really want to talk about it. I'd rather leave the past in the past."

Blaze let out a growl that electrified me, as if he wished he could raise the predator from the dead just to murder him all over again. But he took a deep breath and nodded. "Understood. I'm sorry."

"You don't have to apologize," I said quickly. "I like that you'd want to defend me. I—" I hesitated and then barreled onward. "I *am* attracted to you. I'm just not sure…"

I had the feeling if I asked him to turn on his charms again, my body would react instinctively no matter what my mind wanted. But it was hard to picture him putting on the same domineering front the other men either came by naturally or could pretend so easily, like Garrison. I didn't know if that was how I'd want Blaze anyway.

Resolve gripped me. I gave Blaze a gentle push into the back of the sofa and straddled him in one swift movement. He stared up at me, his pupils dilating with obvious hunger. "Dess?"

A sly smile curved my lips. "Maybe it'll work out if *I'm* the one doing the seducing. We could at least see how it goes."

He kept his hands carefully at his sides, but a grin of his own took his face from handsome to stunning. "I've always been a fan of experimentation."

Those words sent a heady quiver right down to my sex. Licking my lips, I leaned over him and looped my arms loosely around his neck. He smelled tantalizing too, with a crisply fresh cologne that reminded me of the ocean.

He was letting me take the lead, waiting to see what I'd take from him. I figured I'd start by stealing a kiss.

I dipped my head so my lips brushed his. Blaze kissed me back, but gently, cautiously, still giving me room to decide how far I wanted to go. Only when I melded my mouth to his more emphatically did he let out a rough noise and let his tongue flick out to play with mine.

I wanted more—I wanted his hands all over me. The thought of directing him to my exact desires sent a thrill racing through my veins.

Tipping back just enough to speak, I murmured against his lips. "Take my shirt off."

He complied without hesitation, a hotter spark dancing in his eyes now. His hands weren't the only thing I wanted on me.

"Kiss my neck," I added, tilting my head to the side to give him easier access. "Until I moan."

"My pleasure," Blaze murmured, and adjusted me against him so that he could bring his mouth to that sensitive slope of skin. His hands slid up and down my bare sides as he worked over my neck with lips and tongue and nips of his teeth.

I was gasping in less than a minute. It wasn't much longer before another skillful swipe of his tongue sent such a giddy surge of need through me that a moan spilled from my lips.

Blaze eased back and winked at me. "Mission accomplished. What next, my lady?"

I grasped the base of his shirt and tugged it upward. "This definitely needs to come off too."

He raised his arms so I could peel the garment off him. I sat there for a moment on his lap, running my eyes and my hands over the toned planes of his torso. He was the leanest of the Chaos Crew's men, but strength emanated from every one of those wiry muscles. I could tell he'd worked hard to build that trimly sculpted physique.

"Like what you see?" he teased playfully, desire burning in his gaze.

"Oh, yes. Very much." I bent forward to claim another kiss, drawing this one out until we were both breathless. My nipples grazed his chest through the fabric of my bra and immediately pebbled.

"My breasts would appreciate your attention," I instructed.

Blaze chuckled eagerly and trailed his fingers up my back to unhook my bra. Then he cupped both my breasts with his slender fingers, his nimble thumbs stroking along the curve and rolling my nipples in tandem. The second time, he pressed a little harder with the perfect flick at the end, jolting another gasp out of me. He clearly knew *exactly* what he was doing.

I arched into him, sucking in a breath as my pussy ground against his groin where his cock pressed rigidly behind the fly of his slacks. A faint groan reverberated out of Blaze in turn, but he kept to his orders, massaging my breasts and alternating between pinching and stroking the nipples until I was rocking against him with fraying control.

I traced a finger down his abs to the waist of his pants. "I need more."

"Fuck, yes." He teased his lips along my jaw. "Tell me exactly what you want, Dess."

"Pants off," I mumbled. "Both of us. *Now.*"

With a rough chuckle, he squirmed out of his own slacks with a little help from my grasping fingers and then lifted me over him to yank down my sweats. As I stood there with my feet braced on the sofa and his face level with my pussy, a deeper, hotter urge came over me.

"Kiss me," I demanded. "Right—right here."

I brushed my fingers over my panties, and a grin of pure delight sprang to Blaze's face. "It would be an honor," he said, wetting his lips, and pulled my panties down too.

He gripped my thighs and swept his tongue over all of me, from my clit down to my channel. A whimper tumbled out of me at the rush of bliss. But it was only just getting started.

Blaze devoured me, suckling my clit and then plunging his tongue right inside me. His hands squeezed my thighs and slid to my ass. He spread me a little wider, but I barely wobbled in his firm grasp.

"That's right," he whispered against me. "So fucking delicious. I could do this for weeks."

I tipped back my head, my fingers curling into the fine strands of his hair. His tongue was both hard and soft where it needed to be, flicking small circles around me teasingly before dipping inside again, conjuring thrilling quivers through my entire being. My hips swayed toward him, still steadied by his hold. With a pleased hum that reverberated into my pussy, he brought me to the trembling edge of release, eased back just slightly, then repeated the torture all over again.

An ache spread between my thighs, the hunger to be filled more than his tongue could manage. I grasped his hair tighter, whimpering and gasping before I managed to speak.

"Blaze, I want you inside of me."

I didn't have to ask twice. He drew back, licking my slickness off his mouth with a satisfied glance at me, and grabbed a condom packet out of the pocket of his discarded slacks beside me. "Never hurts to be prepared," he said with a quirk of his eyebrows, but his tone was all heat.

The second he'd rolled it over his cock, I sank down and pulled at him so he sprawled over me on the sofa. I wanted him on top of me now, driving us toward our climaxes.

The soft kiss he offered me and the tender way he slid inside me didn't set off any alarm bells now. He was giving me exactly what I'd asked for. I was still in control.

Maybe someday I'd be able to enjoy sex like this without having to call all the shots. Eventually my body had to catch on to the fact that not every man who was gentle with me wanted to hurt me, right?

Blaze dappled kisses across my cheeks, jaw, and neck, bracing himself with one hand and stroking my breasts with the other. His hips pumped his cock in and out of me, deeper and deeper with every thrust. I raised my knees on either side of him automatically and cried out when he hit an even more sensitive spot inside me. My hand came up to clutch his shoulder as if I needed to hold him here with me to make sure he'd stay.

Our gazes locked for a second, nothing but passion and awe in his eyes. They started to haze as his thrusts sped up, and I knew his release was near. I rocked my hips up to meet him, chasing my own. So close—so fucking close—

He slammed into me, and his lips parted with a stuttered groan. We tumbled over the edge together, me quaking against him, his cock pulsing inside me. I clung to him, holding him close to me as the afterglow rolled over my body.

After a minute, Blaze tipped himself into a sitting position, pulling me onto his lap with him. He beamed at me, and my chest filled with the joy of the moment—both the physical release and the fact that I'd found a way to connect with this amazing man too.

I was just about to reach for my clothes when the door to the apartment swung open, and the rest of the crew strode in, stopping with a jerk when they saw us in our naked embrace.

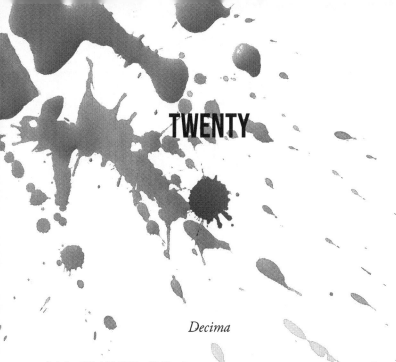

TWENTY

Decima

ALL THREE OF the men now staring at me and
Blaze had seen me in some state of undress before. I
probably would only have felt a little awkward at them
walking in not expecting the provocative sight if those
gazes hadn't looked not just startled but also, on at least
two of them, angry.

"What the fuck is this?" Garrison snapped, taking a
couple of steps closer and then stopping with a grimace.
His face had flushed red.

I grabbed my shirt and pulled it on, not bothering
with my bra for the moment. Blaze scrambled for his
boxers and slacks.

"I'd think it's pretty obvious," I said to Garrison, a
little irritation creeping into my tone at the tone he'd
taken with *me*. "We didn't know you'd be back so soon, or
we'd have taken this somewhere more private." I wriggled

into my sweatpants as quickly as I could, feeling more composed once all my own private bits were no longer on display.

Garrison's furious gaze whipped from me to Blaze and back again. "And that would have made it better—if you'd hidden it and pretended nothing was going on?"

I opened my mouth and closed it again, not just irritated but confused now. Why the hell was he so angry anyway? It definitely didn't seem to be just about getting unexpectedly flashed.

And Julius looked pissed too, in his own way. His stance was as cool and commanding as always, but his jaw had clenched and something in his deep blue eyes had hardened in a way I wasn't used to, at least not when they were aimed at me.

"What were you trying to accomplish with this?" he demanded, looming over me.

I stared at him, now utterly bewildered. "The usual things someone wants to accomplish when they hook up with someone? Was there a rule no one told me about that Blaze is off-limits or something?"

If so, *he* definitely didn't seem to know about it. He was standing there a few feet away from me, just in his slacks, looking tense but uncertain. I didn't think he was totally sure what was going on here either.

"I think you know that's not the point," Julius said, his voice unshakably firm, and I started to get pissed off too.

"I obviously don't," I shot back, folding my arms over my chest. "You didn't seem to have any problem with me sleeping with you and Talon, so I have no idea why getting it on with someone else in the crew would be such a big deal."

Somehow his jaw clenched even tighter, but he held himself with his typical restraint. I couldn't say the same for Garrison.

The younger man's eyes flickered from furious to absolutely enraged. "You fucked the two of *them* too?" he snarled. "And you don't think you have any explaining to do here?"

Blaze made a sweeping motion with his hands. "Let's all chill out for a second and have a reasonable conversation. There's obviously been some miscommunication somewhere."

"No fucking kidding," Garrison retorted.

Julius appeared to simmer down just slightly, but his voice was still taut. "I realize you haven't had a whole lot of experience outside of your missions, Decima, but I would have thought you had some concept of the fact that people generally inform their partners if they're seeing other people."

I blinked at the bunch of them, the pieces slowly connecting in my head. Was that all they were pissed off about? I frowned.

"I mean... I thought we were all already partners. Isn't that what you've been saying, about me being part of the crew? I'm attracted to all of you. You seem to be attracted to me. I didn't think hooking up would be that big a deal. It's not like we made any epic commitments—it's not like we were even going on dates or whatever. It was just sex."

"Just sex," Garrison repeated, rolling his eyes skyward.

"Yes," I shot back. "Just sex. Simple physical gratification. If any of you wanted more than that from me, none of you bothered to mention it. I'm not sure why I'm the only one at fault here when it seems like I'm the only one who actually was clear about what I wanted instead of keeping it a secret that I expected more."

I searched all their faces, even Talon's, who'd stayed silent through the conversation so far. I couldn't read his impassive expression at all, but that was pretty normal. He simply watched the conversation with a slightly stiffened stance as if he'd rather not have been there at all. Wonderful.

Blaze glanced at me. "I didn't realize—I figured if anything had happened with the other guys, you'd have talked about the fact that it wasn't just them. I'm not blaming you, but lack of exclusivity *is* usually the kind of thing people assume will come up."

"We're not usual people, are we?" I demanded.

Julius cleared his throat. "Are you really trying to say that you had no idea this would be an issue?"

"Yes! You're all so close with each other—you share so many things—I didn't think you'd suddenly get all possessive and decide you owned me just because we got off together." I scowled, my frustration growing. "It's not like I've been going around picking up random guys off the street."

Garrison snorted. "Thank God for that."

I glowered at him. "I wouldn't *want* to do that. For fuck's sake. Did you go around announcing that we'd slept together to the rest of the guys?" My gaze jerked to Julius.

"Did you?" And then Talon. "Or you? Seems like no. Apparently it wasn't important enough for you to bring it up, so it doesn't make any sense to me that I should have known I had to."

Blaze reached over to give my arm a quick reassuring squeeze. "She does have a point. She didn't hide this from any of us. It just… never came up."

A rush of renewed affection for him washed through me. I'd have kissed him if I hadn't suspected that'd cause even more explosions around here.

Julius rubbed his forehead as if he had a headache. "We didn't know we needed to bring it up."

"And you did hide it," Garrison added. "Lying by omission is still lying."

"I never once lied," I spat, poking a finger at his chest. "You never asked if I was with anyone else, and if you had —if any of you had—I would have told you. By that same logic, you lied to your friends by not telling them that we had sex. I don't know what you're all so offended about. Is it so horrible that I was with other people you supposedly like and respect?"

For a second, none of them spoke. It appeared they couldn't fully put into words what *their* problem with the situation was.

I wanted to feel bad for whatever hurt I'd caused them, and in a way, I did. But I hadn't done anything in which they hadn't actively participated. I'd never broken my word with any of them, and I didn't understand why they were blowing up about this. I wasn't going to stand here and let myself be lambasted for doing nothing wrong.

"If we knew—if I knew—that this wasn't exclusive, I may have handled the situation differently," Garrison said finally.

I looked at Julius. "What about you?" Then I moved my eyes to Talon. "Or you?"

Neither answered outwardly, and I knew it was a different story for them. They'd taken me together, and it had never been exclusive for Julius. I'd never given the impression that it was. He should have been the least surprised out of all of them, but he still reacted as if I'd done something completely shocking.

"I don't know," Julius replied. "But that's why it'd have been good to have the information."

Talon only shook his head, refusing to verbally respond. Maybe he needed to gather his thoughts first, or maybe it simply wouldn't have mattered to him at all.

I sighed. "Fine. Whatever. You all know now. I find you all appealing, and I'd happily hook up with any of you again, and I don't see what's wrong with that. I'm sure as hell not going to let you force me into a box where someone else is telling me what I'm allowed to think and feel like my whole life before. I don't belong to any of you. I don't belong to *anyone*. I choose who I'm with and when. If you're up for it or not, that's the only part that's up to you. Period."

That was all I had left to say. I grabbed my bra off the couch and pulled it on without totally removing my shirt in a few hasty movements. Meanwhile, the men all eyed each other.

"I think we should discuss this amongst ourselves," Julius said in a definitive tone. "Just the four of us."

He motioned to the others, and they fell in line with him as he stalked to the stairs that led to the rooftop deck. I watched the door shut behind them with a horrible sinking sensation in my gut.

I still didn't see what crime I'd supposedly committed, but if they decided I'd misled them anyway... What if I'd screwed up the good thing I'd found here? The *only* good thing I'd had in my entire life? The way Julius had talked, it was like I wasn't even a member of the crew, only a bystander who'd thrown them off course.

I sucked my lower lip under my teeth and worried at it for a moment before I caught myself and stopped. Instead, I flopped down on the couch and pushed my hands back over my hair.

What were they talking about up there? What were they saying about *me*?

Would they even want me around after this, let alone want to keep helping me?

I hadn't done this out of spite or any intention to hurt them. I'd wanted to be *closer* to them. Because I trusted them. Because I enjoyed their company. Why couldn't they see it that way?

A loud ping filled the room, and I sat up straighter. It'd come from Blaze's laptop, still standing open on the coffee table from when he'd gotten it to stream *Spy Times*. The screen had woken up, now showing a red alert box.

I leaned closer and saw it'd brought up a photograph. The alert contained the words *EXACT MATCH*.

And it was. The photograph showed a dimpled white wall with the bisected teardrop symbol etched into it, exactly as it'd looked when we'd encountered it before. My hand rose to scratch at the back of my neck instinctively.

Where was this picture from? I tapped on the window it'd appeared in and spotted a geolocation at the bottom. My mind absorbed the coordinates in an instant. That was nearby—right here in this city.

A cab could take me there in less than an hour. Julius had shown me how to surreptitiously leave the apartment building a couple of days ago, so I could handle that on my own. I could check out this lead and maybe even get back before the men even finished their conversation.

Or should I interrupt that conversation and fill them in?

I wavered for several seconds, my stomach twisting, and then strode to the door. I didn't even know if they'd want to continue this quest that was really for my benefit. I could handle this one part of the investigation on my own. It was probably better if they had more time to simmer down anyway.

I slipped out the door and hurried down the hall, my heart starting to thump harder. In less than an hour, I might have more answers about who I actually was—or at least who had stolen me from the life I'd been meant to have.

TWENTY-ONE

Talon

"SHE FUCKED ALL OF US, and you don't have a problem with it?" Garrison was griping at Blaze. "Because in all the years I've known you, I never thought you'd be into swinging like that."

He'd been going off on Blaze since the moment we'd reached the rooftop deck, but Julius and I needed a moment to process. I stood back, leaning against the wall and thinking about the signs that I'd noticed and written off as something insignificant. Was Julius thinking the same?

"She's allowed to make her own decisions. If it bothers you that much, don't sleep with her again," Blaze said, stating it as if it was the most obvious solution to the problem. And I supposed it was, even if the thought of not sleeping with her again sent a twinge of loss through me that clashed with the flare of jealousy when I remembered seeing her tangled up in the other man's embrace.

Julius stepped forward, and the two of them fell silent. "How long has this been going on?" he asked in a no-nonsense tone.

Blaze gazed steadily back at him. "Today was the first time we ever hooked up—or did anything remotely close to hooking up. You saw how she reacted to me the first time I got flirty with her." He paused, and a hint of a smile curled his lips despite the situation, one so pleased it provoked a renewed jab of possessiveness in my chest. "We got that all sorted out."

"Wonderful," Garrison groused, and turned to Julius. "It was only once for me too—that we slept together. The evening before the L.A. job. We fucked up here while the rest of you were out doing prep work."

He spoke callously, but I couldn't help noticing that he didn't clarify the way Blaze had about interactions that fell short of "fucking." He'd been the most obviously upset out of the four of us. Just how entangled had the two of them gotten?

At the same time, my mind was doing its own simple calculations. Unless Julius had welcomed Dess into his bed sometime before our threesome, which it certainly hadn't seemed like in the moment, I was the only one who'd been with her *before* we'd known who she actually was. I'd been the first.

Should I feel triumphant about that fact? I didn't really. The brief flickers of jealousy had faded, and now I only felt a dull discomfort when I thought about Dess waiting downstairs, shut out of our discussion despite how much it involved her.

She hadn't committed a cardinal sin. She hadn't betrayed any of us, not really. Our feelings were our own to deal with, weren't they?

Maybe I only thought that because I rarely had much of any feelings to do anything about, but I didn't like remembering the frustration and pain that'd shown so clearly on her face when Julius and Garrison had chided her in their own ways—and when we'd left her behind.

"What about you and Talon?" Garrison asked, his narrowed eyes flicking between us.

"Also once, on the way back from the convention center," Julius said. "It sounds like this hasn't been an ongoing situation then. She's just… given each of us a try."

I couldn't tell how he felt about that idea, but the need to correct his mistaken assumption prickled at me, alongside Garrison's earlier remark about lies of omission. I wasn't sure it'd make a difference, but I wasn't going to leave our boss with the wrong information.

"Actually," I said brusquely, "she and I also ended up getting together once before we found out about her real identity."

Blaze's eyebrows shot up in a surprised reaction that might have offended me if he didn't have way more of a reputation as a ladies' man than I'd ever possessed.

Garrison's eyes only narrowed further. "You got it on with her when we weren't even sure if she was the enemy?"

I frowned at him. "She wasn't, and I didn't compromise the crew in any way."

"Why didn't you say anything?" he demanded.

I gave him an even stare. "Why should I have? I didn't see how it was anyone else's business. It didn't affect the crew."

"Yes, of course you'd see it that way."

"Hey," Blaze broke in. "I didn't hear *you* announcing your involvement with her from the rooftops—even though that's apparently where it happened."

"Because I thought it was just me," Garrison retorted, and sighed. "Which obviously we all did. Well, except you two, it seems." He studied me and Julius in an evaluating way I didn't totally like.

"How we conduct our own private business isn't any of your concern either," Julius replied.

Garrison threw his hands toward the sky. "It isn't just private business anymore, is it? Look at us! We were thinking of bringing her into the crew permanently, and she has us at each other's throats. How can we trust someone who'd create this much turmoil?"

I didn't think Garrison trusted much of anyone anyway. But Julius stirred on his feet with unusual restlessness. "That is a point that's weighing on my mind."

Even Blaze was silent for a moment. The discomfort inside me congealed into a heavier ache.

Dess hadn't done any of this intentionally. From her reaction, she hadn't understood that what she'd done might bother us at all. She hadn't liked that she'd upset us

—I'd been able to see that much in her face—but she simply hadn't viewed the situation the same way we had.

Some core part of me resonated with understanding and sympathy. How many times throughout my life had people gotten pissed off at me for not feeling the "right" way or as much as they thought I should? Teachers prodding me with concerned questions, my fellow soldiers joking that I should be sent to a shrink, friends and lovers from all the way back to my early teens shouting at me or turning their backs on me because I didn't perform to expectations. I'd always wished they could just accept that I simply didn't feel much of anything.

The crew had been the one group where that didn't matter. But they didn't seem to be able to extend that same recognition of our differences to Dess. After the brainwashing she'd been through, she had even more of an excuse to look at the world differently than I did, so why the hell were they demanding she fit their idea of a "correct" intimate relationship?

The strange thing was, I *did* feel something now. That ache, and a heat that pulsed from it with the determination to defend her. She'd woken up more emotion in me than I'd known I was capable of. Even if that still wasn't much, it showed she was something special. She deserved some kind of recognition. Or at least respect.

My brothers-in-arms had started sniping at each other again while I'd been lost in thought. "She's fucked up everything," Garrison muttered. "And we *all* let that happen." He shot an accusing glance at Blaze.

"Including you," Julius said darkly.

My fingers curled into my palms. This was my crew. They had my absolute loyalty, and I'd have killed a hundred men for any of them. But in this moment, I had the intense urge to knock their heads together until I could snap them out of this fit of jealousy they seemed unable to shake off.

Garrison shook his head. "We shouldn't be fighting with each other anyway when it was Dess who did this."

My voice erupted out of me. "Dess didn't do anything wrong. Actually, she's totally right. She *doesn't* belong to any one of us, and we're lucky she wants all of us in whatever ways she does. She's an impressive woman who makes her own decisions, so who the hell are we to try to tell her what to do?"

The other men gaped at me, even Julius in a more subtle way than the others. I guessed I didn't often speak this much or so emphatically.

Blaze let out a low whistle that could have been teasing or approving. I shot him a quick glower before continuing.

"Frankly, after the way she's been controlled and manipulated for her whole life, it's wrong of *us* to even suggest that we have some claim on deciding how she's supposed to feel about us—or sex—or anything. I know she matters to all of us, and you know it too. What's the point in denying it? Do any of you really want to give her up just because you're not going to be the only man she turns to? We're a team in every other way. Why can't we be a team when it comes to taking care of Dess?"

I hadn't known I had quite that much frustration built up in me. Maybe it was flowing over from all the irritations I'd suppressed over the years. After the last words had burst from my mouth, a wave of exhaustion rolled over me, as if I'd scaled a skyscraper rather than making a relatively short declaration. Although for me, I supposed the latter was the more difficult act.

My colleagues seemed to be absorbing my words, each of them studying me in their own way. The animosity in the air simmered down. Blaze was the first to speak up.

"Yes. Everything Talon just said. That's exactly how I feel about it." He gave me a grateful nod.

Julius dragged in a breath. The fresh outside air swept over us with a gust of breeze, and he rubbed his close-cropped hair after the wind ruffled it. "I can see you have a point," he said finally.

Garrison's mouth had twisted. He dipped his head for a second, and I realized he looked almost… embarrassed. I wasn't sure I'd ever seen him show any kind of reaction so humble before.

"Okay," he said, still with a bit of an edge in his voice. "Maybe I went a bit overboard. I mean, it took us all by surprise, right? And *because* she's started to become… important to me, I didn't like the fact that she'd been with all of you too." He hesitated, and then his tone steadied more. "But this crew also means a hell of a lot to me, and I wouldn't be part of it if you weren't people I'd trust to treat her right."

I folded my arms over my chest and frowned at him.

"We're going to be lucky if she wants anything to do with any of us after the way we just came down on her."

Blaze motioned toward the door to the stairwell. "I'd say we owe her a pretty huge apology."

Garrison followed his gesture, and his posture briefly stiffened. But then something softened in his expression. He nodded. "Right."

Julius echoed his nod. The tension seemed to be seeping out of his stance. He drew his back straighter, his usual authoritative presence filling the space. "We obviously need to keep lines of communication more open than they have been, but yes. We can start that process by going down and talking with her to clear the air. Hopefully she'll at least be willing to listen."

I followed the others down the stairs with relief coursing through me. It would all be okay in the end. We could straighten out this mess and get back to the things that mattered.

But when we emerged into the main room of the apartment, Dess had vanished. We glanced around, Julius heading over to the workout room that'd become her bedroom, Garrison poking his head past the door to the bathroom which stood ajar. As they both turned away with expressions that told me they hadn't found her, Blaze leapt toward the sofa.

He snatched up his laptop. "Oh, shit."

We all spun toward him. "What?" Julius asked.

"My image search turned up a match for that teardrop symbol," he said. "It's near here... I'll have to check exactly where… She must have gone out to take a look while we had our heads up our asses."

My gut dropped. "The pricks who want her back are still hunting for her, aren't they?"

Blaze nodded, looking miserable. "And there might be a few mercenary groups who haven't stopped looking to collect the bounty. I know she can handle herself… but she's completely on her own out there right now."

"Then we need to get to her *now*," Julius commanded, flinging open the cupboard near the front door to grab his bulletproof vest. "Gear up and move out. We're not letting her face any kind of trouble alone."

TWENTY-TWO

Decima

I ASKED the cab to drop me at an address several blocks from the geocoordinates. It wasn't the greatest part of town, a lot of the shops around me were closed up with FOR RENT or old CLOSING SALE signs hanging in the grimy front windows.

As I strode along the sidewalk, careful to keep my head down, I watched for other activity on the street, but no one much seemed to come out this way. Even in the few stores that remained open, I didn't spot any customers.

None of that detracted from my mission necessarily. The factory where we'd found the first match for the symbol had been rundown and abandoned too. But the quiet felt a little eerie. I wasn't sure I'd been in any part of the city before where there hadn't been at least a little more traffic just passing through.

The coordinates led me to a massive storage facility

surrounded by a chain-link fence. I studied it from off to the side, not spotting any guards standing watch near the gate and only a few dingy looking cameras mounted on obvious posts. Several of the garage-style doors I could see had padlocks on them. Shouldn't there have been more security here if this facility was still active?

Maybe the owners were too lazy and their customers not concerned enough to hassle them about it, but I didn't like that either.

I obviously wasn't going to break open the gate and waltz in within full view of the main camera. Instead, I scaled the fence where it veered closest to one of the rows of storage lockers. In a matter of moments, I'd scrambled over the edge and was crouched on the building's flat, corrugated-metal rooftop.

I scanned the area again, taking in the aisles of matching buildings with their rows of doors and the utter stillness of the scene. In the middle of the day, no one was monitoring the gate in person, and no one was bringing stuff to or from their unit. I had no idea how normal that was, though.

Checking my phone, I determined that the exact geolocation from the image must be one of the units a few rows over at the dead end of the aisle. If I dropped down to the pavement below and walked over, I'd be boxed in once I reached it, with no easy avenue to climb to a better vantage point. Thankfully, I should be able to make my way over there across the rooftops. Most of them were connected, and those that weren't had only a narrow walkway separating them, which would make for an easy leap.

I started over, walking around one aisle and making my way along the far end of the facility toward the one I needed. The whole time, I kept searching my surroundings for other security measures.

As I came up on the one camera at the back of the facility, I slowed, preparing to figure out a way to avoid it. It was hard to tell from this distance, but it might have captured an angle that would show the unit I needed to get to.

I eased closer, careful to stay out of range for now. If I blocked the view, there was always the chance that would alert an off-site security force that something was wrong— not that it looked as if the storage company cared enough to have hired someone for constant surveillance. I might be able to duck under the camera's view with a quick roll and stay out of its sights the rest of the time...

As I drew closer, my forehead furrowed. I paused, studying the camera—and in particular its lens—more intently. There was something odd about the glass. It looked... smudged, or wet?

I edged even closer, and my pulse kicked up a notch with a surge of apprehension. Someone had sprayed a liquid on the camera's lens that'd left behind a thick film. It would be blurring the view and making any recording taken useless for identifying the figures it captured.

Normally, that would have worked in my favor. I could sashay right by and no one would be the wiser. But the film had clearly been purposefully added. And...

I knelt down and touched a droplet I'd noticed on the roof beneath it. My finger smudged the damp spot. Still wet. The substance had been sprayed on the camera *recently*.

Why would someone else have been here, in this desolate area of town, wanting to obscure the cameras on this exact afternoon? Where were they now?

None of this felt right to me. Every aspect of it was starting to scream *setup*. Someone had ensured there'd be no staff on site and obscured the camera lenses so they could get away with something awful.

After the way we'd been attacked at the meat factory, I couldn't help suspecting it was something awful they wanted to do to *me*.

This was a trap. I didn't know why the teardrop symbol was here, but the people responsible must have known about it too and realized we'd come here soon. Maybe I'd slipped up somewhere along my journey and they'd figured out I was headed this way right now.

It didn't matter which was true. The only important thing was getting out of here before that trap was sprung on me.

I turned, intent on marching to the closest spot where I could easily leap to the fence and vanish without a trace, but at the same moment, the thump of several footfalls reached my ears from the direction of the front gate. With a hitch of my heart, I ducked as close to the roof as I could get.

There was a rattling sound by the gate and a murmur of low voices. I flattened myself, braced to make a run for it as soon as I was sure I had a good opening. Then the gate swung open, and it wasn't enemies but the men I'd left back at the apartment who strode into the storage facility.

They didn't throw caution to the wind. I saw Blaze make a gesture toward the nearest camera and them all adjust their course to avoid it, and their heads swiveled to watch for any threat around them. But they marched quickly toward the aisle with the unit I'd already determined the geocoordinates pointed to with less stealth and wariness than I wished they'd used. They didn't notice me where I was crouched on the roof a few aisles away.

I straightened up and waved my arms, but they didn't glance my way again, already finished with their scan of the rooftops. They were focused on the environment at their eye level now. My chest itched with the urge to yell, but if this was a trap, that would only alert whoever was waiting to spring it that I was on to them. Shit.

Continuing to gesture in the hopes of getting the crew's attention, I darted along the roof with feet set as silently as I could manage. If I could just get in front of them instead of off to the side, they'd have to notice me. My pulse thudded through my veins.

Maybe I was wrong about the trap. Maybe there was a normal explanation for everything that'd unnerved me. I desperately hoped that was true—but I couldn't stake their lives and mine on that hope.

Why weren't they picking up on the same clues? I guessed I couldn't blame them for missing the cameras, since I hadn't spotted the oddity with them until I was up here. But coming through the front gate had been a bold move. It was as if they were in so much of a hurry that they'd set aside caution for haste. What was so urgent about this investigation?

Me, I realized with a jolt of shock. That was the only conceivable explanation. They'd obviously realized I'd come here following the alert on Blaze's computer, and they'd rushed after me. The bigger question was why exactly it'd mattered so much to them, but I could ask them that after we were all out of here safely.

They veered down the aisle they needed. I dashed faster. I was just coming up on that same aisle, preparing to start flinging pebbles at them if need be to shake them out of their intense focus on the unit ahead and judging the distance to where they were now halfway down the aisle, when a horrible screeching sound shattered my own attention.

Locker doors were flying open at the opening to the aisle—and at the far end, where we'd expected to find the symbol. At least two dozen men charged out, all of them with guns in their hands, surrounding the Chaos Crew in an instant.

In the same instant, my mind blanked with panic. I couldn't do anything but muffle a rising scream as the attackers fired. The guys threw themselves toward the nearest locked doors, ducking to the ground and rolling into the small indents of the entrances to avoid being hit. Then my instincts kicked in and launched me into action.

No one had noticed me still—my friends or their attackers. I snatched up the gun I'd brought in a concealed holster under my arm and took aim at the larger group closing in on the crew from the only direction they could make their escape.

As I fired my first shots, dropping one and then another man in quick succession with bullets to the head, someone in the crew tossed a small round object into the middle of the aisle. I braced for an explosion, but instead, smoke billowed out of it with a quavering hiss. In a matter of seconds, most of the aisle was clouded with a thick gray fog. Even from above, I could only make out the slightest impressions of the figures within it.

The men were flattening themselves into the alcoves of the locker doorways, which provided only a tiny bit more cover on top of the smoke. I couldn't tell whether they'd noticed my shooting amid what was coming from their attackers.

The attackers had halted on either edge of the expanding cloud. Several of them glanced my way and took aim, and I leapt behind a low protrusion on the roof. Bullets battered its metal surface.

More shots rang out below. Some must have been from the crew and some from their attackers aiming at them, but any sense of their direction was lost in the general blare of sound.

I scooted out from behind the protrusion with my own pistol at the ready. From that awkward angle, it was hard to aim well, but I managed to pick off a few more of the enemy before they disappeared into the edges of the fog. Apparently they'd decided it was better to tackle the crew in the midst of that than risk losing them altogether, although where they thought the men might escape to, I had no clue.

Since I could barely see them, I knew they couldn't make me out either. I eased out and scuttled over to the edge of the roof, still keeping low just in case. I had a vague sense of where the crew had been holding their ground before, but I wasn't totally sure they hadn't moved. The smoke had thickened around the spot where the bomb had burst to the point that I couldn't make them out at all.

I did catch glimpses of other forms at the edges of the fray. Whenever I got a clear enough view to be confident it wasn't one of *my* men, I took the shots I could. When I ran out of bullets, I swapped cartridges with a flick of my wrist. Gunfire continued to blare on the ground below me.

A gust of wind washed over me and cast some of the smoke even farther, thinning it on the ground. The smoke bomb must have finished spewing out the stuff, because no more rose up to thicken the cover in its place.

Now I could just make out the crew near their original positions. Garrison and Talon stood on one side, shooting relentlessly at the crowd pressing in on them. Julius crouched nearby, still pressed against the wall as he shot into the other side of the fray, and Blaze aimed his own bullets over the other man's shoulder.

They couldn't keep up their fire constantly. As I watched, Julius paused to reload, and Blaze increased his fire to stop any attackers who'd drawn too close. But then they both had to dodge back against the locker door when a hail of bullets careened toward them.

Squinting through the fog, I pointed my pistol at each attacker who got close enough to the crew to target them. I took shot after shot, counting down my bullets as I made the rest of that clip count, only taking the shots when the men got close enough to the guys. We'd only held them off this long because of the smoke, and I only had one clip left. We were still way too outnumbered.

I reloaded once more and then lost a few bullets when someone aimed their shots at me again. My own went wild as I flung myself down on the roof. I picked off that bastard, but I only managed to take down a couple more and partly injure one or two others before I was totally out. Gritting my teeth, I shoved the temporarily useless gun back into its holster.

A few of the attackers had pushed close enough to the crew to tackle them hand to hand. Talon engaged first, swinging his knife, as Garrison continued firing at the more distant people to keep them at bay. Talon wove between the two attackers unlike anyone else, but they were good, and they managed to land a few minor blows through his defenses.

It said a lot about their training, but Talon didn't even flinch. He dispatched one and then the other with well-placed stabs, taking a third man on when he charged in.

Julius gave a shout as several more attackers converged on him and Blaze. He shot one and punched another. Talon and Garrison swung around, both preparing to defend their comrades, and I spotted one last man from the group who'd come from the far end of the aisle slinking toward Talon's back through the lingering smoke.

He was already raising his knife. The boom of several more gunshots drowned out any noise his footfalls might have made.

"Talon!" I hollered, but my voice was lost in the cacophony too. The man sprinted forward with a final burst of speed, and I did the only thing I could: I lunged off the roof straight at the prick.

No one was going to get away with hurting my men.

I soared through the hazy air and smacked right into the guy, my momentum and my well-positioned tackle knocking him to the ground. I moved on instinct, relying on my years of training to guide my hands as I deflected his defensive blows and yanked the blade from his grasp.

He caught my wrists, holding the blade at bay for a long moment with shaking limbs. The flex of his arms, twice as broad as mine, nearly forced the knife into my own chest. But I put my body weight into my thrust, forcing the blade down inch-by-inch until it plunged into his throat.

He gasped and gurgled, his body going slack beneath me. I hunched down, scanning the smoke-laced air around me for more attackers. In the midst of my own struggle, the gunfire had faded away.

A few more shots rang out as the crew took on the final attackers. Those men collapsed, and for a second, relief rushed through me.

It was over. We'd taken them all down.

Then I noticed that Blaze had dropped down onto his

belly. He still had his gun braced in his hands, his eyes intent on the men he'd just helped stop, but a crimson pool was spreading from beneath his stomach.

A cry of dismay broke from my mouth. As I dashed over, his head lolled to the side, and he sagged against the pavement.

TWENTY-THREE

Decima

NONE of us seemed to know what to do as Julius and Steffie patched up Blaze the best they knew how. The bullet he'd taken to his abdomen had passed through his body rather than lodging inside, and Julius had confirmed that it hadn't punctured any major organs, but the hacker was still clearly in a lot of pain. He alternated between groaning, hissing, and mumbling incoherently in a choked voice. Julius hadn't thought it was a good idea to give him any painkillers until they'd determined the extent of the damage.

"So damn lucky," Steffie murmured, a refrain she'd repeated more than once already, alongside phrases in what must have been her native language. She was stitching up the entry wound now with brisk but careful tugs of the thread. She and Julius worked well together, coordinating their actions with minimal speaking as if they'd done this a dozen times before.

Maybe they had.

Still, I couldn't stop myself from turning to Talon where we were watching from the far end of the room and asking, "Are you sure we shouldn't get an official doctor or something?"

Blaze cried out, as if punctuating my question. Then he grumbled something about "fucking needles, I'll pierce their goddamn eyeballs" which didn't make a ton of sense but was at least more understandable than the babbling before.

"Julius got some medical training through the military," Talon said. "And Steffie… The men who had her made her do first aid when they needed it, so she had some experience already. After she came to us, Julius saw that she got a more in-depth education so she'd be able to help in situations like this."

"She's practically a qualified nurse," Garrison put in from where he was standing beyond Talon.

I eyed the younger man warily. I hadn't asked him even though he generally had more to say than Talon because I wasn't sure where we stood after the way he'd laid into me this morning. So far, no one had mentioned anything about that argument, which was understandable given that we had much bigger things on our minds. I had no idea where I really stood with any of the guys, but Garrison had been by far the most furious.

Their comments reassured me a little when it came to Blaze's survival, as did Julius's a moment later. "We would get him to a hospital if I felt it was necessary. But he just needed some patching up." He pressed a sterile pad over the stitched wound and taped it in place. "As soon as we're finished getting on the bandages, you can have the good pain meds," he told Blaze.

The other man nodded rapidly, his mouth pressing flat. I wouldn't have thought he was capable of that much patience.

"Someone could go get that stuff now," Steffie suggested, and Talon moved before she'd even finished speaking. The woman shook her head as she looked Blaze over. "An inch farther, and the bullet would have torn through a handful of organs. I'd love to have the luck that sticks with you boys."

"You're with us," Blaze said with a rasp. "Very lucky. Wanna trade places?"

She snorted and finished her work on the exit wound. As they let Blaze roll fully onto his back on his bed, Talon reentered with a small case. Julius opened it, took out a syringe, and applied the contents directly to one of Blaze's veins.

The effect was almost immediate. A sigh rushed out of the hacker, and he settled a little more loosely into the bed. A crooked smile crossed his face. "Now we're talking." Then he cracked his eyes open a slit, glancing from me to the other guys. "There should be more talking. You all need to tell Dess what idiots you were being."

Steffie raised her eyebrows. "I don't think I'm needed for this conversation." She nodded to Julius. "I'll stay at the apartment until you're sure you don't need me to monitor him further."

"Thank you." Julius watched her go, closing the door behind her, and then shifted his gaze to me. Under his authoritative stare, my mouth went dry.

Was this really a conversation we should be having right now, while Blaze was half-dead from his injury? But then, it was Blaze who'd prompted it. He let out an impatient grunt when Julius didn't speak right away.

"I apologize," Julius said, with a shamed twisting of his mouth. "I made unnecessary assumptions and acted out of possessiveness when I didn't have any right to. I shouldn't have spoken to you the way I did. None of us should have." His eyes flicked from me toward the other men, focusing longer on Garrison.

I kept my attention on the crew's commander, my arms coming up to fold over my chest. I held them back from hugging myself the way I wanted to. "No, you shouldn't have."

He exhaled slowly. "It isn't an excuse, but I wasn't prepared. I do understand that you shouldn't have to rein yourself in from what you want—even if that's more than one of us. I have no interest in taking away your freedom. Hell, I'm dedicated to making sure you get more of it. I trust my crew, and I know you'll be in good hands with them." One side of his mouth curled up. "And I'll continue to be happy to contribute my own hands if you'd like to have them in the mix too."

My own lips pulled into a small smile. "I'll keep that in mind."

Talon cleared his throat. "I agree with everything Julius said. I should have spoken up sooner and not let them badger you the way they did. Thankfully I didn't have to go as far as cracking skulls to get them to see sense."

Had he been the one to force them to understand my perspective when they'd all been talking on the deck? Given how little the taciturn man normally spoke, I wouldn't have expected that, but his words and his solid presence steadied me as they usually did.

Maybe I shouldn't have been surprised. Talon didn't talk much, but he'd always been a sort of calm in the storm of chaos the crew thrived on.

My gaze slid to Garrison. He met my eyes for a second before his own jerked away, his mouth slanting at an awkward angle. His expression tensed and released as if he was grappling with himself. I braced for more snark or another accusation.

"You don't have to make yourself apologize if you're not really sorry," I couldn't help saying. "If it's just to get the other guys off your case, it won't mean much."

His gaze flicked back up to hold mine again. He swiped his hand across his mouth.

"I *am* sorry," he said. "Just not very good at saying it, obviously. Because I mean it."

The words echoed back to our conversation at the fundraiser in a way that sent a pang of understanding and relief through me.

Garrison tipped his head toward me and went on. "You never lied to me or broke any promises, and I shouldn't have accused you of anything like that. I only—I only got so angry because I thought *I'd* screwed up by trusting you. But you haven't done anything wrong, and I'm sorry I went off on you like that." He paused, and a hint of his usual smirk touched his lips. "I guess I should have known you're too much woman for any one of us to satisfy on our own."

Blaze chuckled lightly from the bed. "It's a good thing there's four of us."

A laugh tumbled out of me. "I don't know if that's a compliment or an insult."

"A compliment. Definitely a compliment," Blaze insisted.

Garrison's smirk grew. "Absolutely. Hell, if being with *all* of us makes you happy, who am I to argue with that?"

"Here, here," Blaze said with a wobbly nod.

Julius shot him a sharp look. "I know this is a difficult ask, but if you could manage to stay still for another twelve or so hours at least, I'd really appreciate it."

Blaze let out a huff, but he rested his head back into the pillow.

With that, the tension that had been wound through me since this morning started to dissipate. It didn't vanish completely, but at least the crew felt like a consolidated unit again and not one fracturing under strain. I wasn't sure whether things would actually play out so smoothly going forward, once they had to put that newfound generosity into practice, but it wasn't as if I was planning on hooking up with anyone in the middle of this mess. We had more important things to focus on.

"Now that we've determined that you're not all pissed off at me still," I said, "should we talk about what happened at the storage facility? It was obviously a trap."

Julius grimaced. "Yes. One you spotted well before we did. We rushed when we shouldn't have."

"We were worried about you," Garrison said quietly.

I shot him a baleful look. "And because of that, you made me way more worried about all of *you*."

"I should have known," Blaze muttered. "For the search to come up with a result this close to home after it's already been running for days... It should have popped up much earlier if it'd been there all along."

"Do you think someone planted the image specifically for us to find?" I asked.

Talon hummed. "It wasn't in the storage units where we thought it would be."

"Right," Blaze said. "No symbol there at all. They faked it as bait to get us to come while they prepared their ambush."

Julius sighed. "After our standoff at the meat factory, the organization behind Dess's capture must have realized we were looking for their symbol, that we were using it to track them down. They turned the main lead we have against us."

A gloom settled over me, seeping into my gut. A similar shadow had crossed Garrison's face.

"If *that* was faked..." he said. "If they've figured out that much about the way we're working... can we trust *any* of the leads we've gotten? Almost everything we've found has been through the image recognition app. All of it could have been manipulated to leave a false trail—the images and videos of Dess's trainer, the ones of the people we saw her with, the symbol…"

"The symbol is definitely real," I jumped in, even though a deeper sense of hopelessness was swelling inside me. "It's on my neck—it was in the mansion."

"But we don't know much other than that for sure," Julius said, frowning. "We can't trust any information that came to us from outside sources, no matter how innocuous it seemed at the time."

My heart sank. "Then what *do* we have, really?"

Garrison made a face. "We're basically back to square one."

Silence fell over all of us, even Blaze the chatterbox. I swallowed hard. After all the effort we'd gone to and the danger these men had put themselves in for me, we might not be any closer to answers than when we'd started this mission.

And I had no idea where to go from here.

TWENTY-FOUR

Blaze

PAIN PULSED through my belly from the bullet wound that'd hit just shy of my intestines. Every time I shifted my position in the bed or, well, breathed, it turned into a sharper jab. The painkillers had numbed the worst of it, but this was hardly the most comfortable I'd been in my life.

I hadn't let Julius dope me up too much. I could handle a little aching, and we had even more work to do than before now that all our previous leads had been called into question. Focusing on the data I could chase down and sort through on my laptop helped distract me from my physical discomforts anyway.

First I prodded at the image that had led us into the trap at the storage facility. It'd been well-positioned, but after several minutes of intensive prying, I dug up the evidence that it'd been posted to the internet only a couple of hours before the search had picked it up, not the many months the post that had held it had been designed to suggest. If we hadn't been in such a hurry to make sure Dess was safe, I probably would have investigated further and noticed that before we'd left.

Of course, if we hadn't rushed in there and Dess hadn't been so cautious herself, those men would have taken her out easily while she was on her own. I might have saved myself from this stupid injury if I'd trusted her instincts more, but... it was hard to feel that racing to protect her had been a mistake. I liked the idea of standing back and expecting her to figure out all the threats on her own even less.

We couldn't afford to step into any other traps, though. There weren't any new image results so far anyway. Our best bet was something totally unrelated to the investigations our enemies were already aware of. Something that would never have occurred to them to use as a trap, since they didn't know it'd appeal to us as bait.

There *had* been one line of inquiry I'd just started following up on the other day. I hadn't mentioned anything about it to the others yet since I'd been half convinced it'd lead nowhere.

I dove back into tracing that thread, uncovering one bit of information and then another, examining each of the pieces from every angle to make sure it was legit before moving on. As the picture started to form in my head of what exactly I'd uncovered, a slow smile spread across my face.

This could be it. This could be the answer—an answer

the pricks who kept attacking us couldn't interfere with. Of course, there'd be a whole lot of other challenges to overcome, but the Chaos Crew had never shied away from danger. Still…

A knock sounded on my door. "Hey," Dess's voice carried through. "Steffie brought some fresh lemonade by. Do you want a glass?"

"Sure," I said, though I was more interested in setting my eyes on Dess's face than getting a drink. I'd been way too isolated in here thanks to my invalid status.

Dess slipped inside and set the glass of pale yellow liquid on the end table next to where I was propped up on multiple pillows. She took in my expression, and hers relaxed a little. "How are you doing? Can I get you anything else?"

"This is great," I said to reassure her, and took a gulp of the lemonade—which was the perfect combination of sweet and sour; excellent job as always, Steffie. Dess had come in to check on me more than any of my other comrades, worry always darkening her eyes when she looked me over.

Now, she stepped closer and tugged the fleece blanket draped across my legs a little higher on my body. "Julius and Steffie said you wouldn't want to let your muscles stiffen up with a chill."

"I'm warm enough," I said gently.

She backed up a step, her hands clasping in front of her with an awkwardness I hadn't generally seen from her. Dess was usually so focused and self-possessed. I liked her that way… but I had to admit there was a certain appeal to her new role as concerned caregiver. I could see how hard she was trying to make things better for me even though she wasn't sure how. Watching her like this set off a warm glow in my chest that told me I was falling for her even harder than before.

There was definitely no chance of me giving her up now, so it was a good thing the other guys had gotten their heads straight.

"How's the pain?" she asked. "Do you need any more medication?"

I shook my head. "Less, I think. I can handle it. And I want my head as clear as possible. I think I've found a lead we can actually use—one that can't be faked."

Her face brightened, and she eased right to the side of the bed to peer at my laptop screen. "What is it? Did you find out something about the symbol or Malik?"

I shook my head. "Something totally different, which is why it should be safe from traps. Not that I didn't examine it in minute detail to make sure it was legit on top of that. It's not at all connected to anything else we've been doing, so there's no way the people after you could know we're looking into it now."

Dess cocked her head. "If it isn't connected to anything else, how useful can it be?"

I chuckled, glad to have the chance to surprise her. But I felt the need to clarify first, "It'll be dangerous. Probably incredibly dangerous. But I think it'll be worth it, because if we can pull it off, there's a decent chance of us finding out *exactly* who you are."

She sucked in a startled breath, her eyebrows rising.

"Okay, now you really have to tell me. I don't think dangerous is going to be a problem. It seems to be all of our middle names."

"True. That's why I bothered to track this down anyway."

I swiveled the laptop toward her and motioned to the screen. It showed a blueprint for a four-story building in the shape of a segmented cube. Dess studied it, knitting her brow. "Where is this, and what's so special about it?"

"From what I've been able to determine," I said, "this is a secret, high security government facility that holds *all* the genetic information collected by various governments, law enforcement agencies, and companies around the world. Every record our government could get their hands on, by both legal and not-so-legal means."

"Genetic information," Dess repeated. "Like DNA. I thought you said running a test on that would be too risky."

I nodded. "With any commercial company it would be. Your former captors could easily get access to those and put up alerts to notify them if anyone ran your DNA. But they may not even know this facility exists. I didn't for sure until a few minutes ago. And even if they did, they wouldn't have been able to plant code like that in its systems without the intrusion being detected quickly and destroyed."

An eager gleam lit in Dess's eyes, much better than the shadow of worry that'd lingered there before. "Then we could test my DNA after all."

"Exactly." I grinned at her. "Now, it isn't a guarantee

that someone related to you will also have their sequence in this database, but there's a better chance of it than any other database in the world, since this is by far the most extensive. And it doesn't put us or you in view of anyone who has it out for you."

"That all sounds great. I'm guessing there are a few 'but's you haven't mentioned yet."

I waggled my eyebrows at her, my rising spirits making even the pain of the gunshot wound feel distant. "I'll talk about your butt all day if you'd like."

Dess snorted. "You know what I mean. What are the catches?"

I'd have pointed out that she was quite a catch, but then she might have smacked me even in my invalid state. I turned the laptop back toward me. "Well, for starters, I don't know how to sequence your DNA myself, and the other guys sure as hell haven't got a clue. So we'll have to outsource that. To a private individual who's capable of it, someone we can be sure isn't compromised."

"And?" Dess prompted, obviously picking up on the fact that the element I'd just mentioned couldn't be the highly dangerous part.

"And in order to compare that sequence against the database, we'd have to actually get into the building and run the processes ourselves," I said with a wince. "And it is a top secret, high security facility, as I might have mentioned before. There'll be guards out the wazoo. Not to mention locks and other technical safeguards."

Dess exhaled in a rush. "Okay. So we'd just have to get past all of that."

"Yes," I said dryly. "That's all. Well, okay, that's not totally all."

She glowered at me. "What else?"

"I don't think I'd be able to go in with you," I admitted, as much as it pained me to say it. "Even at the best of times, I'm not the most physically coordinated guy around. With my injury on top of that... I'm not sure how well I can walk, let alone dodge a pack of elite security guards."

"But wouldn't we need you to get past the tech stuff and tell the computers to do what we want to search for the DNA match?" Dess said.

"Yeah. I can program some things ahead of time, but quite a bit I'd have to be talking you through remotely. Which does make it a more difficult proposition. More chance of human error. I'd try to cover every eventuality, of course, but it's harder when I'm not right there."

"Understandable." Dess's expression turned pensive. She gazed into space for a long moment as if gathering her thoughts.

I knew that figuring out who she was had always been the largest driving force behind her quest. She wanted to take the people who'd kidnapped her to task, sure, but mostly she wanted to know where she'd come from. What family she'd once belonged to. Even if it turned out they were jerks, I could only imagine the release that knowledge would give her. I had no idea what it'd be like to feel so adrift with no human connections to the most primal part of your past.

"I'm sure we could manage it," she said finally. "You've

had to instruct the rest of the crew from a distance for other jobs before, haven't you?"

"Yeah, now and then. It's not my ideal approach, but sometimes it's necessary. Never in a situation quite this complex, though."

She shrugged, a smile coming back to her face. "So it'll be a challenge. We haven't backed down from any of those yet. Unless *you* think we're not up to the task?"

I shook my head. "It's not that. I just—I hate the idea of all of you going in there and taking all the risks for a plan that's totally my idea, while I get to hang out somewhere safe and sound."

She patted my side, carefully avoiding the bandages there. "I think you've already proven very clearly in the past couple of days just how much danger you're willing to put yourself in for me and the crew. No one's going to criticize you for not being up to a high-stakes breaking-and-entering mission. I trust you to get us past anything we need your help with, and I know the rest of the crew will have no problem counting on you to look out for us too. If you believe we can pull this off, then I'm all in."

Her words sent a strange sensation unfurling through my chest, a little giddy but also so unfamiliar I wasn't sure what to make of it. I'd always been someone the guys could turn to for technical support and information, of course, and I'd helped in my own ways on the ground when I could, but the idea that people would trust me to protect their very lives made my pulse wobble.

I wanted to be someone my crew could count on that

much, though. And this time—this time I'd do a good job of protecting everyone under my care.

Resolve rose up through me, and I shot Dess another grin. "All right, then. I'll talk it over with the guys, and then we're going to need to call in a favor. That DNA won't sequence itself."

TWENTY-FIVE

Decima

"IS THIS... a kind of job that you guys normally take on?" I asked, holding the leash of a small corgi that walked in front of me as if he was the one leading *me* down the sidewalk. I'd never thought much about how I felt about dogs, but this one had stolen my heart the moment we'd picked him up from the breeder.

I wished I could take him home with us, but I imagined the guys would have something to say about that. And he was kind of essential to our plan.

Julius shook his head where he was walking by my side. "Not on a regular basis. It's definitely not within our typical range of services. Only for special circumstances like these."

Like a genetic scientist who didn't happen to have anyone she wanted chaotically murdered as payment for her services.

I couldn't suppress a laugh, and the corgi looked over his shoulder at me without slowing his pace. He ran into the back of Garrison's heel and stumbled over his sausage legs before correcting himself and walking a few paces behind Garrison.

Garrison shot the dog a look, but from the twinkle in his eye, I didn't think I was the only one taken with this bundle of brown fur.

"It seems pretty simple for the complex work she's going to be doing for us," I had to point out.

Garrison snorted. "For her, sequencing DNA is a piece of cake. We had to locate a dog that's a near-perfect match for hers, and now we've got to sneak it into her ex-boyfriend's house and retrieve the real one without him having a clue. It's a stealth mission that takes a lot of skill and prep-work, so I'd say she's getting one hell of a discount for our services."

At his tone, I couldn't resist gazing down at the dog and sticking out my bottom lip in an exaggerated pout. "And you're sure that we can't keep him?"

Julius looked over at me, and a chuckle escaped him. "He's already been assigned to a home, Dess."

I sighed. "Fine. But don't blame me if I find I'm unable to stop myself from bringing a different one back to the apartment one of these days."

Garrison shook his head, but his lips twitched with amusement. I glanced around at the quiet suburban neighborhood through my sunglasses, still alert within my disguise even though traffic cams were in shorter supply here. We had no idea how close our enemies might be to finding us, so we'd pulled together this job as fast as we could.

But at the same time, a sense of calm had settled over me, taking the edge off my nerves. We'd all worked together, making a convincing case for dog ownership when we'd picked up the pup, driving out to the edge of the suburbs while keeping our charge in a good mood, and now approaching our target's home like a group of friends out for a stroll. It was like nothing had changed, despite our argument a couple of days ago. No matter what our enemies might have in store, that knowledge filled me with relief.

"That's the house," Julius said without looking at it as we crossed the street. "Three down from the corner."

I took it in from the edge of my vision as we ambled by. It was one of the larger buildings on the residential street, white with beige shingles and a big porch. "Got it," I said.

We made a longer circuit, coming around to where Talon was waiting in our getaway car. Julius nodded to him, and the other man started the engine to drive over to the house on the opposite side of the block from our target's. Garrison headed back around to the front of the house, while Julius and I followed Talon on foot.

"You're sure you want to do the inside work?" Julius asked me.

I nodded. "I'm the smallest out of all of you—it'll be easiest for me to stay unnoticed. And he seems to like me." I bent down to scratch the dog behind the ears. "Hopefully his counterpart will too."

"All right. I'll be waiting by the fence for the handoff. Get in there as soon as you hear Garrison at the door."

We walked up the driveway of the house that backed onto our target's backyard as if we belonged there. We'd already confirmed that the owners and their neighbors would be at work. Too bad we couldn't say the same for our target, but apparently one of the reasons our client had broken up with him was that he'd decided to laze around at home all day playing video games while living off an unexpected inheritance.

Unfortunately, that'd also made it impossible for her to get the dog herself. He'd paid for one of its vet bills once and had found some lawyer who'd insisted he could make a case to sue if our client tried to take the dog with her, even though the dog had been hers for years before they'd ever met. I knew all about vindictive pricks, even if I'd never been in a relationship with one, and this guy was clearly a massive one.

I scrambled over the wooden fence with the help of a lawn chair, and Julius handed the corgi over the top to me. The dog squirmed a little when I tucked him under my arm, and I made a soft clucking sound that had seemed to soothe him in the car. When he went still, I gave him a quick pet. "Good boy." Then I stole across the overgrown lawn to the back door.

At least it looked as if this dude didn't treat the current doggie resident too badly. There were a few toys scattered in the yard, and when I peeked through the window in the back door, I made out a full water dish and a food bowl that looked recently cleaned of its contents.

No sign of the actual dog, though…

I couldn't see the supposed owner, but chances were he was camped out in the living room in front of his widescreen TV jabbing at a controller. Stroking the dog's fur comfortingly, I used my other hand to quickly pick the lock so I'd be ready to move as soon as I got the signal.

All good, I texted Garrison.

A minute later, the doorbell pealed out. The floor creaked as the occupant must have walked over to answer it. I eased open the back door at the same moment.

It let out a faint squeak, and I froze. But the guy was already swinging open the front door and didn't appear to notice. I slipped into the mudroom and set down the new corgi.

"You stay right there," I murmured to him, setting a few treats in the food dish. As he started gobbling them up, I stalked farther into the house.

"Here, Terry, Terry, Terry," I whispered, careful to keep my voice much lower than those carrying from the front of the house. I wasn't sure what story Garrison had come up with to keep the guy distracted, but it obviously involved a lot of talking. I clucked my tongue under my breath for good measure and waggled the toy that the client had told us was his favorite with the faint jingle.

To my relief, the click of little claws reached my ears a few seconds later. Another corgi, which did look remarkably like the one we'd picked up, came trundling over to meet me. I'd have thought our original one had left the mudroom if it wasn't for the collar around this one's neck.

"Good boy," I told him, and jingled the toy for him to follow me back to the mudroom.

There was an abrupt silence from the front. I halted in my tracks again, my nerves prickling, prepared to simply snatch up the dog and run for it. But then Garrison's laugh pealed out, the other guy's echoing it, and my breath rushed out of me.

We were okay, for now.

It took some wrangling and a couple more treats to get the original corgi to allow me to unbuckle his collar, and the new one huffed as I fixed it around his neck. Then I was darting out the back with a different but equally cute doggo under my arm.

The dog gave a small woof just as I closed the door, which Garrison must have heard because all of a sudden he gave a loud exclamation to draw the guy's attention. I dashed across the yard, narrowly avoiding tripping over a rubber bone, and lifted my cargo so Julius could take him over the fence. I clambered after him, and we both loped down the drive to jump into the waiting car.

I rubbed under the corgi's chin as we swung around to pick up Garrison farther down the street and shot a teasing glance at Julius. "Are you sure I can't keep *this* one?"

He gave me a mock-glower. "I think our client might have a few complaints about that."

———

No doubt Julius had been right, because the client was absolutely ecstatic from the moment she opened the door and saw the corgi in my arms. She took him from me, whirling around with him like he was her soul mate, and peppered kisses all over his furry head for the better part of a minute.

"That's right, Terry," she murmured. "You're back with Mommy now. No more meanie Kevin. You're all right."

The dog's tail was wagging so hard I was surprised it didn't fall off his body. Clearly he was happy to be back with her too.

Finally, the woman sat down at the desk in her living room and looked up at us. "There's no chance my ex will realize Terry is gone?"

We shook our heads. "We found a suitable replacement," Garrison said with a smirk. "From the sounds of things, he won't notice the difference."

She let out her breath. "Perfect. He was being such a scumbag about it." Then her face settled into a more professional mask. "I guess it's time for my side of the bargain. Whose DNA am I sequencing?"

I stepped forward and then stopped, not sure what she needed from me. "Mine."

She nodded and set the dog down at her feet with a fond pat. He stuck close to her legs as she retrieved some equipment from a case under the desk.

"I'll just need a small sample of your blood for the most accurate sequencing. I'll have to wait until I have the lab to myself for a long enough time, but I should be able to manage it in the next couple of days. After that, you want me to send it to the man who set up the exchange, if I understand correctly?"

"That's right," Julius said. "We appreciate your assistance."

"I appreciate having my dog back."

She motioned for me to hold out my arm. I tensed a little as she swabbed disinfectant over the vein she meant to use, my body automatically rejecting the idea of being handled by a stranger. I'd been pushed around so much during my time in the household that any touch I hadn't sought out felt like an imposition.

But I needed this. This was my ticket to finding my family. At least, it'd better be after the lengths the crew was going to on my behalf.

The woman knew what she was doing. The needle gave only the smallest pinch as she inserted it. The tube attached to it quickly filled with the dark red blood she was drawing. The whole process was over in an instant.

"There you go," she said, smoothing a bandaid over the spot. "I hope you find what you're looking for with this."

"So do I," I replied, and I'd never meant anything more.

TWENTY-SIX

Decima

"I AM *NOT* SHARING a bed with Blaze," Garrison said, pointing to the bed where Blaze lay sprawled, laptop on his chest and three pillows propping up his head. He tipped his head to the side, a sly glint coming into his eyes. "I'll share with Dess."

Julius shot him an unamused look. "This is not the topic we need to be discussing right now, but I'll remind you that if all goes well, *none* of us will be spending the night here."

"I just figured I should make my position clear now, just in case," the younger man muttered, and reached toward the array of weapons we'd all been assembling our arsenals from.

I fixed a few more tactical items to my belt and added another holster under my arm. We were loading ourselves down with even more equipment than when we'd taken on the Funhouse, but for good reason. We had to navigate the entire four-story building and eliminate any guards who got in our way… without actually *eliminating* them. Julius didn't feel right about mowing down random people who were simply doing their jobs working for the government, and I was inclined to agree.

The computers that would allow us to run the analysis on the DNA sequence now stored on a flash drive stood in the very center of the building's top floor, because of course they did. Each stage of our entry would have different difficulties. Some of them we'd need to handle on our own, and others Blaze would be talking us through from the hotel a mile from the facility, over the headsets we'd all put on.

"Remember," Blaze said for the dozenth or so time as he tapped at his keyboard, "*don't* split up. I don't have access to the cameras inside that place, and it'll be almost impossible for me to help two of you with two different problems at once."

"We promise if we split up, we won't get into any trouble," Garrison shot back.

Blaze glowered at him. I knew how nervous he was about having us go in alone while he was blind to what was happening, relying on only the bits of data he'd been able to dig up on the facility's layout, GPS trackers clipped to our belts, and our reports through our headsets. He'd told us everything he could to prepare us until Julius had finally—gruffly but gently—informed him that at the rate he was going, we'd mess up because we had too much information stuffed into our heads.

"We're in good hands with you here guiding us," I said, adjusting my bulletproof vest to make sure it was perfectly positioned and then going over to the side of the bed. I tucked the stuffed tiger I'd brought along—"For luck," I'd told the guys—closer to his side. If it'd come from my former family, maybe in some weird way, it'd help us take the final steps to getting me back to that family.

"And we've been through a hell of a lot of other difficult missions," I added. "You don't really think the Ghost would fail even at a challenge like this, do you?"

Blaze opened his mouth and paused, probably torn between protesting and not wanting to diminish my past accomplishments. Before he could decide which to go with, I bent down and pressed my lips to his. He settled on a pleased hum as he leaned into the kiss.

"We'll be fine," I repeated, pressing a finger to his mouth as I pulled away. "Trust me."

He kissed my finger gently, grabbing my hand and flipping until the palm faced upright. He kissed the palm too before exhaling a long breath. "Just be careful," he insisted as I pulled away.

"I don't think any of us wants to be in more danger than we have to be. And I know how prepared *you* are. We've got this."

I wished I felt as confident as I managed to sound, but at least my words seemed to reassure Blaze. He nodded and gave us a little wave as we headed out the door.

We marched to the elevator in a formation that'd come instinctively: Garrison and Julius in the lead with me in the middle and Talon bringing up the rear. Blaze should have been walking next to the cool-headed killer, but I didn't let myself dwell on that.

His injuries were healing. He'd managed to walk a few steps to grab a glass of water and a snack today. Soon he'd be back to his former energetic self.

As the elevator door stood closed, Garrison raised his eyebrows at me. "Why does *Blaze* get a kiss? He's the one lounging around on a bed while the rest of us do the hard work."

His tone was grumbly but with a playful note underneath. I rolled my eyes at him. "If you want something, there are nicer ways to ask."

Heat flared in his eyes. "Oh, I could come up with something *very* nice if we had a little more time."

"I'm sure you could." I stepped closer to him and gave him a quick kiss, one he turned hot and firm with a hand on my waist. Not wanting to leave anyone out, I turned to Julius and reached up to touch the massive man's cheek. He smiled, his dark eyes smoldering, and met my kiss for him with equal enthusiasm.

Talon touched my back before I'd even turned to him. He pulled me around and kissed me so soundly my panties were damp by the time he let me go.

"There," I said, folding my arms around my chest. "That evens things out." The desire now tingling through me wanted more, but my nerves were too keyed up by the mission ahead to give in. We had a lot of work to do, and any distraction could get us killed.

The easiest part of the job was getting *to* the facility.

Beyond that, there was nothing easy about it. It was late enough that not even the hardest working lab technicians would remain, but security was tight and difficult to infiltrate at any time. From rotations on the perimeter to interior security, we'd detected no gaps in coverage. On top of that, Blaze had determined that the building held alarm systems that were sensitive to noise and probably the wrong sorts of pressure as well, although he couldn't figure out the specifics without going in.

"I see you're just outside," he said through our headsets as we crouched in the shadow of a nearby art installation, his normally easygoing voice terse with the tension. I could imagine him watching us as little blips on his laptop screen.

"Ready to move," Julius confirmed. In the glow of the security lamps that cut through the night, the building before us looked like a plain block of concrete, nothing high tech about it. I'd bet no one passing by gave it a second glance. But apparently the windows dotting the cement exterior were only for show. There wasn't any real way to look inside from out here.

Blaze spoke with total efficiency. "There are four guards on constant rotation around the entrance, as I expected. You have about a minute between them, and the fourth one is checking in with the supervisor every twelve minutes like clockwork."

"He's the one we need to avoid," Julius said, his whisper coming through my headset clearly.

"Exactly. You can't be seen by the fourth security guard, and he can't suspect that anything's wrong, or a ton of backup will come down on you. Don't make a noise knocking out the other three and get them out of sight, and he won't have any idea something's wrong until the guard rotation in an hour."

I eyed the entrance, which a man was striding by right now. "Which one is off-limits?"

"He's the lead, so he should have a golden patch on his left sleeve," Blaze instructed.

Thirty seconds later, another man rounded the corner, a rifle in his hands. I spotted the gold patch immediately. He surveyed the entire area with a keen eye. We'd definitely need to be extra careful with leaving evidence, as this man would spot any discrepancies.

"When he passes, you have four minutes max to deal with the other guards and get inside the door." Blaze's voice became even harder as he gave careful instructions. "Dess, I showed you how to use the keypad cracker. The rest of you, work to disable the guards and hide the bodies. Hide them *well.*"

Four minutes. I could do this in four minutes. When I'd practiced with the cracker on various doors around the city for practice, it'd never taken more than a minute to find the right combination. But Blaze had warned me that this one would likely take longer, and we didn't want to cut it too close. I only had one shot. If I pulled it off before it was done decrypting, it could set off the alarms in the building.

The second the lead guard turned the corner out of view, the next guard had come into sight. Julius leapt forward silently, capturing the weapon first, then muffling the man's gasp and knocking him out with a jab of a syringe. Maybe the same stuff the crew had used on me when they'd first taken me home. He pulled the man toward the sculpture where he'd restrain and more carefully hide him, and Talon moved forward to deal with the next guard.

The second the guard was unconscious, I bolted toward the metal front door, yanking the keypad cracker from its spot on my belt. With a glance at the lock, I stuck the device to the base of it and pressed the necessary buttons. It flashed, and the orange light began blinking, showing that it was scanning for possible combinations.

I looked toward where the rest of the crew stood by the modern sculpture, waiting for the next man on duty to come into sight. The seconds slipped by, and the steady rhythm of guard's footsteps reached my ears.

The lock cracker was still blinking. I tried to tune out the anxious twisting of my stomach. "What are we doing the second we get inside?" I whispered into my mic as I heard the faint scuffling of Talon effectively incapacitating the other guard.

"Go directly to the right, staying as close to the wall as you can and then keep going in that direction until you reach the stairwell door," Blaze replied in my ear. "The automatic lights will alert security if you go forward. You'll need to get to the employee's stairwell at the side of the building."

"Got it," I whispered. One more guard left. Well, that and the damned tracker. I stared at it, willing it to switch to green, but it just kept blinking that orange dot at me.

Julius had gotten into place to take down the third guard. Talon was still concealing the second. Garrison slunk over to stand at my shoulder like a guard dog, ready to bolt inside with the rest of us the second we could.

"We have time," he murmured into my ear, taking in my stance.

But we *didn't*. If this stupid box of circuitry didn't perform fast enough, the entire mission would be a bust before it'd even started.

The third guard's footfalls sounded. Julius was on him in an instant. Talon joined us at the door, Julius following seconds later. The fucking light was still orange.

"Blaze," I hissed. "It's almost time for the lead guard, and the cracker hasn't—"

The light blinked green, and the lock clicked open. At the same moment, I heard the lead guard approaching. He hadn't turned the corner yet, but we had the space of a few heartbeats to get out of sight.

I yanked the device from the door, shoved it open, and flung myself inside and to the right, just as Blaze had said. The others had heard his instructions too. We all flattened ourselves against the wall in the sudden, thicker darkness that had no streetlamp glow tempering it.

The door shut with a faint tap. I held my breath, braced for thudding footsteps and an angry shout.

Nothing came. More seconds ticked by with the pounding of my heart. The lead guard must have walked right by with no inkling that anything was wrong.

Next to me, Garrison gave me a gentle nudge. I

nodded even though he couldn't see me and started sidling on down the righthand hall.

I couldn't make out any of the technology that made this place so special in the pitch black we'd found ourselves in, but I could hear it. An electronic hum droned through the air as if from all around us. It sent a shiver down my spine.

The seemingly endless corridor finally brought us to a push-style door. A dim light on the other side showed a narrow stairwell.

"We've reached the stairs," Julius murmured to Blaze under his breath.

I could almost hear Blaze nod. "Go up. There aren't many other guards until you get to the top floor, and the ones who are on the lower floors aren't likely to be on the stairs. If you do run into anyone… you know how to handle them."

Julius had another syringe ready in his hand. Garrison brandished a stun gun. I flexed my fingers, mentally rehearsing the move Noelle had taught me that could briefly knock out a man if you applied the right amount of pressure on just the right spot by his neck.

We slipped up the stairs one after the other, giving the doors we passed on the second and third floor a cautious glance before hurrying by. Several steps down from the fourth landing, we paused again.

"We're just about at the top," Julius reported quietly. "What are we facing up here?"

"I couldn't find out all that much specific detail, unfortunately," Blaze said. "But since the control room is up there, it's where the most security presence is concentrated. Avoid any loud sounds and try not to touch anything I don't tell you to. The control center is in the middle of that floor, with data banks all around it. Make your way to it as quickly as you can, and any guards you need to deal with, do your best to keep them out of sight afterward."

That sounded a whole lot easier said than done. I dragged in a breath and glanced at the others. They all nodded.

"I'll stay in the lead," I murmured, and darted to the door.

I edged it open just a smidge, enough to spot a row of machines on the other side that stretched to the high ceiling and flickered with a multitude of tiny lights—and two guards waiting in the hall just a foot from where I was standing. I held up two fingers to the men and then leapt forward.

I threw myself at the man farther away so the guys could tackle the closer one. One hand clamped around his mouth. The other dug into his flesh where I would find just the right nerve.

I squeezed hard, flinging a leg around his to bring him to the ground so he couldn't buck me off him. A second later, he slumped over.

Talon was already on the second guard with a needle, and Julius gave mine the same treatment, since the effect I'd produced would be short-lived on its own. After a moment's silent debate, we dragged them into the corner of the stairwell, figuring that was the safest place for them.

"There's a pattern marked on the floor farther down the hall," Garrison murmured, and eased a little closer to describe it to Blaze in more detail.

The hacker hummed. "That'll be one of those touch-sensitive alarms. That's got to be the way to the control center. But you'll have to disable it to get past it."

"And how do we do *that*?" I asked.

"Look around. There should be a small utility room to your left. The wiring will probably run through there."

I spotted a discreet doorway past another row of humming, flickering computer units and hustled over. "I found it."

"Good, go inside, and I'll direct you. We have to be careful not to cut the wires for the wrong devices, or it'll trigger an alarm. We can't afford that."

No kidding. I reached the utility room, unlocked it with some jabs and twists of my lock picks, and slipped inside. The others crammed into the small space after me to avoid being seen. Garrison glanced around.

"We could chuck a few bodies in here too," he remarked.

"Not right now," I muttered, and stared at the mess of cables that covered the wall in front of me. "Blaze, I'm going to need some serious guidance."

"Okay. You want to find a cable labeled 4J. A place on this level, they've got to be up to code. Do you see it?"

I scanned the cables in the thin light and caught sight of it partway down the wall. "Here. I cut that one?"

"Not so fast! There'll be a dual trigger. If either of them shuts down without the other, we're screwed."

My heart started thumping faster again. "What's the other one?"

"Usually it'd be a switch… They like to use blue ones for this type of system. Do you see any blue switches?"

I did, but there was a slight problem. "Five of them."

Blaze muttered a curse under his breath. "Okay… They would have it lower than the cable's entry point, and to the left—no, no, to the right. Lower and to the right."

There was only one blue switch that met that description. I rested my fingers on it. "Are you sure?"

"Yes. Cut the wire and flick the switch at the exact same time."

I pulled a knife from my belt and braced it against the cable. My fingers curled around the switch. Then, in unison, I jerked both hands into action.

The cable split. The switch dropped. My jaw clenched, but no blare of alarms filled the building.

"Did it work?" Blaze asked in my ear.

I exhaled shakily. "I don't like that you're asking me that. It seems like it. Let's check the hall."

I'd just said that when Julius and Talon leapt out ahead of us. I understood why a few seconds later when they dragged two more unconscious guards past me into the stairwell. We were certainly leaving a trail of bodies behind us, if not in the typical way.

"The pattern on the floor has vanished," Garrison reported.

Blaze let out a little cheer. "You're good to go then. Well, as far as that's concerned anyway. Still proceed with extreme caution, watching for a set of glass double doors to your right that'll lead into the control room. If you're quick, maybe you can make it there before any more patrols reach that part of their circuit."

We weren't quite that lucky. I'd just spotted the double doors between two stretches of looming data storage units when another two guards rounded a corner up ahead. Apparently on this floor they worked in pairs.

Julius dashed forward with a speed I wouldn't have expected from such a massive man if I hadn't seen him in action before. He mashed their faces together, muffling their shouts of alarm against each other's flesh as Talon and Garrison dove in with syringes.

We dragged the limp bodies into the control room with us and then paused to stare at the array around us. It looked like something Blaze would have wet dreams about. Screens and computer towers filled every inch of the walls. Beneath one cluster of monitors sprawled a vast black keyboard with five times as many keys as usual. Or, well, when I got closer I saw that many of them were actually round buttons or rectangular switches.

"We're in," I said. "Here goes nothing."

Blaze had already gone over this final part of the plan in detail, because he'd mostly been able to predict what to expect ahead of time. He'd also warned us that the control room was probably checked by guards at least every ten minutes. We had to work fast.

I pulled the flash drive that Blaze had given me from the secure pocket where I'd kept it. Garrison motioned to a port that would accept it on the base of the keyboard. I jabbed it in and tapped the power button. A few of the screens blinked on immediately.

"The drive is in," I whispered.

"Good. Is it already working on the password?"

"Looks like it." Blaze had set up the drive to run its sequence of operations automatically on contact. A window had appeared on the main screen, letters and numbers whipping by too quickly for me to make out more than a blur. Abruptly, that screen vanished, and a spread of icons appeared. A program opened as if of its own accord.

"I think it's starting the search now," I said.

"Good." Blaze's relief rang through his voice. "It'll take a couple of minutes to get through all that data, but it's got to be one of the most advanced systems in the world. This laptop of mine would take a hundred times that long." He chuckled.

I leaned against the nearest console and inhaled deeply. "I think we did it."

Julius shot me a crooked smile. "Let's not get cocky. We've still got to get out of here."

The computer next to me whirred faintly, and a spiral of DNA showed on the screen. My pulse hitched. "I think it found a match."

"Perfect. It'll be downloading onto the drive now. Wait until the screen stops showing any activity, then grab the drive and get moving."

Abruptly, a beep emanated from the console where I'd inserted the drive. I frowned. "Is it supposed to beep when it's done?"

"What? I wouldn't think so, but—"

I missed whatever else Blaze said when the screen flared all at once with blinking red letters. *UNAUTHORIZED ACCESS*. I jerked back, just as the blare of a siren screeched through the room.

TWENTY-SEVEN

Decima

"SHIT, SHIT," I muttered to myself over the alarm's siren wail. Around me, the men's hands flew to their weapons.

Blaze could obviously hear the alarm on his end without us needing to tell him that something had gone wrong. He mumbled a curse of his own. "Get the drive, and get out. *Now.*"

I yanked out the flash drive and shoved it into my secure pocket. We whirled toward the doors—just in time to see another metal door slowly sliding out over them to seal us in. It'd already covered a quarter of the second door's surface, including the handle.

"There's a secondary door, steel, closing over the first," Julius said into his mic. "There's got to be a failsafe to shut it off somewhere."

Blaze swore again. "I don't know what it'd be without

more information than you have time to give. There'll be at least a dozen guards coming at you. Can you get past it by force?"

I threw myself at the glass pane on the door, but it only jarred in its frame. The thunder of racing footsteps carried through it. Talon motioned me aside and hurtled past me, taking a few shots at the glass to crack the thick layer before slamming his elbow into it with the full impact of his body weight behind it.

The pane shattered. Talon burst through, and the rest of us charged after him, Julius dragging Garrison the last few inches before the automatic security door pinned him to the frame.

We didn't have any time to appreciate that narrow escape. Squads of guards burst into view at both ends of the hallway.

We ducked low instinctively. My fingers closed around my gun. We didn't want to kill anyone just doing their job, but if it was us or them, we wouldn't have much choice. We'd agreed that we'd shoot to injure rather than kill if that would be enough, but it was going to be hard with this many opponents.

"Stay close to the data storage equipment!" Blaze shouted through my headset. "They won't want to risk damaging the machines."

We all flung ourselves upright and pressed tight against the towering machines with their blinking lights. The guards slowed as they approached, their guns drawn but silent. Blaze had been right.

"Hands up!" one in the lead barked at us. "Drop your weapons. You're surrounded and outnumbered."

That might be true, but I'd be willing to bet that these men hadn't been in quite as many tricky situations as I had. I'd never let the hopelessness of a fight stop me from giving it my all before, and I wasn't going to start rolling over now.

As my pulse thudded behind my ears, my vision narrowed down to the most important details of the figures around me—how they were spaced around each other, which hands each had on their guns, what sort of protective gear they wore that could deflect a bullet. Then I sprang into action.

Keeping my back against the computer equipment, I fired into the squad of guards closest to me, hitting a wrist, a hand, a bicep, a thigh. Weapons clattered from fingers that could no longer hold them; arms sagged, and legs staggered. Julius started shooting at the bunch in the opposite direction, and Talon squeezed his trigger too, adding to the injuries on both sides.

A couple of the guards farther back that we hadn't been able to hit immediately took a few shots at us, but they were so careful about the machines and their colleagues across from them that we managed to dodge. Then they barreled straight toward us, barging past their wounded comrades—but that gave us time to deal out a few more shots precise enough to crumple them to the ground without outright killing them.

"Come on!" Garrison yelled, motioning for us to leap over the slightly smaller squad and get out of there.

I thought a silent mental apology at the men I'd had to shoot—and who I now kicked and stomped on to fend off their snatching hands and waved batons as they tried to stop us even in their blood-soaked state. Someone was hollering into a radio that Julius shot out of his hand to a yelp of pain, but we had to assume that more backup was on the way.

We dashed down the hall the way we'd come—only to discover that another steel security door had already snapped into place over the entrance to the stairwell. There was no escaping that way. But the alarm's wail had faded away, maybe so the security officers could track us easier, and more footsteps were pounding toward us. The guards must have had another route through the building.

"Blaze," I hissed. "The main stairwell is sealed. How do we get out of here?"

"I'm trying to find—the blueprints must have been altered after the version I have—shit." He was typing frantically enough that the clatter of the keyboard sounded over the headset.

"Get out of sight," Julius ordered the rest of us, jerking his hand toward the utility room we'd used to disable the floor alarm.

We dashed into the room and tugged the door shut. Only seconds later, guards stomped by outside. I had a brief moment of hoping that they'd forget about this room, but the government didn't hire any slouches for their top-secret facility. Someone grasped the handle and turned. There was no way to lock it from the inside.

Talon grabbed the inside handle and hauled backward,

holding the door shut with his considerable strength. Unfortunately, the men on the other side had clearly figured out that someone was in here. There were more shouts, and a couple of shots rattled the handle. They were less concerned about sending bullets in here. There must have been backup elsewhere in the building for the vital electrical systems. Maybe we'd have been safer staying in the hall.

And now we were trapped in a box of a room, hardly bigger than a coat closet, with a horde of furious armed men on the other side.

As my gaze darted around the dark room searching for some kind of answer, an uncomfortable knot formed in my stomach. We'd ended up here because I'd wanted so badly to know who I really was—to figure out what family I'd been stolen from and why. But had it really mattered so much that it'd been worth putting not just myself but the men who'd supported me in this much danger?

I could have decided I was simply Decima and walked away. Focused on taking down anyone who tried to capture me again until they gave up. Instead, I'd gone chasing danger with the only men I'd really cared about— the only people who'd ever really cared about *me*—by my side, and now we could all be screwed. I was good, but even I knew that maximum security prisons weren't a piece of cake to break out of.

Julius had braced himself with his gun ready. I supposed we had a small advantage from the fact that we had a wall at our back and only a narrow doorway that our enemies could come at us through. Our enemies who were now managing to jostle Talon in his rigid position despite the strained bulging of his arm muscles.

Then my eyes caught on the edge of a rectangle on the ceiling, mostly hidden by the shadows and the top of the cabinet beneath it. My breath caught.

"Blaze, are there air vents that reach the utility room?"

On the other end of our connection, he sucked in a breath. "That isn't shown on the blueprint I have either, but it'd make sense for them to add one. Every room with a door should have adequate ventilation. It'd be a tight fit for Julius, though."

"I'll make it work," Julius said grimly. "I've squeezed through tight spaces before. It's all a matter of angles. But we have to get up there without getting shot on the way."

"Move the cabinet," Garrison said quickly.

We heaved at it together and managed to shift it toward the door. Julius gave me a boost toward the ceiling, and I unscrewed the grate covering the vent in less than a minute. Talon let out a grunt where he was still pulling back the door with all his might.

"You and Garrison get up there," Julius ordered. "I'll knock the cabinet over, and it'll block the doorway long enough for me and Talon to jump off it to follow you. Just keep moving."

"I think once you're in there, you just need to head left and you should find a connecting vent that'll take you down to the first floor," Blaze said helpfully in my ear. "One good thing about it being narrow is that you should be able to brace yourself against the sides and scramble down without falling. Just don't get stuck."

"No fucking kidding," Talon muttered.

I grasped the edge of the vent and dragged myself up into it on the left-hand side. Immediately, I crawled forward on my hands and knees. I didn't think Julius would be able to manage more than an army crawl in this tight space. Good thing he'd have gotten professional training at that.

There was a thump as Garrison clambered up after me. Then a clang resonated from below as Julius must have shoved the cabinet in front of the doorway. With a grunt, the other two men hauled themselves into the vent in quick succession.

Gunfire rang out below as I scuttled forward as fast as I could go. But the cabinet must have blocked the entrance long enough to shield Julius and Talon, because I heard three sets of breaths in the passage behind me, terse but not pained.

"Everyone okay?" I murmured, just to be sure.

"I've had more enjoyable nights," Julius retorted. Talon simply snorted. I decided to take both of those responses as a yes.

"Stop joking around and get the hell out of there," Blaze chided us. "I've just picked up on transmissions in the neighborhood—there's going to be a whole army on the doorstep if you don't get out in the next five minutes."

My heart hiccupped. I pushed myself forward even faster and nearly toppled right into the downward vent before I realized I'd found it. In the total darkness, the only warning was a slight ripple of the metal lip around the opening.

There was no time for negotiating who'd go first. I wedged myself around the corner so I could drop my legs in and then slid the rest of the way, balancing myself between my back and my feet with my knees brushing my chest.

With little hitches of jumps, I careened several feet at a time, catching myself and then doing it all over again. The rasping and thudding above told me the men were following me using the same strategy, although the bigger guys wouldn't be able to move as swiftly.

Blaze was already planning our next steps. "It bottoms out over the first-floor ceiling. You'll want to go back in the same direction you reached the vertical vent from. About twenty feet along, you should find a grate that's just a short dash from the main entrance."

"Perfect," I said around a gasp for breath.

With a few more jumps, my feet smacked into a metal surface below me. A metallic *clunk* rang out, making me wince. I couldn't hear any voices filtering through the ceiling of the hall below me, but it was only a matter of time before the guards who'd swarmed us upstairs figured out our strategy and caught up with us.

Contorting my body, I squirmed around until I could crawl through the horizontal vent passage and hurried onward. Garrison, Talon, and Julius followed me with a soft grunt for each landing.

"I could hear the guards rushing down through the wall," Julius reported. "They've got to be at least to the third floor by now."

Crap. I shoved myself farther and spotted a glimmer of light just up ahead. There was the grate.

I caught hold of the metal rectangle and brought my tools to bear on the screws. My fingers flew, and in a matter of seconds, I was tossing it aside. I poked my head into the hall below to look around, and my heart all but stopped.

"We can't get out," I said, jumping down into the open, currently empty hall so I wasn't blocking the men's way. I stared at the door we'd come through—which was now completely sealed off by another one of those steel security doors. No handle, no clear controls. And we only had a minute or two before a mass of guards would be surrounding us from both sides.

Garrison dropped to the ground and came over to stand beside me. "There's got to be a way to get it to retract."

"Do you see any panels in the walls nearby that you could open up?" Blaze asked.

I stared at the walls around us. "There's nothing."

Talon and Julius leapt down and studied the door in turn. A distant thunder reached my ears—the thudding feet of the multitude of guards who'd be on us in mere seconds now.

We'd run out of options. In less than a minute, they'd be shooting us down. Even if we could manage to take on all the guards in here, despite the fact that we couldn't rely on any nearby equipment to prevent them from shooting us, by the time we'd accomplished that, the army Blaze had warned us about would be gathered outside.

We were all going to die.

I didn't say the words out loud. They felt like a betrayal of everything the Chaos Crew had done to get me here. The risks they'd taken for a mystery that only really mattered to me. I swallowed hard.

"I think there's another exit," Blaze said, but his excitement vanished an instant later. "Only it's on the other side of where the secure staircase has to be. All those guards are between you and it now."

The answer came to me like a signal flare in the dark. This was my quest. I should be the one to make the ultimate sacrifice. I could dash over and draw the guards' attention, get them to chase after me, and buy the men enough time to escape.

They'd done so much for me. Given me so much. They shouldn't have to give their lives too, especially not when it was my fault we were here at all.

Who I was didn't matter if I was dead, especially not if the men around me died too.

I gathered myself, preparing to race toward the sound of the stomping feet with an explanation shouted over my shoulder, and my gaze inadvertently caught on Garrison's.

I should have known better than to look at him, the man who made a living out of reading people's deepest secrets.

The moment my eyes met his, he narrowed them, detecting something in my expression that I hadn't thought to keep hidden. In the time it took for me to push all my thoughts down, I was afraid he'd already seen what I was planning.

Garrison took a discreet step closer to the door and shook his head lightly—too lightly for the others to notice. I countered by shaking mine.

"You can't—" he started, and then his attention jerked to something over my head. I might have made a break for it then if a hopeful light hadn't brightened his expression.

"Paper!" he said abruptly. "Who's got a piece of fucking paper?" He snapped his fingers, fishing something out of a pouch on his belt at the same time.

I had no idea what he was talking about, but the other men responded automatically, trusting that their comrade had a good reason for his request. Talon's hand jerked to his own belt, but Julius was already thrusting a piece of folded notepaper from his pocket toward the younger man. Garrison scraped a match against its book, brought the flame to the paper, and held the now-flaming sheet up... to a sensor next to a sprinkler system fixture I hadn't noticed mounted on the ceiling.

The first floor must be all regular offices, no high-tech equipment the government workers would be too worried about getting wet. And they'd wanted to protect the ground floor from any sort of fire that might spread upward to all those precious hard drives.

A different sort of alarm careened through the air, and a burst of water sprayed down over us. In an instant, I was drenched.

In the same instant, the steel security door began to whir open.

A bellow reverberated through the hall behind us. We leapt toward the front door as one being.

"Thirty seconds until the first cars reach the building," Blaze called through the headset.

It took ten for the door to open all the way. Julius and Talon fired a few shots down the hall, and then we dove out into the night.

Our feet pelted across the pavement. We hurtled down the sidewalk and around the block, dove into the waiting car, and didn't properly breathe until Talon was gunning the engine to tear down the road away from there.

I sagged into the back seat, drenched and chilled but giddy with relief. "Oh my God." I glanced at Garrison next to me. "How did you know that would work?"

He shrugged, a pleased gleam in his eyes. "I didn't know. I just guessed. It wouldn't make much sense to allow the employees to be locked up in there if the place caught fire. Like Julius said, there's always a failsafe."

"Thank fuck for that," Julius rumbled, a sentiment we all echoed with a round of exhausted laughter.

TWENTY-EIGHT

Decima

BLAZE GREETED us at the door to the hotel room, his eyes wild with manic energy. "What took you so long? I had about five panic attacks thinking they'd surrounded you and gunned you down on the way back."

Julius gave him a baleful look as we all tramped inside and nodded to Talon, who swiftly but gingerly picked up Blaze and hefted him back to his bed.

"There's this thing called traffic," the leader of the crew said dryly. "And I didn't figure it'd be a good look to speed the entire way back here once we'd gotten away from the scene. Trying not to draw undue attention to ourselves and all that."

Blaze huffed but sank back into the pillows, tucking my tiger under his arm. "You did practically die about ten times in the past hour. I think a little concern is understandable."

"You shouldn't be on your feet," I told him. "You didn't pull your stitches, did you?"

He threw his hands up in the air and then winced, which made me worry that he'd done it right then if he hadn't already. "Pull my stitches, when you were facing off against a thousand highly trained government security officers—"

"I don't think it was *quite* that many," Garrison put in.

Blaze glowered at him. "It would have been if you'd gotten out of there even ten seconds later."

I sighed and sat down on the edge of the bed next to Blaze. "But we didn't. We're okay. We're back now. And a lot of that is thanks to you, you know."

The worry fell from his face enough for him to smile back at me.

Garrison cleared his throat. "That last brilliant brainstorm was all *me*, I'd just like to point out."

I rolled my eyes at him. "And you get full credit for it. But right now..." I pulled the flash drive out of my pocket. "We went through an awful lot of trouble to get this loaded up. Let's see if it actually finished processing and made all that trouble worthwhile."

I spoke casually, but as Blaze grinned and snatched the drive from my grasp, my pulse started to stutter almost as badly as when we'd had a horde of armed guards on our tails. We *had* gotten out, and not even with any serious injuries, but I was still going to feel massive guilt if we'd gone through all that craziness for nothing.

And it wasn't as if we'd be able to break in *again* for a second try. This had been my one chance.

Blaze tossed his computer onto his lap and jabbed in the drive. His fingers raced over the keyboard so quickly they were almost a blur. Julius came up behind me, setting a firm hand on my waist as if to steady me while we both watched the screen. Garrison and Talon gathered on the other side of the bed.

The hacker let out a whoop of excitement. "There was a match!" A record sprang onto the screen. "A close one too. Parental—paternal." He skimmed down past several paragraphs of data that apparently weren't relevant to him. "Your dad's name is…"

I was so keyed up with anticipation that when he trailed off into sudden silence, I couldn't keep quiet. "*What?*"

Then my eyes settled on the name in bold partway down the screen. I blinked at it, read it again, leaned closer, and read it a third time. It didn't change.

Damien Malik.

My lungs seized up. It was a few seconds before I could breathe again. I kept gaping at it, my thoughts whirling in my head.

"That's why Noelle and the people she worked with were interested in him," I said as the pieces slowly came together. "Because… because he was related to me. But how can he be related to me? Did he have some secret kid that somehow the media didn't find out about in the two years or whatever before I got kidnapped? What the hell is going on?"

My voice got louder with each question. Julius lifted

his hand to squeeze my shoulder instead. He and the other men were staring at the screen too.

"I don't know," Blaze said. "This doesn't make any sense. Unless—" His eyes widened. His fingers darted over the keyboard again.

He brought up an article with the headline *State Rep Malik Loses Daughter to Car Crash*. Nodding, he tapped the date. "I never checked the exact details because it didn't occur to me that they'd be relevant. That's just a week before that first video we found of you being trained, Dess. She was the right age—twenty-one months, just shy of two years old."

"What are you talking about?" I demanded. "I'm not some zombie who got raised from the dead."

Blaze turned to look at me, his eyes shining with a mix of excitement and sympathy that made my gut twist up. "No, you're not," he said. "I'm saying that Damien Malik's daughter never died at all. Your household people must have staged the accident, left remains that were a convincing enough match that anyone would believe you'd died. But instead, they kidnapped you. It's a near-perfect crime. If the parents think a kid is dead, then they're not going to search for them, right?"

"But I… Could it be some kind of mistake?" I was still having trouble accepting this new version of events. I'd been wondering if Malik was the one who'd *stolen* me, for fuck's sake, and now he was my dad? "If there was a family resemblance, wouldn't we have noticed?"

Blaze brought up some photographs, flicking through them until he found one he was satisfied with that showed

Damien Malik and his wife just a few months ago. "There aren't any of the daughter. Usually the press is a little sensitive about showing photos with young children." He cocked his head and zoomed closer. "His eyes are kind of like yours. The same color. I never noticed before because I wouldn't have thought to compare. And she has black hair with a similar wavy texture to yours."

"So do lots of people," Garrison pointed out. "Otherwise, there aren't many similarities." He squinted at the photograph, and his eyebrows rose slightly. "Although… see if you can find any pictures of the wife when she was a lot younger. I think she must have had work done to her face a while back."

"You mean plastic surgery?" I asked as Blaze dove back into his searching.

Garrison nodded. "The signs are only subtle—it was well done—but it's hard to hide the evidence completely if you know what to look for."

After a few minutes while we waited in tense silence, Blaze crowed in victory and brought up a slightly grainy photo of a dark-haired woman in a robe. "Her high school yearbook photo, senior year. Holy shit."

My jaw went slack. The woman in the picture wasn't a perfect match for me, but I felt as if I could have been looking at a younger sister. She had not just the same wavy black hair, but a long nose and thin lips that made her face echo mine.

"That's her?" I murmured.

Blaze nodded.

"Looks like she had her nose done to give it more of a

cute ski-jump thing," Garrison observed, and glanced at me. "I personally think the version you've got is more elegant." His gaze darted back to the photograph. "And a little plumping to her lips. Enough that the resemblance was obscured. But there's no denying it seeing that picture."

My mouth had gone dry. There really wasn't any denying that this woman was related to me. I had no idea what to say or do about it. My whole body had frozen in place.

Blaze looked over at me. "Are you okay, Dess?" he asked in a gentle tone.

"I—I guess." I rubbed my temple. "This all still seems so bizarre." I paused. "Even if the household did kidnap me, why would they still be keeping tabs on Malik *now*? It's been over twenty years. It must be obvious he doesn't realize I'm alive."

Julius frowned. "Maybe there's more to their plan beyond simply kidnapping you. Let's take a look at his recent activities again with the new perspective we've just gotten."

Blaze typed away without any further prompting. A list of search results popped onto the screen—and the first one made my heart lurch to the base of my throat.

Damien Malik, Majority Whip, Victim in Brutal Attack. And the time stamp next to the headline was just this evening.

ABOUT THE AUTHORS

Eva Chance is a pen name for contemporary romance written by Amazon top 100 bestselling author Eva Chase. If you love gritty romance, dominant men, and fierce women who never have to choose, look no further.

Eva lives in Canada with her family. She loves stories both swoony and supernatural, and strong women and the men who appreciate them.

Connect with Eva online:
www.evachase.com
eva@evachase.com

Harlow King is a long-time fan of all things dark, edgy, and steamy. She can't wait to share her contemporary reverse harem stories.

Made in the USA
Las Vegas, NV
13 December 2021

37545298R00180